LOSING
JUSTICE

PETER O'MAHONEY

The fight for justice has begun...

Losing Justice: A Legal Thriller
Tex Hunter 8

Peter O'Mahoney

Copyright © 2022
Published by Roam Free Publishing.
peteromahoney.com

ALSO BY PETER O'MAHONEY

In the Tex Hunter Legal Thriller series:

POWER AND JUSTICE
FAITH AND JUSTICE
CORRUPT JUSTICE
DEADLY JUSTICE
SAVING JUSTICE
NATURAL JUSTICE
FREEDOM AND JUSTICE

In the Jack Valentine Series:

GATES OF POWER
THE HOSTAGE
THE SHOOTER
THE THIEF
THE WITNESS

In the Joe Hennessy Legal Thriller Series:

THE SOUTHERN LAWYER
THE SOUTHERN CRIMINAL

PETER O'MAHONEY

LOSING JUSTICE

TEX HUNTER LEGAL THRILLER BOOK 8

PETER O'MAHONEY

<u>CHAPTER 1</u>

CRIMINAL DEFENSE attorney Tex Hunter hated politics.

He hated the games politicians played, the backroom deals, and how the powerful played with the lives of the innocent like they were worthless. He hated how the corrupt hid behind veils of media spin, how the rich influenced decisions with the promise of campaign donations, and how the players made a mockery of moral decision-making. He did his best to avoid it, he did his best to steer clear, however, in his world, the world of law and justice, politics was an inevitable dilemma.

The soft northern sun gleamed off one of the upper windows of the George N. Leighton Criminal Courthouse, and a breeze blew through the parking lot, bringing with it the smells of a thick and humid summer's day in Chicago. The smell resurfaced a memory, causing Hunter to stop in his tracks, the memory resurfacing like a savage punch to the stomach. It'd been five months since he walked his father out of prison, five months since he beat the system that was determined to squash his father's innocence.

Alfred Hunter's death still held a powerful grip on Hunter, one that was taking months to work through.

He'd finally achieved a goal he'd pursued most of his life, an achievement a lifetime in the making, but it quickly turned to grief after his father passed away within a week of his release. He'd achieved his life's work, his life's passion, and he'd felt lost ever since, wandering through his days in an apprehensive fog.

"Rest easy." Hunter looked at the deep blue sky as the sun's reflection began to dissipate with the arrival of a cloud. Another warm gust blew through. In the middle of July, summer had well and truly arrived, delivering hot and steamy days. After hibernating for much of the winter, Chicago exploded into life in July with long evenings, outdoor dining, and days by the lake. July meant festivals, music, art, and fabulous food. It meant weeks of sweat-soaked humidity. And for Tex Hunter, this July meant the start of another murder trial.

"Mr. Hunter."

The person's tone didn't sound friendly. Hunter turned to see two men walking toward him, crossing the parking lot, both of their eyes fixated on him.

Hunter didn't respond. He stood still, waiting for them to continue.

The first man was older, into his late sixties, and Hunter recognized the face—Walter Charman. He was the son of a mobster, just a young man when his father was shot dead by police in the 80s. Charman had used his father's connections to step into the world of politics, becoming an influential political lobbyist, wheeling and dealing behind closed doors. Although he never fronted an election campaign, his influence was marked on many. He was stocky, with a barrel chest and solid shoulders. His white hair was thinning, his skin had an olive complexion, and a smell of Old Spice followed him. The second man was younger, only in his early twenties, tall and skinny. He was well-groomed—his fitted suit was new, his tanned face was clean-shaven, and he didn't have a hair out-of-place.

"Callum, wait for me back at the car," Charman half-whispered to the other. His tone was laced with textbook arrogance.

The well-dressed younger man didn't hesitate, nodding with obedience before turning back in the direction of the courthouse's parking lot. Walter Charman waited for the other man to walk out of earshot before turning back to Hunter.

"It's been a while since we talked, Hunter. Quite a lot has happened in your life since then," Charman pointed towards the courthouse. "Your father's re-trial and release made quite the news story. You had the entire city on edge for months."

"I'm a busy man, Charman. What do you want?"

"I gather that you're on your way to see former Assistant State's Attorney prosecutor Michelle Law," Charman stated the name of Hunter's newest client. He gestured to the younger man waiting by a black sedan fifty yards away. "That kid's name is Callum Strauss. It was his ex-girlfriend that they found in Michelle Law's trunk."

"I'm sorry for his loss," Hunter said. "But he doesn't appear to be too broken up about it. Her body was only found this morning, and he's already back at work with you?"

Charman took a step forward, lowering his tone. "People grieve in different ways, but I don't want to discuss the grieving schedule of broken boyfriends."

"What is it you want?"

The older man's eyes narrowed as he watched Hunter. "I'm here to offer you some friendly guidance and give you the chance to avoid getting yourself into trouble. My job is to give people advice, and I'll give you some for free—let this case pass by."

"Why would I do that?"

"Because you value your career in the justice system." Charman considered Hunter for a moment, before a grin took hold at the corner of his mouth. "Michelle Law isn't a client you need to defend. That's all you need to know. Turn around, go back to your office, and leave this case alone. Tell Michelle that you're sorry, but your schedule is full. She's got money. She can afford another good lawyer."

Hunter glared at him for a few long moments before he stepped past him, brushing his arm into the shorter man.

"I'm running late for my client," Hunter said as he continued towards the courthouse's main entrance. He didn't look back.

He continued through the courthouse security, through the marbled foyer of the grand courthouse, and to the elevators, waiting to take him to see his client before her bond hearing. As he walked through the halls, thoughts of the case flooded his mind.

He knew what a high-profile murder case meant—it meant months of scrutiny, burnt-out energy reserves, and media around every corner. It meant seventy-five-hour weeks in the office, sleepless nights, and endless stress. It meant pressure from political powerhouses, threats to his office, and danger in every shadow.

But despite the pain that lay before him, despite the risks, he'd made a promise to Michelle Law, and he wouldn't let her down.

CHAPTER 2

THE JUSTICE system never changed.

Even with reforms, even with all the money poured into improving services, the massive machine that was the Cook County justice system still churned on, spitting out anguish and agony to anyone unfortunate enough to pass under its judgment. Every inmate had their own terrible story to tell, every person had a past full of trauma, but the machine didn't care—it was there to deal out punishment, and in that, the machine was extremely successful.

As Hunter handed over his identification to the desk assistant, as he'd done many times before in the preceding two decades, he felt a rush of panic that the memories he had of his father's release were nothing more than a dream, and at any moment, he would be back in the visitor's cubicle watching the old man get wheeled in before him, staring back at him with sunken eyes, his mouth slightly ajar as he drew in each labored breath.

"Mr. Hunter? Hello? Are you with us?"

The officer's voice pulled him from the daydream. She handed him a form to sign, and he thanked her, before turning and following the corridors through to the pre-bail conference room.

He greeted the guard, who looked up at his

towering presence, grunted, and then opened the door, pointing to cubicle number five. Inside, the meeting room was dark, stale, and unforgiving. There were five narrow cubicles for defense lawyers to meet with the recently accused before the bail hearing, with only a thin wooden panel separating each meeting space. It was Monday morning, and the room was full, all the other areas occupied by recently charged women, with more lined up outside waiting to take their place. The smell of fear, mixed with mold and body odor, was overwhelming.

Hunter looked at the ceiling to check the ventilation system, but he couldn't see or hear any movement. Maintaining a room used by defense lawyers and the accused wasn't a high priority for the jail. A woman screamed in the corridor outside, and Hunter could hear guards rushing to subdue her. It didn't work. Her howling scream, coming from the depths of her soul, continued for another twenty-five seconds, before she was dragged away, banging on the walls as she went.

Everyone was on edge. Everything was at its tipping point. And in the middle of it all sat Assistant State's Attorney Michelle Law. She sat on the other side of the desk, reserved for those arrested under felony charges, dressed in a dark blue shirt and pants. Hunter barely recognized her. The dark blue prison uniform contrasted with her pale skin. Her impeccable make-up was gone. Her black hair was messy. She was shaking.

She could've passed for several clients Hunter had visited inside prisons, right down to the look of distress and defeat in her eyes. As Hunter sat down, Michelle didn't greet him. She turned her attention to the scratches on the table, long and deep, not taking her eyes off them, her head shaking slightly from side to side.

Another round of shouting commenced outside, and, although muffled to a certain degree by the steel door, it was a constant reminder of where they were.

"Courtroom 101," she said, still not raising her eyes to look at him. "Central Bond Court."

"That's right." Hunter was soft in his approach, careful not to scare her. "That's the first step in this process."

"I know how it works, Hunter," she snapped, finally raising her bloodshot eyes to look at him. "I've tried hundreds of cases here. I'm a prosecutor. I know how this whole machine works. I know every step of this process. And I shouldn't be here. I shouldn't be here on this side of the desk. It's a mistake. One great big mistake. I shouldn't be here."

"That's what we're going to sort out," Hunter responded. He considered opening his briefcase and taking Michelle through the paper diagrams he had ready for new clients to explain the process, but he knew, at best, it would be a waste of time, and, at worst, completely patronizing. "Judge Wallace is on today. He's lenient on people who have strong ties to the community, and that should work out for us, given your employment history. Looking at his history of similar cases, 'D' Bond is likely to be set at $500,000. If you want to make bail, you'll have to put up 10% of that amount, $50,000. Do you think you can do that?"

She nodded, her head dropping again, staring at the table. "I can do that."

Hunter watched her, looking for any hint of guilt.

Two decades earlier, they had attended law school together, and through years of interactions in the courtroom, he'd come to know her, but their conversations were always on the surface, never quite touching on anything personal. He only knew snippets about her past—that she was adopted by a cold-hearted couple when she was a baby, never met her birth father before he passed, and her birth mother was a convicted killer. He knew her as a hard worker, a woman who put her career in the State's Attorney's Office before everything else, but he didn't know what was behind the façade.

"How are you feeling?" Hunter softened. "Are you ok in here?"

"As well as expected," Michelle drew a deep breath. "But ok."

She looked up at him again, and they paused for a second, each aware of what the other was thinking. As a defense attorney, Hunter understood that new clients needed to hear a plan, any plan, as long as it sounded half-plausible and would end their torment as soon as possible. But Michelle Law wasn't just any client. She knew the process inside out, and any spin on the truth would appear condescending and demeaning.

"Usually, I'd spend this time taking the client through the bond court process, talking about the next steps, but I don't need to do that for you," Hunter said. "So, we should use this time productively. While everything is still fresh, we should start with exactly what happened. Start from the very beginning and try not to leave anything out."

"The body they found was—" Michelle began, but Hunter cut her off.

"No, please," he said. "Right from the very beginning. Right now, I'm not interested in what's in the police report. I'm not interested in what they have on file. What I'm interested in is what you can tell me. It's important we discuss this case as early as possible while everything is still fresh in your mind. I need to hear it from you. Everything. No matter how minor or how insignificant you think it is. All of it, Michelle, or this won't end up the way you hope."

She sat up straight, as if her strength had suddenly awoken. Her face turned to concentration as she tried to go back into the recesses of her memories, not an easy task for a woman who'd experienced such a traumatic episode.

"That afternoon, I was working in the office, and a young man I'd been working with, twenty years my junior, came past and asked if I wanted to grab a drink with him. I was flattered, you know? He was young, and handsome, and charming, and he'll be successful one day. He dressed well and smelled like heaven. How could I say no to that?"

"But you've been sober for years."

"That's right. I've been sober ever since my birth mother was locked up." She drew a long breath. "She's back here, you know? In Cook County Jail. I haven't seen her yet, but I'll probably get a chance to see her soon."

"Don't get too comfortable. We'll apply for bail, and given what's in this report, it's a fifty-fifty chance we'll get it."

She swallowed. "Thanks, but you don't need to make me feel better. Based on what I know, I don't like our chances."

The woman in the cubicle next to them raised her

voice, yelling at her lawyer that he was a drunken piece of trash, until the guards stepped forward. Under threat from the guards, the woman sat back and lowered her voice, but the tension remained in the dimly lit room.

"Why don't you just continue to tell me what happened?" Hunter lowered his voice. "A handsome young man asked you out for a drink. What was his name?"

"Callum Strauss."

Hunter's eyes narrowed. "Callum Strauss, that works for Walter Charman?"

"You know him?"

"We met in passing this morning," Hunter said. "Go on."

"He was always around the State's Attorney's Office, working with Charman. Charman is so connected, and Callum was following him around like a little lost puppy." She blinked back a tear. "I didn't know it at the time, but he'd just broken up with his girlfriend. That's who they found dead in the trunk of my car. Amanda Ford. She was beaten and suffocated, they told me. I thought Callum asked me out for a drink, to, well, you know. I was flattered. I don't often get asked out on dates, and he was so charming."

"And did you end up getting that drink?"

"We did," she nodded. "At the Five Cocktails Lounge Bar in River North. I should've known that I couldn't just have one drink. I should've known better. I'd struggled for years with getting sober, and I should've known better than to think I could have just one glass of wine. It's never just one glass."

"What happened next?"

"I don't know." She shook her head. "I know that a solid alibi is the quickest way out of this mess, something watertight and able to stand up to any scrutiny, but I've got nothing. I don't remember anything. I'm an idiot. I should've known better." Her fists clenched into balls, and her jaw tightened. "After we arrived at the bar, we had maybe two or three gin and tonics over the course of a couple of hours before things get hazy."

"Hazy?"

"Hazy, as in my memories of the later part of the night don't seem real."

"Were you drunk?"

Michelle looked away and didn't respond.

"Michelle?" Hunter pressed.

"I don't know if I was... I really don't. But I remember nothing past that third gin and tonic. I'm an idiot. I shouldn't have done it." She clenched her right fist and tapped it against her forehead. "What I can tell you is that the drinks I remember having were not enough to tip me over the edge, not by a long way."

"Are you saying you were drugged?"

She hesitated to answer, taking her fist away from her head and staring down at it. "When I used to drink, I had a problem with blackouts. I used to tell myself that I'd have just one drink after work, and then all of a sudden, it was 5am, and I'd passed out on the couch with a bottle of spirits as a pillow. That night with Callum, all I know is one moment we're having a drink, having a laugh, and the next thing I can recall is lying on a park bench in the early hours of the morning, and my head's pounding, and there's a bottle of cheap vodka next to me."

"Go on," Hunter said as she paused again.

"So, I woke up, got my bearings, and somehow managed to make it back to my car. I remember that. I knew I couldn't drive, so I jumped in the driver's seat and fell asleep. I got a phone call from a source that I've used several times, Jake Berkeley, and that woke me up. He said something about a contact, but I didn't really hear him."

"And who is Jake Berkeley?"

"An ex-felon I've been using as a contact with drug cases. He calls me sometimes with information."

"And what happened after the phone call?"

"I fell back to sleep and woke up about 7am. Once I realized where I was, I drove out of that parking lot, and I made it a block away from the bar before a cop pulled me over. He said he pulled me over because I was driving erratically. Then he says there's blood coming from my trunk. He pulls his gun, I step out, and that's when he found a dead body in my car."

"Was your car in the parking lot all night?"

She nodded. "That's right. I drove there with Callum after work."

Hunter quietly tapped a finger on the table as he considered her situation. He watched as Michelle's body language changed for a split second, something she wasn't quite ready to share temporarily springing forward. It didn't take long for her to regain control.

"All I know is I should've been more than capable of handling the drinks I had, and yet I somehow passed out with no memory of what happened." She punched her fist against her forehead again. "I can't even remember leaving the bar in the first place. The cops said that the bartender told them that Callum and I had left together, and I had a bottle of vodka in my hands. I can't believe I was so stupid."

"Do you take any other medication? Anything that could interact with the alcohol?"

Michelle shook her head. "Not now. I used to, but I haven't needed to in years."

"What about recreational drugs? Ever do any?"

"Alcohol was more than enough for me, thank you," Michelle said. "I didn't have room for more."

"Did the cops submit you to a rape-kit test when they brought you in?"

"I insisted on it, but nothing was detected."

"And a drug test?"

"I did one, but there was no evidence of anything other than alcohol."

Hunter drew a breath. "GHB is a well-known date-rape drug. It only has a urine test window of twelve hours," he looked at his watch. "Which, given the time, the drug would've already been out of your system. However, we can test hair follicles for up to a month later, but it's unreliable, with only a twenty-five percent accuracy rate."

"If there's a chance, I need it done."

The woman in the cubicle next to them started screaming again, breaking their concentration and filling the air with more tension. She screamed that she was innocent, that the cop who arrested her was trying to seduce her, and that she had the right to walk out of the prison. The older attorney did his best to settle her, but the woman's rage continued until the guards stepped forward. Two guards grabbed the woman, but she yelled louder, her desperate voice reverberating around the small room.

Once they took her outside, slamming the door shut behind them, Hunter turned back to Michelle.

"Do you need anything?"

"Just get me out of here," she said, then turned to look up at him. "And thanks. Thank you for helping me."

"I owe you one," Hunter replied. "I'll get started on the bail hearing, but I can't make any promises. We'll be called in the next two hours."

He gave her a nod, picked up his briefcase, and stood confidently.

He turned and walked to the door, waiting a moment for the guard to let him out before stepping out into the corridor. With the door closed behind him, he stopped to lean against the wall. He threw his head back, looked up to the ceiling, and took a moment to calm himself.

With what he knew about the case, with the evidence he'd already seen, they had little chance of winning.

<u>CHAPTER 3</u>

CENTRAL BOND Court in Chicago moved fast.

It had to. There was a seemingly endless line of citizens desperate to tell their story before a judge. There was always another murderer to consider, always another violent gang member's case to review, always another sexual predator's charges to assess.

Consolidating all of Chicago's felonies at the George N Leighton Criminal Courthouse, in the neighborhood of Little Village, twenty-five minutes from Downtown, made it easier for lawyers, judges, and assistants to work, but it also transported the worst of the city into one location, creating a melting pot of anger and violence. Chicago had more than its fair share of dangerous felons, and they all needed their day in court.

Prosecutor Pradesh Baron lingered in the hallway outside Courtroom 101, leaning against the wall opposite the courtroom doors, waiting for his chance to protect the system. The courthouse hallway was busy, filled with the echoing sound of shoes tapping on the marbled floors. Baron ignored all the frantic action and focused on a file, drumming his finger on the cover while he read through the details.

"Morning, Pradesh," Hunter said as he approached and then saw the name on the top corner of the file. "You have Michelle Law's case?"

"I do." He looked at Hunter, and as a fellow alumnus of the University of Chicago Law School, he shook Hunter's hand firmly. "And I guess that she's asked you to defend her?"

"She has."

Pradesh Baron was an Asian-Indian prosecutor with an attention to detail few others could match. Coming from a family with a background built on hard work and dedication, he carried himself in a way that exuded professionalism. He was short, thin, and had a thick mustache that looked like it had been shampooed, conditioned, and brushed daily. His cologne was punchy, almost offensive, and his blue suit was crease-free and spotless.

As a career prosecutor, Baron developed a reputation as one of the calmest operators in the business, despite his daily dealings with murderers, thieves, and sexual predators. His relaxed face showed no signs of stress, despite the seventy-five-hour weeks and intense pressure of the job.

"This one is tough for the whole office. Michelle Law?" Baron shook his head. "Well, who would've thought this could happen? We all knew she was a loner and a bit of an odd woman, but a killer? Nobody expected that, Hunter. I couldn't believe it myself. It's always sad when high-profile people fall off the wagon like this. We're all under so much pressure, and so much media scrutiny, that I can understand why she snapped. She was even receiving death threats thanks to the case about your father. That takes its toll. It can drive a person to do some very strange things."

"She hasn't been found guilty yet," Hunter said as

he stepped towards the courtroom doors. "Right now, she's still an innocent woman."

"You don't believe that, do you?" Baron stepped closer. "You've talked to her. You've looked into her eyes. You know she's got a violent streak in her. You know she could've done this."

Hunter didn't answer, stepping through the doors into the frantic nature of Bond Court. Lawyers and assistants pushed past, stepping forward to file their client's cases. Judge Wallace moved through case after case, and the lawyers struggled to keep up with the long line of arrestees waiting outside in lock-up. The air was electric, filled with hustle and bustle, tension and anxiety. Lawyers spoke in hushed tones in the back of the courtroom, trying to hammer out a deal, the judges and bailiffs talked loudly, trying to figure out which case was next, but the long line of defendants were quiet, too scared even to cough.

"Criminal Case 22-CR-7515." The bailiff at the front of the courtroom called out, his voice booming across the room, trying to be heard over the hum of the busy courtroom.

Hunter followed Baron to the front of the room, stepping through the waist-high gate, as Michelle Law was escorted into the dock. Judge Wallace greeted them and then exhaled as he read the file. He turned to look at the defendant, her head low and black hair draped over her face, trying to disguise herself from the shame and embarrassment of standing in the dock. Judge Wallace confirmed the defendant's name and asked the lawyers to identify themselves. They did so, and he moved to the next stage in the process.

"I assume you both have arguments prepared before I make a determination?" Judge Wallace asked.

"And if you do, please make it brief. We have many cases to move through today."

"We have an argument prepared, Your Honor," Baron's response was fast. His tone was callous, and he avoided looking at Michelle. "The State moves to request that bail is denied. This is a violent and callous murder of a young woman, and it deserves to be treated the same as any other murder of this nature. We all know the defendant is an employee of the State's Attorney's Office, and we cannot be seen to hand out favors to our own. We have evidence that she intended to commit this act, and she should not be allowed to walk the streets. We must treat this act as we would any other murder of this nature."

"That's extremely provocative language, Your Honor," Hunter argued. "Ms. Law has never been charged with a crime and is a respected member of the Cook County State's Attorney's Office. In this case file, I see no eyewitnesses to the event, there's no video footage recorded as evidence, and I'm yet to see a motive put forward by the State. Ms. Law is a prosecutor, a graduate of Chicago Law School, and has great admiration and respect for the justice system. We ask that bail be set at $100,000."

"Your Honor, this is a murder case, and Ms. Law is clearly a flight risk. She has access to funds, a passport, and is a regular traveler to the Bahamas. She's a flight risk, and we cannot allow her to skip the country before her trial. We must ensure that she faces the consequences of her actions. We cannot be lenient in this case."

"Ms. Law is anything but a flight risk," Hunter continued. "She's a member of the Bar Association, a dedicated representative of the law, and, through her tireless commitment to justice, she has built deep ties to this community. She's no flight risk."

"All valid statements, Mr. Hunter." Judge Warren read over the file in front of him. He grunted and huffed. "However, the prosecution has a point. The court cannot be seen handing out favors to their own. Considering all this, I will set the 'D' Bond at five hundred thousand dollars, with the conditions that the defendant surrenders her passport, has an electronic monitor fitted, and will have a curfew to be set at 7pm. She may continue to work, if required; however, she's not to leave the state of Illinois."

"Thank you, Your Honor," Hunter said.

Judge Warren dismissed them, and turned to the bailiff, who then called the next case number.

Hunter looked across to Michelle Law in the dock and offered her a nod. She didn't respond. Her cold eyes were staring straight at Pradesh Baron, focused on the man who had just tried to keep her behind bars. Her jaw was tight, her shoulders were raised, and her fists were clenched.

When asked by the bailiff to move on, Hunter closed the folder in front of him, questioning how well he really knew the woman standing in the dock.

CHAPTER 4

WAITING FOR the 'D' Bond paperwork to be processed seemed to take longer than anything Michelle had experienced. Minutes seemed like hours, lost in the vast vacuum of prison time.

Before she had the chance to absorb the judge's decision, and process why Pradesh Baron was so determined to see her remain behind bars, she'd been herded back into a holding cell, and then pushed and prodded as they moved her to the release center. While she waited in her cell, she could see officers walking back and forth behind the main desk, glaring at her like she was a piece of trash.

Her headache was all-consuming, helped in no part by the abrasive environment around her, from the smells of stale body odor and fresh urine, to the bright fluorescent lights near blinding her. But worse than the smells, worse than the sights of pain, were the sounds, the endless groans, the yells of the mentally ill screaming for assistance. The place was bustling with activity, yet Michelle had never felt more alone than she did waiting for her release.

After two hours, she was pushed through to a processing room where her ankle bracelet was fitted. The officer who attached the monitoring device on her leg had the empathy of a brick, ignoring

Michelle's whimper when the skin on her ankle was pinched between the clasps. As she returned to her previous holding cell, she wondered whether a noticeable limp would develop because of the extra weight. A woman staring at her through the window of her holding cell jeered, then licked the glass. Michelle ignored her.

It took a further three hours to be processed, five hours in total since her bail decision, and after being thrown out the doors of the jail without a care for her safety, she struggled to find a taxi. As the night set in, she was approached by numerous men outside the prison gates, each offering a ride home for a long list of sexual favors. Michelle did her best to ignore them, walking to the nearest main road and hailing a cab. Many cabs slowed, but when they spotted her ankle bracelet, they continued. When a cab finally stopped, she questioned whether it was a legitimate cab at all—the taxi company's name and logo had been mostly scraped off, the side-view mirror was missing, and the back seat was ripped in five different places. She knew it was a risk getting into the cab, but after the day she had, she was defeated, with very little fight left in her.

After the driver told her how pretty she was, numerous times, Michelle made it back to her apartment in the West Loop, a stone's throw from Downtown, without further incident.

She had spent one night behind bars before her bail hearing, and she felt like it was one night too many. She spent the entire time on edge, watching as the other inmates sized her up, appearing like they were ready to pounce on her at any moment. She was surprised that she came through the night with no injuries.

At the front entrance to her apartment building, embarrassment crept up again as she imagined her face splashed on every news bulletin in the city. She wondered which photo the media outlets would use—her profile picture from the State's Attorney's Office, a professional shot, or would they scrape through their records and find the worst picture of her, one that made her look like a killer.

Physically exhausted and mentally drained, she set the feelings aside, thinking of nothing else but cleansing the past day from her skin with a long, hot shower. With her head down, she walked through the foyer to the elevators, avoiding eye contact with a passing resident before she arrived at her floor.

"Michelle?"

The voice jarred her as she walked through the wide hallway to her apartment. She turned to find her neighbor, James Heath, standing inside the doorway to his place. The surprise on his face told Michelle he didn't need filling in on recent events.

"James, hey," she whispered in return. He took a step out into the hallway.

"Are you ok?" he asked. "I saw the news."

"I'm ok. I just need a rest."

Michelle had known James for more than five years. He was the first person she'd met when moving into the upmarket apartment building. He'd introduced himself in much the same way as he now approached her, during one of her many trips past his front door.

At the time, James had also been a recent arrival in the building, freshly divorced from a wife who had found comfort in the arms of another man. He'd introduced his two children the following weekend, twin girls. He had Italian heritage, and it showed in his dark hair, dark eyebrows, and olive skin, but he wasn't traditionally good-looking—his nose was slightly too large for his face, and his jawline was soft, but he was confident. He had a stable job in finance and had climbed high up the corporate ladder. He often worked late, and they sometimes found each other walking into the building at the same time.

Despite never coming out directly and saying it, Michelle felt James' interest in her and, given different circumstances, she may have acted on them. But their lives seemed to be headed in opposing directions, and with Michelle's career demands dominating her days, there wasn't much time left for pursuing relationships.

Michelle's avoidance was also hiding her greatest demon. Self-doubt had haunted her for decades, pushing her towards alcohol for most of her adult years. Her demons had held on tight, and anytime she tried to break free of them, she could hear the call back to alcohol, holding her back from any kind of relationship.

"Listen, I'm making some pasta for dinner and—"

"No, thank you, James." She barely looked at him, that in itself sending heat through her cheeks. She didn't want to be alone, loathed it, in fact, but she stood accused of murder, the evidence firmly shackled to her ankle, and any company would only make things worse.

"You sure? I've made plenty," he called after her, unwilling to give in to defeat. "I can drop some past. I'm sure you don't want to cook."

"I'm ok. I have some leftovers in the fridge," Michelle said over her shoulder, already feeling the emotions boiling to the surface. "Control it," she whispered as the first tear broke free. She ignored the tear, thrust the key into place, and angrily forced the door handle down.

Before she stepped inside, James called out a final offering, a last-minute message of hope. "I'm here if you need anything."

Michelle didn't answer, instantly hating herself for it as she stepped inside and closed the door behind her. As if trying to lock her own pain out in the corridor, she slid the secondary lock across, ensuring the door was firmly secured.

Before she had a chance to step further into the apartment, a second tear rolled down her cheek, followed by a third. The emotions began to bubble up inside her, and as her legs began to give out, she leaned her back against the door and slid down to the floor. Sobs rocked her body, the tears falling freely as the emotions finally surfaced in a torrent of grief.

She wiped her eyes with the sleeve of her shirt and looked at the emptiness of her apartment.

The fifth-floor dwelling could've been photographed for a stylish living magazine—the slick glass dining table, the black Swedish leather lounge, the expensive, and recently redesigned, kitchen. It was open plan living at its best, with the living room, dining room, and kitchen effortlessly blended into one large space with high ceilings. The apartment smelled of cleaning products, it always did, without a speck of dust to be seen. The appliances on the kitchen counter were stainless steel, yet spotless, the walls were covered in art, and the windows were sparkling and streak free.

It was a nice place, almost perfect, but at what

cost? More than monetary, Michelle thought, she sacrificed everything to have the perfect home. Her focus had been on success, on winning, going further in her career, but at the end of the day, when it all meant nothing, the reality of her choices hit hard.

Her mind gave in to the nightmares revolving around inside, the loneliness, embarrassment, fear, anxiety, all swirling through a storm of panic and uncertainty. Yes, she wanted James to hold her close. Yes, she needed his arms around her, to reassure her that things would be ok. But as she sat with her face hidden, legs pulled close against her chest, all Michelle could do was give in to her torment.

People would give up everything to lead the kind of lifestyle she'd achieved through hard work and dedication. With a beautiful apartment, a nice car, and a career most could only dream of, on the outside, she looked successful. Her life looked perfect. Admirable. But after two decades of her career, it was finally sinking in that professional success was not the path to happiness.

With nobody to share her triumphs with, with nobody to comfort her when she was down, it all felt like nothing more than display windows at an expensive department store. All her achievements were right there in front of her, and yet, somehow, happiness still felt out of reach.

There was no shower that night. After stumbling back to her feet, Michelle made her way through the dark apartment, dropped onto the bed, curled into a ball, and cried for a long time. The shadows helped shield her from the outside world, and only when she finally drifted off to sleep a little after 5am that morning did the apartment fall back into silence.

CHAPTER 5

PRIVATE INVESTIGATOR Ray Jones pumped out his fiftieth push-up, pushing hard to reach the last one in his fifth set. The morning sun had burned through a thick layer of gray clouds, bathing the outdoor gym equipment in bright light, filling the air with summer warmth. Jones loved the outdoors. Even in summer, even when the heat and humidity was really starting to bite, he preferred to be outside.

Next to Lake Michigan, Burnham Park was situated along the edge of the waterfront, hugging the shore south of the city. A calm refuge away from the chaos of Downtown, the space was one of the four parks that were part of the Chicago Lakefront Trail, an 18-mile-long path for walking, jogging, skateboarding, and cycling, constantly busy in the warmer months.

Jones stood and stretched his arm over his shoulder before jumping on the chin-up bars and pumping out another set, pulling his 260-pound muscular frame towards the bar. The heavy metal music blared in his earphones, ensuring his energy level stayed high, and his yellow tank-top had patches of sweat.

After he finished another set of chin-ups, he stretched again, watching as a BMW sedan pulled into the parking space next to the gym equipment. His friend and colleague, Tex Hunter, stepped out, dressed in a fitted European suit. Hunter stopped, looked up to the sky, and then removed his jacket and tie, throwing them back into the car.

"Always exercising," Hunter called out, rolling up his sleeves as he approached. "It's good to see you, Ray. How's life?"

"Life's good, but something happened to my neighbor this morning," Jones said. "Cops were all over the place."

"Oh yeah? What happened?"

"He got caught stealing from his job as a road worker," Jones smiled. "I didn't think he was a thief, but when I looked over the fence, all the signs were there."

"That's good," Hunter laughed. "How's Trixie, the new girlfriend?"

"I had to break up with her."

"Already? You'd only been dating her a few weeks. What went wrong?"

"She opened the car door for me."

"What's wrong with that?" Hunter asked, putting his hands in his pockets and leaning against the chin-up bar. "It's a modern world. Women can be courteous as well."

"Yeah, well," Jones chuckled. "It would've been a nice gesture if we hadn't been going twenty-five miles an hour."

"Ha!" Hunter laughed again, slapping him on the shoulder.

Jones laughed with him before he wiped the sweat from his brow with the back of his hand and then reached for his water bottle, taking a long gulp.

"I've got a folder for you about Amanda Ford," he said, picking up his gym bag and throwing it over his shoulder. "It's in the truck."

"Find out much?" Hunter asked as he followed the investigator. "Anything that could point us in the right direction?"

"A few things of interest. The preliminary information is mostly about how she was working for political lobbyist Walter Charman, and he's certainly an interesting character. Charman's name comes with a lot of warnings, but I can see why people take the risk and work for him." Jones fished the keys out of his bag and unlocked his truck. "Many of his previous interns have gone on to lucrative jobs, not the least of which includes both state and federal politics. He's made a lot of high-level connections that way. If I had to say one thing about him, it's that he's connected all the way to the top."

"Explains his arrogance," Hunter said. "I had a run-in with him yesterday, and he warned me off defending Michelle."

Jones opened the passenger-side door, dropped his bag on the seat, and grabbed a folder. Turning back to Hunter, he handed it over. "I've got all the preliminary information about Amanda Ford in there. By the looks of things, she had a good life. Nice parents, nice middle-class upbringing, nice friends. She had a decent social media profile, but nothing that points to any trouble. She studied political science and was top of her class at the University of Chicago. That's how she landed the intern job with Charman, and her boyfriend of a few months, Callum Strauss, was also working for Charman. And from my initial look, she had no previous interactions with your client, although I'll have to dig deeper into Michelle's past."

Hunter opened the folder, placed it on the hood of Jones' truck, and glanced across several reports on Amanda Ford. "The connection to Charman is going to present a problem. He has a lot of connections, and he can be very influential. It means it's going to be hard to source information about her work, because everything he does is closed off." Hunter looked back down at the top report, a small photo of the victim staring back at him. "How tough is the internship?"

"It's a wonder any of the interns make it out of there unscarred. Just in her group alone, six keen interns were vying for the top job, with second prize a very rare thing." Jones reached across and slid the top pages aside, revealing a second report with Callum Strauss's photo attached. "That's the kid she'd been dating for the past few months." He paused, ran his hand over his bald head, and then continued. "You know, I always find it interesting when people who work together begin dating."

"Interesting how?"

"Strauss and Amanda Ford were in direct competition with each other for the top job."

"You think one of them tried to get the upper hand somehow?"

"From what I could find on social media, it looks as if Strauss was the one who started the relationship. He might've been trying to get the upper hand on her. He posted a picture of them together with the caption, 'I've been trying to get this date for months.'"

"Callum spread his wings further than just

Amanda Ford."

Jones looked at Hunter, his head tilting curiously. "How so?"

"It was Callum Strauss who joined Michelle for drinks on the night of Ford's murder."

"You mean they went out for drinks that night?" Jones raised his eyebrows. "Coincidence?"

"I don't think it's a coincidence that the victim's ex-boyfriend just happened to be drinking with the suspected murderer the night his ex-girlfriend was killed."

"Sounds a little too convenient to me."

Hunter closed the folder and looked back at Ray. "Anything else?"

"Yeah, you might want to look into a man named Jake Berkeley. He's an ex-con, now working as a private investigator." Jones nodded. "I'd heard that Michelle Law was using him as a contact. He was arrested a year ago but dealt out on a drug charge, and from what I've heard, she's been using him again and again as a contact on the street. I can't imagine he was happy about it because no private investigator wants to get used by the State's Attorney's Office. If there was something going on in Michelle's life that we don't know about, then he may be able to help."

There was a pause in their conversation as a police cruiser slowly drove past the two men. The officers inside appeared to check them out, slow a little more, then turn their attention to a couple walking along the path beside the road. Hunter watched the cruiser continue before turning back to Jones.

"Think she's guilty?" Jones asked. "Think she snapped when she found out about Callum's ex-girlfriend? Perhaps she wanted the young man all to herself?"

Hunter paused and looked back out at Lake Michigan. "I don't know. After what she did for my father, I hope she's innocent, but I also don't really know her. I don't know if she could've done it."

"Then start with Berkeley," Jones said. "He'll be the person who could answer a lot of questions for you."

CHAPTER 6

HUNTER LOVED the people of his city—mix big-city hustle with small-town generosity, and you get a Chicagoan. Even the elite had a rust-belt blue-collar edge to mix with their chic swagger.

Summer brought out the best in the people of Chicago, with smiles and laughter abundant on every block. Every time the sun was out, the residents rushed out of their homes, desperate to soak in the vitamin D before the inevitable long winter set in again. And as Frank Sinatra once put it, 'Chicago is why I grin like a clown. It's my kind of town.'

But there was a dark side to Chicago—everyone knew it, and everyone did their best to ignore it.

Michelle Law dealt with the dark side of the city every single day of her working life. Every month, she'd see more gruesome, horrid, and repulsive behavior than most people experience in a lifetime. She saw the worst the city had to offer, coming face to face with gang members, mobsters, and cartels. That had to affect someone eventually, Hunter reasoned.

As Hunter followed the flow of traffic towards Berkeley's office west of Downtown, a recurring thought continued to rise, perhaps to draw his attention to a fact he'd overlooked. It was the expression Michelle had when she spoke about her alcoholism.

He remembered the quote, 'Alcohol is a well-documented reaction to unresolved grief,' and from what he knew of Michelle's past, she had more than her fair share of grief. While he saw a hint of shame in her eyes, there was something else there, the woman doing her best to hide another emotion from him.

Was she guilty? Her birth mother was a convicted killer, so was it genetically in her blood to do the same? He'd seen court cases where the prosecution wheeled out genetic specialists to convince the jury that there was a genetic link between murderers, trying to convince the audience of a pseudo-science that had little backing.

Hunter had faced those questions all his adult life. He'd seen it in the way people looked at him, in the way people treated him, and in the way people feared him. When he was ten years old, his father was arrested and convicted of the murders of eight teenage girls, and his life changed after that moment. Mothers took their children off his sports teams, his friends were forced to move schools to get away from him, and people in the shops refused to serve him. At only ten, at such a tender young age, his life was forever changed due to his father's conviction.

When he was fifteen, he was approached by a researcher from the University of Chicago who asked to study his brain patterns to see if there were any indications of a murderous intent. His Aunt, who was his guardian at the time, yelled at them and told them never to bother the Hunter family again.

Hunter pulled into a parking lot in the

neighborhood of North Lawndale, a struggling area near the Cook County Jail. He parked between an old white van, which appeared to be lived in, and a twenty-year-old red Chevy sedan, which didn't look road-worthy.

He glanced across the street to where Jake Berkeley's office sat above a tattoo shop, complete with bars across the windows. A large tribal face had been painted on the metallic security shutter covering the tattoo shop's entrance, showing off the tattooist's artistic talent. Looking up and down the street, Hunter could see that all the shops along the strip either had bars, boards, or broken windows. A trash can was overflowing on one side of the entrance to Berkeley's office, and a homeless man had tucked himself in the doorway of an empty shop on the other side.

As he waited in the parking lot across the street, one eye on the second-floor office, Hunter pulled out his cell and typed Berkeley's name into Google, soon staring into the eyes of a private investigator who'd done time for fraud and assault. He shook his head as he wondered why Michelle would put her trust in a man with such a checkered past, especially when her role required nothing but the highest amount of integrity and honesty.

After a ten-minute internet search confirmed he was dealing with a dodgy investigator, Hunter climbed out, locked the car, and crossed towards the single glass door which led up to the second floor. As he crossed the street, the man Hunter had just seen in a news article on Google emerged from the office carrying a half-empty bottle of Jack Daniels with blue tape wrapped around the neck of the bottle.

"Jake Berkeley."

The man stopped, his hand reaching for his hip, no doubt where a concealed weapon hung under his black leather jacket. Berkeley was an older man who looked like he still hit the gym, with a solid jawline and weathered skin. He'd given up trying to save his hair, shaving it into the stubble, the same way he'd left his beard. His nose was crooked, no doubt from a bar fight, and his blue eyes were steely.

"Who's asking?" he stepped forward, then grinned as recognition dawned on his face. "Oh, it's you. Tex Hunter. The famous lawyer that got his killer father out of prison. A lot of people weren't happy that you put a serial killer back on the streets."

"My father was innocent. That's why he got out of prison," Hunter responded. "We proved that in the courts."

"You might've convinced the courts, but you didn't prove it to me. That man killed those girls," Berkeley said, eyeing Hunter's tall figure up and down. "I heard about Michelle Law, and I wondered when you were going to show up here."

"What can you tell me about her?"

"About Michelle? That evil witch is a piece of work. She made me sign a deal to avoid some drug charges and then used it against me every day for the past two years. I'm glad she's out of my life," he spat the words out with venom. "Is she a killer? I'm sure of it. I've seen the look in her eyes. I've seen that look many times, and I'm sure she's a murderer."

Berkeley turned and began walking away from Hunter.

"Wait," Hunter said. "I have questions about Michelle."

"I'm sure you do," Berkeley paused. "But I'm not answering any more questions."

"I need you to answer my questions. And we can either do it here, or we can do it in court."

"You'll subpoena me?" Berkeley turned and smiled. "You lawyers always think you can bully us little guys, don't you? You think we're scared of your courts, like we hold the same sort of value to your system. I'll tell you something, lawyer man, most people don't care about your courts. We think the whole system is a joke. I think you're a joke, and I think Michelle Law is a joke."

"If I subpoena you, you'll have to answer questions under oath. I don't think that's a situation you want to be in." Hunter closed the space between them. "I need to know what Michelle was asking you to do?"

Berkeley raised his chin, squaring up to Hunter.

"I've got nothing for you." He took a step back. "All I can say is that I'm glad she's gone. That State's Attorney's Office was using me. I signed one deal, and then they kept coming back for more. It was killing my work. Everyone knew I was working with them, and nobody wants to hire a snitch. And now, she's gone."

"Berkeley," Hunter was firm. "What were you investigating for Michelle?"

"I can't help you," he snapped. "Michelle Law isn't what I'd consider a high priority. She could've killed the woman, and if she did, she deserves to go to prison. I won't cry about it."

Without bothering to hear Hunter's response, Berkeley turned and continued down the street.

Hunter remained where he stood for a few more

seconds before he headed back to his car. A minute later, he climbed into the driver's seat, and left the troubled streets of North Lawndale behind.

It was clear that Berkeley was withholding information. And he needed to find out what it was.

CHAPTER 7

HUNTER'S MOUTH dropped open the moment his assistant, Esther Wright, walked into the office.

The blonde looked dazzling in her black skirt and white shirt. Somehow, despite being dressed in everyday office wear, she looked like she'd stepped out of the pages of a fashion magazine. The skirt hugged her waist, running down to her knees, highlighting her long legs, and her blonde hair draped just over her shoulders. Her skin was tanned and glowing with health, and her feminine curves were accentuated by the outfit. As she stepped closer, Hunter caught a whiff of her scent, a hypnotic aroma of floral perfume with hints of jasmine.

"Don't be a pervert," Esther smiled broadly when she caught Hunter staring at her legs. "I'm more than a piece of meat, you know?"

"Yes. Of course. Sorry." Hunter swallowed hard, trying to compose himself. "You look amazing, Esther. I just… um, you look…"

"Put you in a courtroom, and you're full of words and wisdom, but when you try to compliment a lady, you turn into a nervous little schoolboy." She smiled and squirmed a little, happy to have impressed him. She pulled a strand of blonde hair behind her ear, and the grin on her face broadened. "But I like that."

Esther Wright had been blessed with the gift of beauty, along with a smile that could make the most hardened crumble, and it had been both a blessing and a curse. While she attracted the attention of just about every man she passed, she struggled to find the right man despite endless attempts at dating. Tex Hunter was that man. Went she first met him in an job interview almost ten years earlier, she knew right then and there that she'd found the right man. It took Hunter a lot longer to realize it. While he felt their connection, while he felt his heart skip a beat each time she stepped into the room, his world had been consumed by the need for justice, pushing his emotions aside for his quest.

When he finally stepped up and asked her out, their connection was like two planets colliding, an explosion of passion, lust, and love.

After five months of dating, they were still in a beautiful honeymoon period, that sweet mist that covered every thought, and Esther was happy she could still take his breath away. She adored him, not only for his looks and charm, but for his unshakeable commitment to honor and integrity.

They stood in awkward silence for a few long moments before she stepped forward, leaned over, and kissed him on the cheek. "I know we said no romance at work, but sometimes you're just too handsome not to kiss."

He tried to contain his smile, but his dimples gave his feelings away.

Since they had started dating, they'd been trying to find the balance between work and home life. Hunter knew in his heart that he had found the one. He knew when he looked at her. He knew it when he heard her speak. He knew when she laughed. Everything about her was perfect—even her constant bad jokes.

"When I caught up with my friend at the bar last night, we met a rich 65-year-old man with a smoking hot 22-year-old wife," Esther smiled. "So, I asked him, 'How did you convince her to marry you?' 'It's simple,' he said. 'I lied about my age.' 'Did you tell her you're 50?' I asked, but he shook his head. '40?' I said. 'It couldn't be younger than that.' 'Nope,' he smiled. 'I told her I was 85.'"

Hunter tried not to smile, but a slight grin escaped his lips.

"Which had me thinking about my age, and now that I'm getting older, I've been thinking about all the people I've lost along the way." Esther stopped and shook her head. "I guess my job as a tour guide wasn't such a good career move."

Hunter grinned, his dimples showing off his smile.

"And just this morning, my friend asked me to pass her a lipstick, but I accidentally passed her a glue stick," Esther started laughing at her own joke. "She's still not talking to me."

Hunter laughed and moved back to his desk.

"I thought you could do with a laugh, given what we're about to face," Esther smiled. "It's going to be a rough morning."

"Almost time?" he asked, looking at his watch.

Esther nodded. "Any minute now."

"If there was one part of the job I could do without, it's this."

"Tough, huh?"

"Tough is an understatement. It's only been a few days since the funeral, so I can't imagine how raw their pain must be. I know crimes don't exist without

49

victims, but every victim has a family, and it's normally the family who brings the greatest stress with them."

"You didn't have to meet with them," Esther said. "You could've said no."

"I know," Hunter sighed. "But they've lost their only daughter. I should listen to what they have to say. It's the right and honorable thing to do. "

Before Esther could continue, the door to the reception area of their office opened. Esther left Hunter's office and went to greet the visitors. A moment later, she walked them through to where Hunter was waiting and made the introductions.

"Please, take a seat," he offered, standing up and waiting for the pair to accept his invitation.

In their late sixties, the couple still had a bounce in their steps. Ian Ford looked like he still swam two miles a day, and Valerie Ford looked like she could still lace up her shoes and run a sub-four-hour marathon. They were dressed well—Ian in a white shirt and black trousers; Valerie in jeans and a blue shirt, but their expressionless faces spoke of an unspeakable pain.

"Thank you for seeing us, Mr. Hunter," the father said. From his heavy tone, Hunter could tell the grief remained raw. "We had Amanda later in life, and we never expected we'd be the ones to bury her…" He stopped for a moment and sat down, holding back the emotions. "We never expected we'd see her pass. After having her in our late-forties, we thought she would outlive us by many, many years."

"I understand," he said. "Can we get you a coffee?"

Ian shook his head. "No, thank you. I'd like to get

straight to the point, if you don't mind. Valerie hasn't been feeling well, and I'd really like to get her home." Ian looked at his wife with sympathetic eyes, and she squeezed his hand in return. She was sitting in the chair opposite Hunter's desk, leaning forward and clutching her arms across her chest. "Valerie's got cluster migraines," Ian continued. "She hasn't had them for a decade, but Amanda's death has brought them back with a vengeance. What we're going through is still very raw."

"I can't imagine how hard it is for you right now." Hunter's tone was soft. "How can I help you, Mr. Ford?"

"You can help us by walking away from this case."

Hunter drew a deep breath. He knew that statement was coming, but he had to respect their grief. "No parents should ever go through what you're enduring right now, but this matter needs to be dealt with in open court. This is a long process that you'll go through, and it's only been a week."

"We buried her yesterday," Valerie whispered. "Do you know what that's like? We had to bury the child that we thought would grow up with hopes and dreams and wishes and goals. Now it's all gone. It's all gone. And it's all that jealous lawyer's fault. We don't want you defending her."

"What Valerie is trying to say," Ian squeezed Valerie's hand tighter. "Is that we respected and admired the determination you brought to your father's case. We watched it all, and we even remember his first trial in the 80s. We know about your family history, and your father, and how he spent thirty-six years in prison for a crime he didn't commit. And we also know how good you are in the courtroom. We've seen what you can do. We watched it on television."

"Thank you, but—"

"I know you're a defense lawyer, but I also know that you're driven by honor and justice," Ian continued. "You're a man of integrity. I can see that. I saw it on television, and I can see it now. Valerie and I are here because we think we can appeal to your sense of integrity and ask you to walk away from defending our daughter's killer."

"Mr. Ford—" Hunter tried, but again his words were cut off by the grieving father.

"We need justice for our baby girl, and justice will be to see her murderer go to prison forever. You're a good lawyer, Mr. Hunter, but Michelle Law murdered our child because she was jealous of her. We need to see her behind bars. Can you understand that?"

Hunter nodded, doing his utmost to comfort the father as best he could. The man was heartbroken, and grieving people didn't always see the sensible side of an argument.

And no pain was as commanding as a grieving parent.

"I understand what you're saying, Mr. Ford, and I'm very sorry for your loss. Yes, somebody murdered your daughter, but locking an innocent woman up for that crime will not bring Amanda back. As a defense lawyer, my job is to make sure that the truth comes out." As Hunter spoke, he watched a tear slowly roll down Valerie's face, her eyes turning down into her lap. "My team and I are investigating several leads, and I can assure you we won't—"

"Is Callum Strauss one of those leads?"

"You've met Mr. Strauss?"

Valerie nodded as Ian took over once again. "Twice, and I can honestly say it was twice too many times."

"You didn't like him?"

"Not from the moment I laid eyes on him."

"Why was that?"

"Amanda wasn't herself around him. Reserved mostly, as if she couldn't let go. She was such a happy girl before she started that internship alongside Callum. They were dating for a month before something happened with Callum, and she changed overnight." He snapped his fingers. "Our happy girl disappeared one night, and we never saw her happy again."

"What makes you think it was because of Callum?" Hunter asked his questions to them both, but Ian took each as his own, continuing to control the conversation while Valerie sat quietly beside him.

"Because we know our daughter. She was a free spirit, loved to laugh, always looking at things positively, but when Callum was in the room, she was quiet, barely raised more than a smile, and just sat by as he took the floor."

"If it helps set your mind at ease, yes, Callum is someone who we're looking into." Hunter leaned forward, folded his arms on the desk, and lowered his voice a little. It was time to be firm, but fair, with the grieving parents. "My job is to defend my client. That's an essential part of the justice system. If the prosecution has the evidence that proves Michelle Law is the culprit, then nothing will stop the process, but if there's doubt, if there's a hole in the evidence, then that needs to be investigated."

"You're not going to change your mind, are you?"

Ian leaned forward, staring at Hunter. "You're going to defend that jealous killer, aren't you?"

"That's my job."

"Then we won't waste any more time here," Ian stood, the emotions becoming too much for him. "Valerie, it's time for us to go."

Valerie nodded to Hunter, wiped a tear from her cheek, and then followed her husband to the door. Ian stopped for a long moment at the door before he turned back to Hunter. "Whatever you do, remember that it's the 'justice' system. Don't betray that."

CHAPTER 8

DESPITE ALL the record-keeping, despite all the cameras, despite all the information available online, the greatest way to know a person, to really understand them, was to watch them in their daily routine. Tex Hunter knew that better than most. He followed Callum Strauss, the ex-boyfriend of Amanda Ford, staying half a block behind on the warm Saturday morning, and not for one moment did he like what he saw.

After spending the previous day researching the young man, Hunter had information, he had his history, but that only told part of the story. The son of a surgeon and a housewife, Strauss appeared to be earmarked for a career in politics. He had finished his law degree at the University of Illinois, but he never practiced. From what Hunter had read online, working as an assistant lobbyist for Walter Charman was the quickest way to ensure a career in politics succeeded.

Dressed in a white polo shirt, pink cargo shorts, and boat shoes, it was clear that he'd come from money. His aviator glasses were new, as was his Cartier watch, and his soft and moisturized skin didn't look like it'd experienced a hard day of work in his life.

In Lakeview, a safe and wealthy neighborhood on Chicago's North Side, Callum Strauss walked from his apartment to the nearest café. According to his regularly updated social media profile, it was his usual Saturday morning routine. The morning air was fresh, heavy with the scent of summer dew, implying that fall wasn't far away.

Hunter followed Strauss from his apartment, staying far enough back not to be noticed. Hunter watched as Strauss snapped at numerous people during the walk, all in sparks of arrogant filled rage. The first unfortunate person to feel his rage was a woman talking with someone on the phone, smiling as she walked in a happy daze, who accidentally wandered into the middle of the sidewalk. Strauss could've easily stepped past her, but he held his ground and bumped into the woman, followed by a tirade of cruelty about her looks.

His second outburst exploded when a taxi pulled up to the light, stopping slightly over the line. Strauss slapped the hood, pointed his finger at the driver, and then told him how he should learn to drive if he wanted to drive 'in this country' before telling him to 'go back where he came from.' The third, and loudest outburst, came when a homeless woman dared to ask him for a dollar. The disgust on his face was clear, cowering away from her before he told her to move to the south side of Chicago, where 'trash belongs.'

After he ordered a coffee to go from the stylish café, Strauss stepped back onto the sidewalk, only to be confronted by Hunter's looming figure. Hunter waited, leaning against a parking meter, hands in pockets, and raised his eyebrows.

"You again," Strauss grumbled once he had

regained his composure. "I imagine this isn't a coincidence."

"No, it's not, Callum."

"I've got nothing to say to you." Strauss waved him off and began walking again. "Anything that needs to be said is in the police report."

Hunter knew it wouldn't take much to light a fire in the spoiled brat, and it wouldn't take much to produce an angry response—all he needed to do was prod the right area, and he wouldn't be able to control his rage.

"You're a smart man, Callum, but you're not playing this one wisely," Hunter called out. "I'm sure your father wouldn't think your actions are too smart."

"My father?" Strauss swung around. "What do you know about fathers? Not much, I bet." He tried to compose himself, taking a deep breath and looking at Hunter. "Are you going to frame me? Is that what this is? I'm going to be your dummy on the defense stand? You're going to use me as your target in a third-party culpability play? Well, I've got news for you—I've got a law degree, and I'm not going to be fooled like that. I'm too smart to become involved in your defense. Save your time and go harass someone else."

Hunter didn't reply as Strauss stared him down. After a moment of hesitation, Strauss took another step toward him.

"But you'd know about framing people, wouldn't you, Tex Hunter? Here you are—the son of a serial killer—trying to get me to frame myself. I saw what you and Michelle Law did in that courtroom together. You guys are a team, but I don't want any part of it."

"Where did you go after you left Michelle in the bar that night?"

"Home."

"Can anyone verify that?"

"No. I wouldn't think so."

"You just left Michelle Law, a woman you asked out on a date, smashed drunk in a bar?"

"We left the bar together, and we were walking through Ward Park, near the river, but she was behaving erratically, and I'd had enough, so I left her behind. I don't know what she did after that."

"How honorable."

Strauss scoffed and turned away again, throwing the lid of his coffee cup onto the edge of the sidewalk, even though a trash can was barely fifteen feet away.

"Ever use GHB, Callum?" Hunter called out.

"What?" Strauss stopped and turned back. He walked closer, checking over his shoulder at the people watching them, wondering what was transpiring on the street. Strauss came close and lowered his tone. "Why would I use a date-rape drug?"

"They can test hair follicles for exposure to the drug for up to a month after the event."

Panic swept over the young man's face as he worked through the scenario in his head. Hunter studied him and waited for him to make the next move.

"You need to be careful," Strauss whispered through a clenched jaw and pointed his finger at Hunter. "I work for a powerful man. All I have to do is call him, and you're toast."

"Walter Charman? I don't think he'll risk his neck

for an intern that's only been in the job for a few months."

"I don't need him anyway." The anger was raging through Strauss. He lifted his arm and clenched his fist, waving it pathetically at Hunter. "Don't pry into my business."

Hunter stepped forward. "Unless you want that hand broken, you need to put it down."

Strauss faltered for a moment and then lowered his fist.

Despite his arrogance, Strauss held no fear for Hunter. He could tell the young man was weak; not the sort of weakness that came from never going to the gym, nor the sort of weakness that came from never working a day of manual labor, but the sort of weakness that came from a lack of character.

"Stay away from me." Strauss tried to deliver the threat with a sense of danger, but his voice squeaked a little at the end.

Hunter smiled before Strauss stomped his foot, turned, and walked away.

Hunter waited a few moments, watching Strauss until he walked around the corner of the next block. He returned to his car, pondering the encounter and the man himself.

That Callum Strauss had narcissistic traits was unquestionable. He was impulsive, abusive, and quick to anger—the sort of person who could have lashed out at his ex-girlfriend for daring to speak back to him and then callously dumped the body in the trunk of a car.

If Michelle Law didn't do it, then Hunter had found a new suspect. Hunter wasn't sure what his next move would be, but one thing was clear: he hadn't finished with Callum Strauss yet. Not by a long shot.

CHAPTER 9

TEX HUNTER'S law office was an oasis, a retreat from the busy streets of summer in Chicago.

On the twentieth floor of a Downtown Chicago building, off busy West Jackson Boulevard, it was his second home. It was silent in his office, except for the hum of the air-conditioner and the occasional noise from the other offices on his floor. He liked having a quiet office to escape to, a place to think and let his mind drift over the possibilities of the case.

At the start of the second week in the murder case, Hunter unclipped his cuffs, rolled his sleeves up to his elbows, and opened the file on his desk, trying to focus on the missing pieces of the puzzle.

He spent the first hour of his Monday studying the file, looking for any mistakes in the police report, and when he found none, turned his attention to the witness statements. There were inconsistencies, but they were minor and would be easily explained by the prosecution if he presented a motion to dismiss them. Still, it was worth the shot, and he'd take the chance in due time.

At 10.05am, Pradesh Baron arrived, ready to discuss the case in detail. They greeted each other with a firm handshake and talked casually about the weekend before Baron sat down in the chair opposite

Hunter's large oakwood desk.

"This is a pleasant office, Hunter." Baron's eyes drifted around the room, looking over the law books covering the right wall and the brown leather couch to the left. "There's so much room in here that you could play a game of golf. Set up a putting green and spend your hours honing your skills. I don't have an office like this, but I guess that's the price you pay for chasing real justice. Sometimes, I wish I could sell my morals for cash and become a defense lawyer."

"People pay a lot to make sure they receive a fair trial," Hunter smiled. "Especially when facing made-up charges from within their own department."

"I'm sure." Baron drew a breath and crossed one leg over the other. He sat comfortably in the armchair opposite Hunter, confident in himself and his position. "I'll get to the point then—we've got an offer for Michelle Law. We're putting up a deal under 720 ILCS 5/9-1."

"First-degree murder?"

"She suffocated a twenty-five-year-old woman to death and put her in the trunk of her car, intending to dispose of her body. Michelle had a complete disregard for Amanda Ford's life, and there's no doubt she would've known her actions would lead to her death. There's no sign of a struggle, no marks of any kind on Michelle, so there's no chance you'll get her off on self-defense."

"Sentence?"

"Twenty years, minimum security," Pradesh Baron said, brushing a piece of dust off his knee.

"Starting high?" Hunter raised his eyebrows. "That's standard behavior for your department these days, isn't it?"

"Let's not beat around the bush, Hunter. This is first-degree murder, and your client is looking at a lot longer than that if she's found guilty. This way, we can—"

"I'll take it to Michelle," Hunter said, cutting his opponent off. "But there's no incentive to avoid the courts. Michelle knows how this process works, so we both know what she'll do with the first offer."

"Yes, we do."

"Are you not even willing to put up a deal for second-degree murder and concede that maybe there was intense provocation?"

"At this point, no."

"The courts are busy, Pradesh. The system is at its limits, and there's a long line of people to process. If you present a decent deal, then it's beneficial for everyone. The court system doesn't need any more pressure chasing cases that can be dealt with out of the courtroom."

"Michelle's a prosecutor. She's prosecuted some of the biggest cases we've had in the last ten years. She should be the symbol of justice, but the media are making her into a symbol of crime and corruption. That doesn't look good for our department, and you know she can't get away with a slap on the wrist. The entire city is watching this department now, and you know we have to go hard on the deal."

"A good deal would save your Office a lot of embarrassment. You don't need this case being dragged through the courts, constantly up there on the front page of the paper. It'd be better to offer a good deal, sign it off, and then forget about it."

"You know we can't deal low on this. The media are watching. They're going to run every angle they can of her, and it's not going to be pretty. And if we deal low, then the entire reputation of the hard-working State's Attorney's Office is on the line." Baron looked at the bookshelf, his eyes running over the law books. "And your profile isn't helping the case, Hunter. The media loves you at the moment, and they can't get enough of your family's story. Have you considered whether it would be in Michelle's best interest if you stepped aside?"

"That's Michelle's decision to make."

"Of course." Baron rested his hands on his lap. "How are you going to play this? Being drunk is not a cause for not guilty. Need I remind you that diminished capacity is not a recognized legal defense in the great state of Illinois? You can't plead not guilty on the basis that she blacked out from her voluntary drinking. That will never fly, and you know it."

"What if she was drugged?"

"You'd have to prove it, and you have little chance of that. The blood and urine tests showed nothing but alcohol in her system."

"We're working on that."

"I'm sure you are." Baron sighed again. "I liked Michelle. I did. She had her troubles, but she was a hard-working, career-driven woman. We all liked the way she worked hard. But at what cost did it come at? She sacrificed having a family for her career. She sacrificed love for justice. And that led her to killing a young woman because she was jealous that she had been dating Callum Strauss. That deserves to be punished. She cannot be above the law. Jealousy is not a suitable reason to murder someone."

Hunter sat back in his chair. He smiled. "Thank you for telling me about your strategy for the motive.

At least it's out in the open now."

"Come on, Hunter. You must've known we were going to take that angle. Strauss takes Michelle out for a drink, she finds out he's got an ex-girlfriend he still likes, and then Michelle takes the ex-girlfriend out of the picture. I don't know exactly how it went down, but it's clear that's what happened, and it's clear that will be our strategy." Baron cleared his throat. "Just as we know that you're going to plead not guilty by reason of involuntary drugged condition under 720 ILCS 5/6-3, but it won't work here. There's no evidence that she was anything other than blacked out drunk. She told the arresting officer she blacked out, and that's not a defense. All her drug tests show that she must have been very intoxicated."

"We need a list of everyone in the bar that night. I assume that's in the discovery material."

"Ah," Baron replied. "There's a problem with that. The bar is at the end of an old alley, and they protect their privacy there. That's the point of an expensive bar like this. There's no video footage inside the bar or the surrounding streets, and the bar owner prefers people pay in cash, so there are no credit card records."

"And has he told you who was there that night?"

"No," Baron said. "He's refusing to identify them, which is his right. He did confirm that Michelle and Callum Strauss were drinking there and that Michelle had a lot to drink before they left together around 10pm. He wouldn't confirm anything else."

"Sounds like he's protecting someone."

"Maybe, but he's not a suspect," Baron shrugged. "We have the killer, so whoever else he's protecting is not our concern right now."

Hunter paused, waiting for Baron to put a better offer on the table, as was their usual procedure.

"There's no other offer coming," Baron stood. "Please take this offer to Michelle and encourage her to take the deal. It'd be better for everyone, including the reputation of the State's Attorney's Office. If she just took the deal and admitted responsibility for this terrible incident, we can all go home happy."

"I'll take the deal to her and discuss it." Hunter stood and offered his hand. "But it's her decision, and it's not a good offer."

Baron shook Hunter's hand, turned, and walked out the door.

Hunter waited a moment before he sat back down, the realization becoming clearer that he was fighting against a department that was determined to ensure that they were tougher on their own than anyone else.

He needed a break in the case, and he needed it fast.

CHAPTER 10

MICHELLE LAW buzzed Hunter through to her fifth-floor apartment, waiting by her door as Hunter stepped off the elevator.

She looked disheveled—her hair was messy, the bags under her eyes had grown larger, and her skin looked devoid of all moisture. She wore gray sweatpants and an oversized Prada blue t-shirt, looking like she had no plans to leave her apartment any time soon.

"Tell me they've dropped the case," she said as she waited by the door, arms folded across her chest. "Tell me they've come to their senses and thrown this whole thing out."

"No such luck," Hunter said. "But they offered a deal."

Without a response, Michelle turned and entered her apartment. Hunter followed her through, stepping into the open plan living space, gazing out at the view through the large floor-to-ceiling windows that lead to her small balcony.

"Nice view of the city."

"Not worth it," she whispered as she turned on the coffee machine. "None of this is worth it."

Hunter didn't understand the reference, but he didn't press any harder, instead turning his attention to the rest of the apartment. While his eyes drifted over the place, one thing was clear—there weren't many personal touches in her home, photos included. There was one photo of her birth mother on the bookshelf, along with one photo of her adoptive parents. The five other photos were of landscapes, two of beaches in the Bahamas, two of the hills in Italy, and the fifth was of the Eiffel Tower.

"There's nothing important in those photos," Michelle stated when she saw Hunter looking at the shelf. There was a sting in her voice. "They're just moments from the past, and they mean nothing now. The past is just a forgotten piece of time."

Hunter raised his eyebrows. "How have you been keeping?"

"Like a woman counting down the days until I spend the rest of my life in prison." She shook her head and walked to the edge of the living room, looking out over the city before her. The skyscrapers were reaching up to the blue sky, glittering in the summer sun. "I used to stand here and think about all the ways I was helping this city. That's what kept me going many mornings. How I was contributing to the health of this community." She turned away from the window and moved back to the kitchen, pouring two cups of coffee. "And now, I'm as bad as the rest of them. Have you heard what the media is calling me? 'The Killer Attorney.' What a title. I'll never shake that. Even if I get off this charge, that nickname will stick. I'll hear it walking through the courthouse and from every opposition lawyer."

"We can file several gag orders until the case reaches trial."

"It wouldn't do any good." Michelle shook her

head as she walked back into the room, carrying two mugs. "It'll only bring more attention to the case. The media will focus on what we're trying to suppress, rather than whether I'm innocent."

"Has your memory of that night become any clearer?" Hunter placed his briefcase on the floor and accepted the coffee, blowing the steam off the top. "Anything at all that can help us? It doesn't matter how small."

Michelle sat carefully on the black leather couch, leaning forward with her hands wrapped around her coffee, resting her elbows on her knees. "I was working hard in the afternoon, alone in the office, and then Callum Strauss knocked on the door. We'd been working on a fraud case, and his father had contacts that could help us. When he walked in that afternoon, he started flirting with me, saying things like my hair looked nice and how he loved the confidence of older women. He hooked me in."

"How had your relationship been before that day?"

"Strained, I would say. I don't enjoy having lobbyists like Charman in our offices, so I didn't really enjoy having to work alongside Callum. I was hard on him, but when he asked me out, I thought maybe he liked that sort of thing. Who knows what gets people excited?" She placed her coffee down on the glass table and stood, pacing the floor, rubbing her forehead as she went. "But we've been through all this, Hunter. I just keep running that night through my mind. Trying to make sense of it all. Trying to see what I might have missed."

"And you've got nothing more?"

"Not a thing after my third gin and tonic. I don't

even remember leaving the bar. What happened that night shouldn't have happened."

"You fell off the wagon," Hunter began. "It happens."

"No, I didn't," she snapped, turning to face him. Realizing the volume of her response, she apologized. "I'm sorry. This is just getting to me." She rubbed her forehand as she sat back on the couch. "That's the thing—I know alcohol. I know its effects. I know what it does to me in the mornings. I spent more than enough time with it in a permanent one-on-one relationship. What I remember drinking that night… it shouldn't have affected me the way it did."

"At its worst, how bad was the drinking problem?"

"Bad. I used to sneak in drinks in the morning, and then lunchtime, before really hitting it at night," she said. "I used to drink out of desperation. My perfect life, my perfect world, all this, was too lifeless to endure. The misery, the loneliness, the emptiness. Oh, the emptiness. That hurt the most. I couldn't face a night without a drink. I couldn't even bear the thought of it. That hollow pit of loneliness in my stomach was too much to endure alone. Alcohol was my friend, the thing that comforted me. In the end, I couldn't even think about going to sleep without passing out. I couldn't remember going to sleep sober."

"Any prosecutor will look at this as a drunk episode, even more so if they know about the past alcoholism." He paused, waiting for her to answer, and when she didn't, he prodded her a little. "Do the people in your office know the extent of your past problem?"

"I'm not sure. It's not something you talk about

freely, and the place I went for help wasn't in Chicago." She closed her eyes, the hand returning to her forehead. "I took an extended leave of absence during my treatment. I just said that I needed some time out."

"But?"

The silence hung in the air, suspended like a beacon, both aware of its implications. Hunter sat patiently, waiting for Michelle to talk. When she did, she spoke like a witness under intense cross-examination. "But trying to hide alcoholism is like trying to hide a dead body. You might get away with it in the beginning, but eventually? The smell is going to bring the flies every time."

Hunter thought back to his fifth-grade teacher, a man named Douglas Fairbanks. He would roll up each day with glass-shot eyes and an aroma that stung the nostrils of everyone he taught. The smell was whiskey seeping from his pores, unable to be masked at the best of times, and at the worst of times, it was enough to stink out an entire classroom.

"So, lay it on me," Michelle said, closing her eyes. "What have they offered?"

"Murder one and twenty years in minimum security for a guilty plea," Hunter said, watching as the words stung her face.

"Not happening. They can go as low as four years with second-degree murder," she whispered. "And I'm not taking twenty years. If they put up a year for manslaughter..." She opened her eyes and looked at Hunter, gazing at him with a look of solitude. "Maybe, I'll take it. I don't know. All I know is that I blacked out, and they have no evidence of Amanda Ford and me together before they found her in my trunk."

"Callum Strauss stated in his police report that he left you in the street outside the bar because you became very angry about the fact that he still had feelings for his ex-girlfriend. He stated that you went into a jealous rage when he told you. And he said that Amanda Ford's apartment was only five doors from the bar. He even gave you the exact address, he claims. And then you pushed him away and said that his relationship with Amanda would be over by the morning. He said that you then started vomiting on the street, and that's when he left."

"That doesn't sound like me," she whispered. "I've never said anything like that in my life."

She stood and began pacing again, unable to control the nerves. She paced the floor for a while before stopping near the window, leaning against the far edge, staring back out at the city. She tapped her head against the glass, trying to make sense of her situation.

"Jake Berkeley called you at 5.05am that morning," Hunter said. "Does he usually call you at that time?"

"Sometimes," she shrugged. "If he had information, he'd call me at any hour. In fact, I'm sure that he used to wait until the early hours of the morning to call me, just to torture me. He was like that. He was a contact, and I used him, but I couldn't tell you what he told me that morning. I was still too out of it." She spread her arms out wide, pointing to the city. "In a city where half the murders go unsolved, I have to be the unlucky one that gets caught up in a mistake."

"We don't know what happened yet," Hunter tried to settle her. "We've still got a lot of loose ends to work through."

"My whole life, I've dedicated my time to serving justice, and I never really felt like I was making a dent. There are just so many murders and so much gun violence. My job barely made a dent in it at all."

Hunter placed his coffee mug on the table and walked over to the window, standing next to her.

"There are three options going forward here," he said, remaining focused. "And we'll work them all before the trial."

"Option one?" she asked, not turning away from the view.

"That you did blackout because of the extreme stress and alcohol, and you went to talk with Amanda Ford after Callum left. You discussed something with her in her apartment before you hit her, suffocated her, and then carried her body from her ground floor apartment to your car parked on the same block. In that instance, we can push for murder two and try and get the offer down to four years."

"And admit guilt? I can't admit to something I don't know about. I have no idea what happened." She shook her head. "Option two?"

"That your drink was spiked by GHB, and you lost your capacity for reasoning. Our defense in this instance would be 'involuntarily drugged condition,' under 720 ILCS 5/6-3, which has deprived you of substantial capacity either to appreciate the criminality of your conduct or to conform your conduct to the requirements of the law. We'll gather all the evidence and comb through it piece by piece until we find that one fragment of evidence that gives us leverage over the prosecution."

"If we can prove I was drugged," she dropped her

head. "And option three?"

"That someone else killed Amanda Ford and carried her body into the trunk of your car."

"A set-up?"

"Possibly."

"Callum Strauss would be suspect number one. He's the one that was with me that night. He's the one that possibly spiked my drink. He's the one that took me to that bar." She turned away from the window and began to pace back and forth for a moment, talking as she walked. "I've been putting away criminals for a long time. The line of people queueing to get back at me would stretch around the block more than a few times. I've put a lot of people behind bars, and not all of them were your typical gun-wielding bank robber. There were more than a few people who would do anything for revenge."

"But there was one case that really made the wrong people angry."

"Your father's case," Michelle agreed. "When I joined the motion to dismiss his charges, there were a lot of angry people. They'd built their reputations on being tough on crime. The case made a mockery of their promises. One alderman had to quit not long after the case, and a number are facing disastrous polls. I expected them to come after me. I expected to be thrown out of the State's Attorney's Office, but this? No, I didn't think they'd do this. How could they? How could any politician do this?"

"I don't think a politician did it," Hunter said. "But who do politicians turn to when they need something done?"

Michelle stared back at Hunter. "Lobbyist Walter Charman."

CHAPTER 11

AFTER THE meeting with her defense lawyer, Michelle Law's spirits were lifted, if only slightly, offering a new sense of hope that, in time, her ordeal would be nothing but a distant memory, a footnote in her career-driven life. She had confidence in his ability. She'd witnessed his skills first-hand—intelligent, quick-witted, and determined. Any prosecutor going against Hunter knew they were up against a challenge.

Instead of returning to the couch once he'd left, she needed a sense of freedom, the kind which could only be found in a place designed to make bad memories disappear. A shopping trip. She grabbed her purse, keys, and cell, then walked to the local mall, taking a shortcut through the small alley running behind Mario's Bar and Bistro. It was a trip she'd made dozens of times, and it felt good to be out of the apartment after too many days locked inside, hiding from the world itself.

The State's Attorney's Office had suspended her, forcing her to take leave without pay, but she had enough investments to live comfortably without an income for a while. That was one thing her adoptive parents taught her from the start—the value of investing ten percent of her income each month. At twenty-five, when she first started full-time work, she didn't see the need to save, but now, over two decades later, those investments had built to a point where she was comfortable, no matter her work situation.

She wore loose jeans, loose enough to cover the fitted ankle bracelet, and a nice shirt with casual shoes. On the way, she stopped in at the nearby Old St. Patrick's Church, sitting inside the calm surroundings for twenty-five minutes, ensuring her outing was a religious one to mark down for the 'D' Bond conditions.

After her prayers, she found herself at the mall, her attention drawn to the many display windows she passed, pausing briefly at some, while stopping at others to just peer inside and feel a part of something else. There was no plan to actually purchase anything, a venture she had a history of making. A man she had once dated would often comment about how frustrating the whole thing was for him, but Michelle had little time for someone who couldn't understand the true meaning of retail therapy.

"It's not always about spending money," she tried to tell him, but the fact was lost on him, and eventually, the short-term relationship was over, ending like all her relationships.

After fifty minutes of trekking past several dozen retail stores, Michelle turned back towards her apartment, finishing her journey at a Goodwill outlet. It was the last store on the strip nearest to her apartment, and the smell of the store brought back memories of her grandma. She stepped inside, and the waft was instantly satisfying—a little bit musty, with a whiff of wool and old cigarette smoke.

The store was filled with goods of all varieties; clothes, books, jewelry, and artworks, but one item caught her attention—a crystal vase that matched one her grandma had owned and kept filled with fresh flowers from her garden the entire year-round. Michelle made a beeline for the display cabinet and, at first, just stood and stared at the antique. When her fingers reached for it, she found them trembling slightly and paused to try and steady them. The last thing she wanted was to drop it, a fate guaranteed to end its life at her feet. The price tag read just five dollars, and Michelle almost laughed when she saw it. Reaching for it, she reminded herself that a lot of people would never lower themselves for such incredible finds, making her discovery even more special.

"Let me wrap that for you," the elderly woman behind the counter said to her as she paid. Michelle thanked her, then handed over a twenty-dollar bill, telling the lady to keep the change. Her smile widened as she took the money, before she placed the wrapped item in a brown paper bag. "I hope you have a fine afternoon," she said, and Michelle nodded her head.

The bag felt a lot heavier than she'd expected, and it only reminded her of the quality of the item she'd purchased. Everything made back then was heavy, as if the weight of an item somehow gave it genuine quality. She smiled again as she turned down the same alley back to her apartment, caught up in her moment of freedom.

She knew that the freedom might not last. Perhaps that's why fate had given her a brief sense of it during her outing.

Maybe, just maybe, she would spend the rest of

her life in prison for a crime she did commit. She didn't know the truth. Did she have it in her to murder someone? The answer, she concluded, was very possibly yes.

That thought was running through her mind when the stranger's voice spoke from almost directly beside her, catching her off guard.

"Decided to come out of your cave, huh?"

Michelle went to turn, but before her eyes had swung around enough to catch sight of the person, pain exploded in her ribs. She saw a flash of metal, perhaps a gun, but the hands swinging at her were moving much too fast, and, before she could react, another fist struck her in the side of the face. Blackness developed around her as something crashed to the ground. A bolt of pain raced through her body as the voice spoke again, finally eliminating the thought this was just a random mugging.

"Watch where you poke your nose. Take the plea deal and go to prison, or next time, things will be a lot worse. Got it?" And then, closer still, "Stop playing with the wrong people."

The footfalls didn't run from where she knelt on the ground, instead walking away as Michelle wiped the tears from her eyes. She looked up, trying to catch a sight of the person, but her vision was blurry. Looking at the ground, she saw the vase that had smashed beside her feet, dropped during the initial attack. All she could do was lift the bag and listen to the crystal shards clinking inside the newspaper wrapping.

After climbing to her feet, she leaned against the wall, then stumbled back to the mouth of the alley, in the opposite direction from her attacker.

She knew this attack was only a warning—and that there'd be much more to come.

CHAPTER 12

DURING A murder trial, Hunter spent his nights at the office.

He preferred it that way. At night, he could think clearer without distractions, focusing on the details that he might've missed during the day.

As the night descended over the city, his focus became the big picture, the tactics, the strategies that might put his cases on the front foot. He enjoyed sitting back, whiskey in hand, staring out the window, and thinking. Not forcing anything, but just letting his thoughts run free, coasting over the steps in the trial. He remembered hearing a Henry Ford quote when he was in school, and it stuck with him, 'Thinking is the hardest work there is, which is why so few engage in it.'

And in summer, he enjoyed watching the long sunsets over his city of Chicago, observing the long dusk as it bathed the surrounding areas in a soft orange glow. After an evening of thinking, Hunter stepped out of his office, locking the door after 10pm, when his cell rang.

"Michelle?" he answered and looked at his watch. "It's 10.05pm. What's wrong?"

"I was attacked today," Michelle replied softly. "Physically, I'm ok, but I'm battered and bruised.

Mentally? Maybe not so much."

"What happened?" Hunter stopped at the end of the foyer next to the elevators. "Have you made a police report?"

"I just finished the reporting. It took five hours to process it all." Her voice was shaky. "A man attacked me when I was out shopping. He must've been following me. And then, when he had me on the ground, he told me to take the plea deal."

"A plea deal?" Hunter repeated. "So, this wasn't a random attack."

"No," she whispered. "Someone targeted me. I don't know who it was, and I didn't get a look at his face. It happened in an alley, and the shops around there said they didn't have cameras in that section either. Nobody saw anything, and I couldn't tell the cops anything about him."

"Did they steal anything from you?"

"No," she said, her voice shaky. "But I was just wondering if you wouldn't mind giving me a ride home from the twelfth district police station on Blue Island Avenue? I'm rattled and not sure who to trust anymore. I don't even know if I should trust a cab driver, you know?"

"I get it." Hunter looked at his watch. "I'll be there in fifteen minutes."

After fifteen minutes of weaving through late-night Chicago traffic, mostly passing cab and Uber drivers, Hunter pulled out in front of the CPD 12th District. Michelle was already standing by the front doors when he arrived. She climbed slowly into the passenger seat. A purplish bruise had appeared down the right side of her face, the edge touching the underside of her eye. Michelle saw Hunter staring at it.

"It looks worse than it feels," she said, avoiding eye contact. "Before I came down here to make a police report, I went to the hospital first, and they said it was fine. They did some checks, and there'll be no long-term damage. Just a bruise."

"I hope so, because from where I'm sitting, whoever attacked you did quite a number."

"You should see me with my shirt off," Michelle said, realizing her words and laughing. The noise surprised Hunter, who at first didn't get the comment. Michelle pulled back her laughter as the pain shot through her ribs, and she cradled her left side. "Oh, that hurts. I have a massive bruise on my ribs. He kicked me like a street thug while I was down."

Hunter sighed, unhappy his client had been targeted. "I know it's not what you want to hear, but maybe in hindsight, it'll be better for you to stay with a family member or a friend until we get things sorted. It'll be safer. I don't want this happening again."

Michelle fell silent. She bit her lip and looked out the car window at the passing building.

When she didn't answer, he pressed on. "Michelle? Is there somewhere I can take you?"

"No," she whispered, still looking out the window.

"It won't be for long. Only a few weeks while we do the initial investigations, then you can return."

"I can't."

"Even just a few days, perhaps a friend or relative—"

"There's nobody," she whispered. "There's nobody I can call."

Hunter looked across at her as he maneuvered through the night-time traffic. He didn't press on. He understood.

In a city filled with millions, in a place surrounded by so many people, she had no one.

Modern city life had created tremendous opportunities, lives of wealth and comfort, but at the cost of community and connection.

They fell into silence as the car continued towards Michelle's apartment. Hunter watched every car that turned when they turned, checking to be sure there was no tail following them.

"They didn't like me," Michelle said as Hunter parked out the front of her apartment building.

"Who?"

"The police. The detectives. The administration teams. Everyone in that building hated me." She bit her lip again. "They told me I shouldn't have let Alfred go. They said by letting him out, I was spitting in their faces. One detective said they work so hard to put criminals away, and I just let them walk back out the doors. I guess that's why it took them so long to take down my police report."

"I'm sorry," Hunter said, turning off the engine.

"It's not your fault. I did the right thing by the justice system, but some people don't see it like that, and now I'm paying the consequences." Michelle looked down at her hands, blinking back another wave of tears. After the weeks that had passed, she was surprised she had any tears left. "It's the price we pay, right? We have to give everything of ourselves to justice, and when the time comes, there's nobody left for us."

"I don't know what to say, Michelle."

"But you understand, right?" She looked across at him.

"I do."

"We give everything of ourselves to this city. We sacrifice blood, sweat, and tears for these people, but nobody appreciates it. No one thanks us. We're not the heroes. The prosecution teams are only on the news when things go wrong. We only get bad news stories, not good ones." She blinked back more tears that threatened to pour out. "And when it falls apart, there's nobody there to back us up. They're so fickle. They just run away the second there's any trouble."

"I'm here," Hunter stated. "I'm with you all the way."

She offered him a half-smile, nodded, and then opened the car door. "Thanks for the lift."

Once Michelle stepped out of the car, Hunter's expression turned to stone as the anger of the attack returned in force.

He didn't need investigative qualifications to know who was behind the beating.

And he decided to go straight to the source.

CHAPTER 13

IF THERE was one thing Hunter hated, if there was one thing that got under his skin, it was the powerful picking on the weak and vulnerable. He had spent his life fighting against corruption, fighting against the dishonesty that occurred behind closed doors, pushing hard against the criminals that thought they owned the game, and he wasn't finished yet.

Hunter raced through the streets. As the night passed 10.35pm, traffic was almost non-existent. After leaving Michelle's apartment, he called Esther and explained the situation, and within five minutes, she had Walter Charman's location.

He was photographed attending a charity function for Cancer Research at the Gleacher Center, only a few steps away from the Chicago River in River North. Esther had found his photo recently posted on social media, a goldmine of information for anyone's whereabouts. Hunter arrived at the function as the night was ending, most of the well-dressed attendees stepping into waiting limousines and town cars.

Hunter snaked through the crowd, using his height to look over the well-dressed attendees until he came to the reception area with around fifty people still mingling, enjoying their champagnes, laughing and smiling. The room had an expansive view of Downtown Chicago, highlighted by the floor-to-ceiling windows. It didn't take him long to find Charman in the room. The man was standing near the bar with a drink in one hand and his arm around one of the leading doctors of the research center, whose face was on the flyer at the door. She was young, pretty, and, by the looks of the situation, remarkably uncomfortable.

"Charman," Hunter said as he approached, raising his voice enough to be heard over the music and the chatter of the busy room. "You and I need to talk."

Charman turned, saw Hunter, and turned back, briefly considering his options. He squinted as he looked at Hunter, trying to understand what was happening.

"Would you excuse me for a moment," Charman said to the young woman as he finished his drink, and set the glass down on the bar. "I won't be long."

Charman didn't bother with pleasantries, passing Hunter and leading them out through a side door into a hallway that led to the restrooms. Once out of the reception area, Charman looked around to ensure privacy before turning back to Hunter. "You got some nerve showing up here, Hunter."

"We can't all aspire to be like you and send men to beat up vulnerable women," Hunter snapped back, taking a step forward as he spoke.

Despite Hunter's towering height, Charman stood his ground.

"Careful," he hissed through clenched teeth, lowering his voice for effect. "You might think you hold some sort of leverage in this whole affair, but let me assure you, you don't. I can end your career with a snap of my fingers."

He grinned after he spoke, in an attempt to look intimidating. Hunter ignored the threat and took another step forward.

"Threaten all you want, Charman, but if any of your thugs touch Michelle Law again, I'll turn my full attention into your affairs, and we both know how that will end."

"You think you want to play this game with me?" Charman snarled. Hunter had rattled him enough for the man to temporarily lose his cool, and once he realized the slip, Charman took a step back and laughed. "I mean, I'll give you credit. You've got bravery. You don't take a backward step, do you? Like a dog chasing a bone."

"That's the only time I'll warn you, Charman." Hunter delivered a threat of his own. "Next time, I'm coming after you, and I'm digging into your affairs."

Charman scoffed and then shook his head.

He moved towards the door but hesitated as he turned to face Hunter again. "Be careful where you stick your nose, Hunter. Not everyone in this city is as nice as me."

CHAPTER 14

HUNTER SPENT most of the following week in his office.

It was the only way to distract himself from the barrage of blame rolling through his head. He considered sleeping in his office one night but decided it was best to head back to his apartment. He arrived at his apartment late, had two whiskeys, then he lay in bed for five hours before deciding that he couldn't sleep. He was back in his office by 7am the next day, scrolling through lines and lines and lines of information. He drafted motions, called in favors, and compiled folders full of strategies for the case. By the time the following Friday had arrived, the whiteboard in his boardroom was filled with notes in various colors.

"So, we have a few options," Esther said, sitting at the end of the table, notepad and pen ready. "What strategy is the leading one at this point?"

"If we were to take the case to trial today, our best option would be to push for a not guilty verdict under the involuntarily deprived capacity defense. We argue she was drugged beyond reasonable capability, and she had no control over her actions." Hunter tapped his finger on the top section of the whiteboard. "The problem is that it's almost impossible to win. If we go down that path, the onus of proof is on us, and we don't have much. All we have is Michelle's statement and the fact that her symptoms the next morning match those who have taken GHB. We've got experts we can call who will testify that her symptoms match a GHB drugging. But all her drug tests were negative for drugs, and we have no evidence of drink spiking in that bar. If we're going with that defense, we need further evidence."

"How about the hair follicle test for GHB?"

"Negative," Hunter replied. "But its accuracy is very low. She could've been drugged, and it wouldn't show on the test."

"That's going to be tough to convince a jury, considering the accused was found with the body in the trunk of her car, as well as the lack of an alibi at the time of the murder." Esther nodded in agreement. "She blacked out. She has no idea what happened during that time. Any jury will think it's just an excuse and that it looks like a jealous woman gone mad. You can be sure that's what the prosecution will present."

"So, we have to introduce doubt by bringing up the ex-boyfriend." Hunter moved to the other side of the whiteboard and pointed to the name 'Strauss,' which was written in the top left corner. "Callum Strauss. Not only was he in a race with the deceased for the top job, but he also began dating her after they met through Charman's job and after he knew she was in direct competition with him. Clear motive." Hunter tapped his finger on the whiteboard to highlight the point, then added, "Plus, he approached the defendant he intended to frame on the afternoon of the murder for drinks at a bar that he's known to be a regular at. There must be something. There must be something we can pressure Callum Strauss with. He's our player. He's the third-party culpability target for our court case. He's the one we have to focus on. The ex-boyfriend who set up Michelle Law and works for Walter Charman. He asked Michelle out, he drugged her, and set this whole thing up."

"But how do we prove it?" Esther asked. "And why would he frame Michelle?"

"He would've acted at the request of Charman, who has a lot of contacts very unhappy with Michelle. They would've wanted to see her rot," Hunter said. "As for how? The fact that Strauss is arrogant enough to get on the stand for the prosecution means he's arrogant enough to make a mistake. We can talk to him about his father and the pressure of expectations. I don't think it'll take much to break him."

"Well, I have something to add to that." Esther flicked open a file. "This information came in this afternoon. According to someone else who attended college with him, Strauss is a regular at the Five Cocktails. The first Tuesday of the month for two years. And he was often seen leaving with a different woman each week."

"Think Amanda Ford knew?"

"Probably. I think it was an open secret, but young love makes people do crazy things." Esther turned the file to face Hunter. "But it led me to think that there must be another reason Strauss goes to that bar, and here's what I've just found out—the bar owner is Elliot Brady, who went to school with Strauss. They're old school buddies."

"What are you saying?"

"I'm saying Strauss was in a protected environment," Esther nodded. "These rich private school boys think they're above the law. These boys both went to a very expensive school, both have very rich parents, and from what I can see, both have been bailed out by their parents every time they get in trouble."

"That's good," Hunter said, turning back to the board. "That's brilliant, Esther."

Hunter walked to the window and gazed across the streets below in silence, his mind ticking over. He stared out at the street for almost five minutes before turning back and picking up his cell.

"Ray, I need you to dig deeper into the Five Cocktails Lounge Bar," Hunter said. "Go there on Tuesday night and see who comes and goes. That bar may give us the break we need."

CHAPTER 15

HUNTER WAITED at the iconic Zebra Lounge in the Near North Side, whiskey in hand, while he listened to the subtle tones of the live piano. Almost a hundred years old, the Zebra Lounge held the third oldest liquor license in the city of Chicago and was eternally popular thanks to live piano playing seven nights a week. Known for secret celebrity drop-ins over the years, the bar was frequently packed with an eclectic mix of regulars, newcomers, socialites, and piano junkies. Under dim lighting, the maroon painted walls, framed pictures, and zebra-striped lamps created an atmosphere of calm, a world away from the city's busy streets outside its doors.

Hunter sunk into one of the red leather booths, watching as the charismatic bartender poured a martini for an older couple, chatting to them about his love for the bar, telling them, 'You can't buy history, and you can't buy cool,' and occasionally disrupting the conversation to sing along with the relaxing piano tunes. The smell was musky, a combination of stale air, tobacco, and spirits.

Ray Jones walked into the bar, folder in hand, and spotted Hunter. Jones ordered a drink and then approached Hunter, sliding into the other side of the booth.

"I got some sad news yesterday—my obese parrot died," Jones said as he placed the folder on the brown table. "Mind you, it's a huge weight off my shoulders."

Hunter smiled, but didn't give the joke the laughter it deserved.

"You didn't like that one?" Jones smiled. "Well, I got an email today telling me how to read maps backward, but it was just spam."

Hunter chuckled slightly.

"Come on, that one deserved a bigger laugh," Jones said but noticed the look of concern on Hunter's face. "Tough week? How's Michelle Law holding up?"

"She's not good. She was attacked in an alley a week ago," Hunter grunted. "Nobody saw anything, but she was badly bruised. Her attacker didn't steal her purse or phone but told her to take the plea deal."

"It was a targeted attack?"

"Exactly." Hunter drew a breath. "I confronted Walter Charman about it and told him to leave her alone."

"I bet he didn't appreciate you confronting him."

"Not one bit." Hunter wrapped his hands around his whiskey glass as the pianist played a Billy Joel tune.

"Charman is as dirty and as nasty as they come. He thinks he can get away with anything. Is there something you need me to do? Bust a few heads?" Jones raised his eyebrows. As much as Hunter loved fighting, Jones lived for it. If there was a chance he could flex his muscles, demonstrate his power, and outwardly display his best skills, he would take it.

"Thanks for the offer, but it's nothing I can't

handle." Hunter shook his head. "But I've warned Michelle to keep her head low and her eyes peeled."

The piano player finished his song, thanked the audience, and walked to the bar to order a drink. His live music was replaced by the gentle hum of another piano track playing over the speakers.

"Excuse me for a moment," Jones said and walked over to the older man. When the piano player noticed Jones, they embraced like old friends, Jones' large frame almost swallowing the shorter man.

Having spent almost twenty years as a private investigator on the streets of Chicago, Jones had enough contacts to fill up his own phone book. People from all walks of life respected him. He was a charming and magnetic man that knew a kind word could bring out as much information as the threat of a punch. The fact he was six-foot-four, muscular, and had a love of aggression also helped.

"An old contact," Jones smiled as he slid back into the booth. "He's a former heavy drug user. I helped him get clean, and I'm glad to see he's doing well."

"That man can sure play the piano." Hunter raised his glass to thank the man for his music. The man raised his glass in return. "So, what's in the folder?"

"Just like you asked, I spent Tuesday night at the Five Cocktails Lounge Bar." Jones flipped open the folder and turned it around to face Hunter. "But first, I did a bit of digging, calling people, talking to some old friends I know."

"What did you find out?"

"The Five Cocktails is a small place, been open five years, but it has a big reputation. Rumors of date-rape drugs being used there have been circulating around the campus of the nearby Northwestern

University School of Medicine. There are some Facebook posts about safety and advising people to think twice before going to that bar."

"Any cases with the police?"

"Not that I've found, but incidents of date-rape drugs can be very hard to get a conviction. Some leave the system within hours, making it almost impossible to prove that the drinks were spiked. The campus had reports from students who were confused after going there, but there was no evidence."

"And inside the bar?"

"I walked in, and the bartender told me it was closed off for a private event every Tuesday night. I explained that I was from out-of-town, looking for security work, and that really, I was just after a beer. He studied me and told me I was in luck—he wasn't just the bartender but also the owner of the bar, and his usual security guy was running late. He offered me two beers to stand by the inside of the door for the next hour until his security guy arrived."

"You don't work that cheap for me," Hunter smiled.

"Hey, you get what you pay for." Jones spread his arms wide. "So, I stand security at the door and watch these guys come in. Five of them, all with young women in their arms. The guys all looked about the same age, all with the same sort of style. They all greeted each other, so it felt like they all went to school together."

"Interesting. Any photos?"

"Well, the security guy shows up an hour later, and I get my two beers. While drinking them, I pulled out my phone and discreetly snapped a few photos."

Jones turned a page on the file, showing several fuzzy photos. "The lighting wasn't good, so I couldn't really get a clear shot of the guys."

"No, but I get the impression. They all look around Callum Strauss' age and wealth."

"Right." Jones tapped the file. "I finish my two beers, and then the owner tells me to move on. He says it's a private party, and his patrons don't enjoy having other guys hanging around. So, I leave and wait in my truck, studying the exit." He drew a breath. "An hour later, the first guy comes out with a girl struggling to walk. He was holding her up. There was no way she could've gotten that drunk within an hour."

"Date-rape drug?"

"That's what I thought, so when I saw the guy was taking the girl to his car, I knew I had to stop it. I jumped out of the truck just as he unlocked his car, with this girl just about limp next to him, and I told him to stop. He made up some story about them being lifelong partners, and she was drunk, but I wasn't buying it. I stepped forward, and the weak little man just let the girl fall on the road while he raced into the driver's seat. I went to help the girl, and the man sped off."

Hunter groaned as he leaned back in his seat, tapping his finger on the edge of the table. "Did you get the girl help?"

"I called the cops, said I found a rich, white girl on the road, and she was drunk, and they were there in five minutes."

"I imagine that the presence of the cops didn't help the others still in the bar."

"It sure didn't. The other four guys in the bar all

left within five minutes, but not with any of the girls. The cops helped the girl on the road, said that they'd take her to the hospital. Just as the patrol car left, four cabs arrived, and I watched as the owner and the other security guard put a girl into each of them."

"They got spooked," Hunter said. "Did they see you?"

"They did. And after that little scare, along with the drama of Amanda Ford's death, I imagine they'll go quiet for a while," Jones said. "But I don't think that'll stop them in the long run. They were too overconfident."

"Thanks, Ray. Let's keep an eye on the place. If we can prove that people in the bar drug their dates, then we might have a hope in Michelle's case."

"On it," Jones said. "So, how's life outside of the case?"

The two large men chatted for the next two hours, listening to the soft tones as the live piano began again, laughing about life, sports, and everything in between. The bartender joined them for a while, happily discussing his business, and as the hours ticked later, just as the bar started to fill with younger people looking to celebrate, Hunter and Jones took their cue to leave. They shook hands at the entrance and wished each other well, heading in separate directions.

With a smile drifting across his face, Hunter walked back to his car.

Life was good.

For the first time since he could remember, life was good. It was Esther. She was his anchor. She was his base that his happiness seemed to blossom from. To have created something so special out of nothing was a miracle.

He couldn't believe that he'd found love. After a life of turmoil, a life of pain and agony, he had closed his heart off to the world. Esther was always there, always supporting him, but he didn't think he had it inside him to let go of his anguish and allow her in. He didn't think he could let down the walls and be vulnerable. But love had a funny way of sneaking up, of building, and then suddenly tearing down all the walls in one beautiful swoop.

It was the distraction of love that kept him from seeing the sedan idling in the shadows.

Hunter pulled the keys from his pocket and listened as the familiar beeping signaled the unlocking of his car. He whistled as he walked further down the street, his footfalls matching the rhythm of the tune.

Twenty feet to his driver's side door.

He smiled as he passed a young couple, walking arm in arm, giggling with new love. He smiled again, shaking his head. He wondered if everyone who found love felt as lucky as he did at that moment.

Fifteen feet.

He whistled as he walked, not spotting the stranger moving through the shadows. Hunter slowly continued, the whistles reaching their inevitable climax.

Ten feet.

The shadow following him paused behind a pillar as Hunter slowed to swap the hand holding the keys with his briefcase.

Just before reaching the door, he reached into his pocket and retrieved his cell phone.

A man in love is a man distracted, and after Hunter opened the door, he threw the briefcase across to the passenger seat and slid in behind the wheel.

The explosion was deafening.

It took Hunter a moment to gather his bearings. Frozen for a second, a flash of light filled his car.

Hunter leaped out, the whoosh of fuel erupting as flames flickered on the back window of his car. As he stood next to his car, he heard faint footfalls running somewhere behind him.

He turned, heard the slam of a car door, then watched as a large black sedan squealed toward him, then banked hard right as it made its escape.

The rear side window of his car exploded with a dull thump, the entire back end now alight. Black smoke billowed from the side window. Hunter could do nothing more than watch his car disintegrate into a storm of flames.

Covering his mouth with his sleeve, Hunter ran to the passenger door, ripped it open, and grabbed his briefcase from the seat.

The thought of the fuel tank exploding didn't cross his mind until he heard the screams of two unsettled onlookers urging him to get away.

Hunter had only made it halfway towards them when the explosion tore down the street.

The force of the blast punched him in the back, lifting him a few inches into the air before dropping him to the concrete several feet further along. Groggy but conscious, he rose, running further down the street.

By the time he turned back to look at his car, flames were streaming out from every window, reaching high into the night.

As the first sirens pierced the warm night air, the

car was engulfed by flames, the sounds of popping glass joining the babble of onlooker's voices.

All Hunter could do was watch as the latest message continued to burn loud and clear.

It was a message he couldn't ignore, but it would be one he refused to obey.

CHAPTER 16

HUNTER SPENT hours upon hours in the police station after the bombing, filling out forms, talking through interviews.

He returned home at 2.55am to find Esther waiting for him. She looked after him, comforted him, and made sure he was ok. He didn't sleep. He tossed and turned, trying to get the thoughts of the attack out of his mind. The next morning, he told Esther to watch her step, and called Michelle to do the same. He told Michelle not to leave the house unnecessarily for the next week. She agreed.

The police investigation concluded it was a homemade Molotov Cocktail. A cheap glass bottle had been filled with gasoline, mixed with roofing tar to create a thickener, and lit by an oil-soaked rag, stuffed into the neck of the bottle. It was designed to explode into a fireball, sending the roofing tar onto its target and then burning brightly until the target melted. And with the items used in the bomb commonly available at any combination of stores, it was also hard to trace. Despite all the information Hunter gave them, the police had no leads.

Five days after the bombing, Hunter received a phone call from an old friend—Chicago Police Department Detective Jemma Knowles. Detective

Knowles called Hunter and asked to meet off the books. That interested Hunter. She wasn't leading the case into the attack, nor did she have any links to Michelle Law's case. He agreed to meet.

The Gold Star Bar, a dive bar in Wicker Park, was quiet on the Friday afternoon, with only a couple near the door making any noise above the gentle tones of jazz playing over the speaker. The dive bar was a constant in the trendy neighborhood, a decades-old locals' retreat where dogs were welcomed during quiet times. The bar ran along one wall, exposed brick on the other. The lighting was dull, especially in the corners of the room, and the smell of beer and nuts filled the air.

As she walked in, Chicago PD Detective Jemma Knowles looked at home. Wearing a black leather jacket over a black top and black jeans, she looked fashionable enough to walk into any bar in the trendy neighborhood. She greeted the bartender and joined Hunter in the booth at the furthest end of the room, well away from any prying ears. There were only a few places where the forty-one-year-old, six-foot-tall, African American woman felt comfortable, but this place was her second home.

"Looking good, old man," she said as she sat down on the other side of the booth. "You're aging very well."

"You look good too," Hunter said, placing his beer on the dark table. "You don't look like you've aged a day."

"Well, I feel it," she said. "One minute, you're young and wild and free, and the next, you're getting excited about buying a new vacuum."

Hunter laughed heartily, more than the quip

deserved. "Did you ever patch things up with your husband?"

"We did." She smiled as the bartender placed a bourbon and coke in front of her. "He went through a mid-life crisis, but instead of buying a sports car and chasing young girls, he drank a lot and stayed home. I guess everyone deals with the mid-life meltdown in different ways, but he's good now. Back on his feet, and there's life back in his eyes. He's the man I used to know again."

"That's great to hear."

Two years younger than Hunter, Knowles had attended the same high school in Logan Square. They'd dated once—Hunter, the son of a serial killer, was seen as the ultimate bad boy, the way a good student like Knowles could rebel against overbearing parents.

Knowles was pretty, she had soft eyes and beautiful skin that didn't seem to age, but her good looks had betrayed her many times. Some men saw her feminine looks and immediately thought she was an easy target. That would be their mistake. With one arm full of tattoos, usually covered during work hours, and a lifetime of mixed-martial arts training, any man that was stupid enough to cross her was in for a shock.

"It's good to see you going well, Tex. I wasn't sure how you would be after... well, after your father passed away."

Hunter looked down at his beer. "It's hard, but I'm grateful that we had the opportunity to prove his innocence in court. That was a lifelong dream of mine."

"Good to hear." Knowles checked over her

shoulder, looking around the room. "And now, after only five months, you're back into the thick of the action in Chicago. Got your face back in the news. You just can't keep away, can you? Always looking for danger."

"Is that what you wanted to talk about?"

"I liked Michelle Law," she nodded. "We've had many interactions over the years, and although we're very different people, she was always on the side of the good guy. There was no politics with her. If she took on your case, you could be guaranteed that she'd be doing it by the books. A real stickler for the rules."

"I'm guessing that you've read the case file against her. Most of the police department would've."

"We were all shocked to hear it, so we looked at what happened," Knowles agreed. She leaned in and lowered his voice. "But this isn't just another case. When Michelle agreed to join the motion to dismiss the charges against your father, she made a lot of powerful people unhappy. The public was divided about your father's case, which meant that people in politics were as well. The case had serious connections, and they aren't strangers to fixing their problems quickly and permanently." And then, as an afterthought, "Without hesitation."

"I've heard that, but I've never been one to back away from exposing the corrupt."

"Hunter, this isn't about corruption," Knowles said, her voice remaining barely audible. "This is connected all the way to the top." She checked around the bar again, and when she saw nobody was watching them, she turned back to Hunter. "The report about your attack last week was flagged with my current case. Your statement after the bombing included a reference to a case I'm working on."

Hunter's interest was piqued. "And what case is that?"

"Just like you said on the record. Date-rape drugs."

Hunter leaned back, nodding.

"Last month, we opened a confidential investigation into the Five Cocktails Lounge Bar," Knowles continued. "We received five reports from women who claimed they were drugged, but in their toxicology tests, we found nothing. Because of the reports, we started monitoring the bar. The owner, Elliot Brady, is a pretty rich boy with more money than he knows what to do with, so he runs the bar. And guess what? The PD has received at least one report per month from women who thought they were drugged there."

"Any hard evidence?"

"Not yet. These guys are smart. They know where the cameras are, and they know which way to walk to avoid detection. We've stopped two couples over the past two weeks, approaching the women before the guys could take them home. But we're stepping carefully, because we're trying to find the source of the drugs before we raid the bar." She leaned in closer. "We need to make sure that this doesn't spread to any other bars. We don't need this type of untraceable drug in circulation any more than it already is."

"Why isn't this in the discovery information about Michelle's case? This is the bar where she was drinking, and it's near where Amanda Ford was found."

"Because there have been no arrests, and we have

no evidence. All we have is the reports."

"And let me guess," Hunter groaned. "Pradesh Baron has called you."

Knowles avoided eye contact, nodding slightly. "He didn't ask us that directly, but he certainly indicated that he would like any raid, or closing of this case, to take over two months. Because the bar owner is the son of a very wealthy and influential man in Chicago, and because of who goes to that bar on occasion, this is a confidential investigation."

"And without an arrest, without any evidence, I can't bring the information forward in Michelle's trial." Hunter gripped his glass tighter. "You know this isn't right, Jemma. There's an active investigation that could influence a murder trial, and the prosecution is trying to sweep that information under the rug."

"I know. That's why I'm giving you a quiet heads up. I can't tell you anything officially, so you need to find another way to expose it and bring the facts out." Knowles removed a piece of paper from the top pocket of her leather jacket. She placed the folded piece of paper on the table and pushed it across to Hunter. "You didn't get this from me. The first list is a list of names that attend the bar. They're all old school friends of the owner, Elliot Brady, and we suspect most of them have been involved in using the drug."

Hunter unfolded the piece of paper and looked at the names. He saw Callum Strauss' name at the top of the first list but didn't recognize any other names. "And the second list?"

"The names of the people that are helping facilitate the arrival of the drugs," Knowles said.

"Know any of the names?"

"One of them stands out," Hunter groaned. "Jake Berkeley."

CHAPTER 17

WAITING OUTSIDE Berkeley's office as the time ticked past 9pm, Hunter sat in his rental car across the street, idling the engine to ensure the air-conditioner kept going. The light was still on, and Hunter could see some movement behind the thin blinds.

Berkeley's connections to the bar were concerning, and after digging deeper, Esther had found that he was involved in a drug bust two years ago. He had connections, he had motive, and he had the means to set up Michelle Law.

It was time to check in.

Hunter stepped out of the car, checked his surroundings, and crossed the street. Hunter stepped through the first door, moving it gently, careful not to make a noise and alert his target. He stepped up the stairs quietly before he rested his hand on the second door, moving it lightly, but it was locked.

He tapped on the door and heard movement behind it.

"Who is it, and what do you want?" the voice called out from inside the office.

"It's Tex Hunter. And you and I need to talk."

Berkeley opened the door halfway, but his right hand remained on his hip, attached to his holster. He stared at Hunter, and then leaned his head out the door, checking for anyone else. When he saw no one, he took his hand away from his hip.

"You've wasted your time coming here," Berkeley said. "I don't have time for you."

"But you will make time to talk about your association with drugs at the Five Cocktails Lounge Bar."

The reference caught him off-guard. He froze for a second and then looked at Hunter.

"Alright," Berkeley conceded and opened the door. He stepped back towards his desk, circling around to the other side, and leaned against the wall, arms folded across his chest. "You've got five minutes to ask your questions."

Hunter stepped in, closing the door behind him. The office was small, dirty, and lit by an annoyingly bright fluorescent light. His desk was messy, filled with loose papers, and the room smelled like stale pizza. Hunter looked around and spotted an old pizza box near the far wall and wondered how long it had sat there.

There was a half-empty bottle of Jack Daniels on the table with blue tape wrapped around the neck and a small glass next to it. Berkeley spotted Hunter staring at it.

"It's a defect batch." Berkeley picked up the bottle. "My cousin works for the production line, and one batch went through with tape across the neck of each bottle. Instead of spending hours removing all the tape, they gave two cases to my cousin for free. He was tight on cash, so I offered to buy it from him." His chest puffed out with pride. "I got two cases of Jack for the price of five bottles. Deal of the century."

"Work must be going well then."

"It's going well enough."

"And that's why it seems odd that a man once prosecuted by Michelle Law was willing to work for her," Hunter said, pushing for a reaction.

"I wasn't working for her. She was using me. I signed one deal because they caught me with some drugs, and then they kept coming back for more. She kept pushing to use me as one of her contacts, or she'd threaten me with prison time. It was endless. She used me like a piece of trash."

"That's motive."

"For what?" Berkeley scoffed. "You think she was framed? I don't think so. She was a psycho, just waiting to snap. She killed that girl."

"Were you at the Five Cocktails Lounge Bar that Tuesday night?"

"What if I was?"

"Did you find someone to drug?"

Berkeley's head snapped to face Hunter. "You think I'm involved in that? I don't do that dirty stuff. I'm not into raping people high on drugs."

"But you deliver it, and you know what happens inside that bar on Tuesday nights."

Berkeley's mouth remained shut, his jaw clenched. He moved around his desk, reached for the bottle of Jack Daniels, removed the lid, and took a swig. "You know, Hunter, in this world, a man needs to do whatever he must in order to survive."

"Regardless of the consequences?" Hunter said.

"Exactly," he tapped the gun on his hip. "And do you know why I like to keep my options open? Because I always like to make sure I'm the last one standing. You've asked your questions, and now it's time for you to go."

"Have you ever used GHB?"

"I said we were done, Hunter."

"Who buys it from you?"

"You must have a problem with your hearing." Berkeley's hand rested on his holster. "And right now, it looks like you're trespassing."

Hunter grunted and turned back to the door. He wasn't going to get what he needed from him, but it was clear that Berkeley knew something more about the case.

"Like I said, Hunter," Berkeley called out. "In this world, a man needs to do whatever he can do in order to survive."

CHAPTER 18

HUNTER CAUGHT a cab into his office the next morning.

Replacing his car was on his list of things to do, but in the middle of a murder trial preparation, he struggled to find the time to make it to the car yard. He ordered a coffee from the new café at the base of his building and caught the elevator to his office, sipping the freshly brewed cappuccino.

Stepping off the elevator, he looked down the hall to the entrance to his office, only to see a large man waiting in the chair nearest his door.

"Mr. Hunter?" The man stood as Hunter approached.

Hunter recognized the face.

Tony Mann was one of the most identifiable men currently serving in the Chicago Police Department. He was not only a Deputy Chief in the PD but was also the leading person known to actively fight for the expulsion of corrupt officials from every facet of government. The media had dubbed him 'The Sweeper,' and although it wasn't a title he admired, he knew it summed his purpose up perfectly. When it came to the general public, Tony Mann was a hero, but he was an ever-present nuisance to the politicians and officials opposing him.

"I've been meaning to reach out to you," Mann said as he held out his hand. "Tony Mann. We've crossed paths a few times, but I don't think we've officially met."

Hunter shook the man's hand solidly. Mann's grip was firm. Hunter respected that.

"How can I help you?" Hunter took out his keys and opened the door to his office. "I rarely have the police waiting for me at 8am."

"I needed to meet quietly because if anybody sees me talking to you, it could spell trouble."

Hunter stepped inside, holding the door open for Mann to follow. "I've been hearing that one a lot lately."

"I can imagine why, with the cases you've been taking on in recent months."

"Everybody deserves justice."

"They do, but when you include people like your father in the mix, it has a tendency to ruffle feathers." He said, then, as if to reach out, added, "I'm sorry for your loss."

"Thank you. But somehow, I don't think you came over here to discuss my father."

"No, I didn't. And this won't take long," Mann waited near the door, not settling into the office. "Although, while on the subject, you might like to remember that there are still a lot of cops upset by his release. A lot of good men are amongst those, and if they should see me now…" His voice trailed off.

"I get it," Hunter said, placing his briefcase down next to the reception desk. He leaned against the desk, waiting for Mann to continue.

"You know, cops are like elephants when it comes to remembering things."

"I don't doubt that."

Mann took a moment to consider his surroundings again, stalling as he second-guessed himself for meeting with Hunter in the first place.

"I need corruption to end in Chicago," Mann said, his voice lower than before. "Walter Charman, and all those like him, are on my hit list. They've had their claws in this city for long enough, and it's time they left for good. It's my job to clean up this city, and people like Charman are at the very rotten core."

"You came to me about Charman?" Hunter asked. "Why would his name interest me?"

"Don't play dumb." Mann looked at him and then around the room. "Why do you think, Hunter?"

"Are you saying he's involved in Amanda Ford's murder?"

"Rumor is that Amanda Ford approached someone in the PD to lodge a sexual assault charge against Walter Charman. She was said to have walked into the 18th District precinct and tried to lodge her complaint, but nobody would take it."

"How long before she was murdered?"

"Two days."

"Do you have evidence?"

"If I did, I wouldn't be standing here. The only note we have about her states that she asked about the process for reporting stolen goods, but the word in the PD is that she went in there to lodge a sexual assault claim, and the cop refused to take it. We've got her on camera walking into the precinct, talking to one of the officers, and then walking back out twenty-five minutes later." Mann lowered his voice even further. "You aren't the only one fighting against the likes of Charman. There are others out there, many others."

"The officer's name?"

"Jerry Stevens. Old-time officer, been in the force for decades, and accusations of bribery have come across my desk against him. Nothing ever proven, of course."

"Would you testify to say that happened?"

"And say what? That Amanda Ford walked into a police station two days before her death? The note says that she asked about the process of reporting stolen items, not sexual assault. All I have are rumors."

"Does the officer have links to Charman?"

"There's a lot of good police in that precinct, but just about all the older cops have ties to Charman. They all love him. He's tight with the police union, and anything that's raised against Charman disappears very quickly."

Hunter lowered his head. "Just because he's connected doesn't mean he should be untouchable."

"I know," Mann agreed. "And that's why I'm here giving you a lead. If I find anything else, you'll be the first to know, but you have to be the one to run with this."

CHAPTER 19

WHEN IT came to unwinding, Hunter had never known a better person to watch than Esther.

She somehow changed from businesswoman to leisure woman in an instant, altering everything about her, right down to the mood she exuded. It was one of the most intriguing things he'd learned about her and added to the mystery of the woman he felt helplessly drawn to.

When he came to pick her up for dinner, he could barely keep his eyes off her.

The sight walking towards him was that of a beautiful woman he barely recognized. Instead of her ponytail, Esther had worked her locks into delicate ringlets, strands gently bouncing around her face. The dress looked to have been made for her, hugging her frame in ways that stole Hunter's breath.

His universe stopped spinning at that moment.

"You… you look amazing," he whispered as she neared, his expression caught in surprise. Blushing, Esther smiled back at him and, once she was close enough, looked up into his eyes. They kissed, Hunter lightly touching her cheek as their lips met, and he could feel Esther's hand tremble a little.

Fifteen minutes later, they arrived at the Michelin-star restaurant, Alinea, for dinner. Praised for its innovative cuisine, Alinea was almost impossible to score a table at. Hunter pulled several strings, landing a coveted reservation in the first-floor gallery.

Half a dozen tables dotted the main area, with a set of stairs curving up and around the wall on one side. They were seated near the entrance and soon were enjoying a quiet drink as other diners engaged in small talk. There was a hush over the room, the atmosphere filled with the anticipation of the food to come.

The detail in every dish, each an individual work of art, and the excellence in every moment created a dining experience like no other. The flavors, the textures, the smells. It was perfection on a plate. The servers were friendly and guided them through the journey of the dinner course with attention. The wine pairings were impeccable, matching each dish completely.

Throughout the dinner, they laughed together, exchanging the best and worst jokes they knew. They talked about the food, the quality of the wine, and the perfect service. Esther talked about the latest celebrity scandal, and Hunter let out numerous sighs. She talked about the latest viral song on social media, quietly singing a couple of lines at the table. He talked about his taste in music, and his favorite bands. They talked about how the youth of today had access to the entire back catalog of music at their fingertips, jumping between decades and genres with ease. They laughed as they remember trying to rewind cassette tapes to listen to their favorite songs. They talked about the instruments they played in their younger years. They talked about the concerts they'd attended, old concerts, and new ones. They talked about anything, lost in each other's eyes, connecting over every word.

"I can't believe you've taken me here," Esther whispered as she set down her wine. "You know, you've really created a problem for yourself, don't you?"

Hunter looked at her curiously. "How so?"

"How are you ever going to better yourself now? This is the pinnacle of dinner dates."

He grinned, sipped his Pinot Noir, and winked at her. "That's where you're wrong. This is just the beginning."

"I remember the first time I went to a fine dining restaurant," Esther said. "I arrived early, and the manager said, 'Do you mind waiting a bit?' And I said, 'Sure.' 'Good,' he replied. 'Take these drinks to table number five.'"

Hunter laughed. "Well, just yesterday, I bought the world's worst thesaurus. It was blank, so I have no words to describe how angry I am."

"Well-delivered," Esther laughed with approval of his joke. She sipped her wine as the waiter removed the last plates from their table.

"So, after five months together and our first Michelin-starred restaurant, I have a question." Esther smiled and then leaned forward. "Are we now officially boyfriend and girlfriend?"

"This isn't high school," Hunter smiled. "I think you could officially be my partner."

"I love the term 'partner.' There's so much ambiguity. Are we dating? Or are we detectives on a case? Or are we cowboys? Or are we cowboy detectives who are dating?"

Hunter laughed.

"Now that we're officially partners, I wanted to talk to you about something," Esther drew a long breath, and then swallowed. "I wanted to talk to you about children."

"Those short little humans?"

"Yeah," Esther nodded. "And I wanted to ask if you had ever considered having children?"

"Me?" The wine glass was halfway to his mouth when he stopped. He held the glass there for a moment before he placed it back down. "It hasn't been on my to-do list."

"That's what I thought," Esther whispered, looking away from him.

"But I feel it's on yours?"

"Aren't you a smart man?" Esther tried to joke, but it was clear she was holding back her emotions. "I, well, I'm ready to start a family."

"Wow," Hunter sat back a little. "That's a big moment."

The silence hung over them like a damp cloth, both feeling pressured to talk but not knowing what to say.

"I can't say I've ever considered having children." Hunter broke the silence. "After my upbringing, I don't think I want to bring a child into that world."

"Your child's upbringing would be very different from yours," Esther added. "Your situation was very unusual."

"I know. I just..." he looked away. "I just don't want to."

"It's non-negotiable for me," Esther kept her eyes down. "It's something I've always wanted. I've always wanted to be a mother and watch my little ones grow. And I'm in my late thirties. I can't spend my time dating men who don't want children."

"Can we talk about something else?" Hunter deflected.

"For now, ok," Esther said. "I'll let you process it all, and we can talk about it at a later time, but it's a talk we need to have."

They didn't talk much on the drive home, each silent as they worked through their feelings.

But as Hunter opened the door to his apartment, he caught a grin from Esther, and the smile broadened across his face. Soon, their discussion about children was forgotten. They embraced each other, the passion gripping both of them.

Maybe, just maybe, love could conquer all.

CHAPTER 20

THE NEXT two weeks of trial preparation went past in a flurry of activity. Days disappeared under a mountain of paperwork and trial strategy discussions.

Michelle was holding on, doing her best locked up in her apartment, while Hunter and his team dug deep into every piece of evidence on the prosecution's lists.

Hunter lodged several motions to dismiss the prosecution's evidence; however, they were all rejected. He lodged a motion to dismiss the arresting officer's testimony after he claimed Michelle was 'driving erratically,' and the footage from his dashcam didn't match that description. The judge considered the motion for a number of days before he rejected it. Hunter lodged another motion to dismiss evidence about the drug tests Michelle took, but the judge wasted little time in throwing it out. And he lodged a motion to strike the entire case, based on a lack of foundation, but it was rejected with little consideration.

Hunter found nothing on Officer Jerry Stevens. There were rumors, but nothing substantial. Hunter attempted to approach Amanda Ford's friends to see if they could confirm the purpose of her visit to the station, but none wanted to talk to the lawyer defending her killer.

While he felt ready to tackle the impending court date, he also knew there was more work to be done on the rest of the case. While introducing doubt was the aim, it was by no means the solution.

Filling the largest cup he could find with strong coffee, Hunter slowly sifted through years of legal reports, court cases, and news articles. His cell rang just before eleven, and when Hunter looked at the screen, saw his older brother's name blinking at him.

"Want to watch the Bears' first pre-season game tonight?" Patrick said as soon as Hunter picked up. "My place."

"7pm?" Hunter responded.

"Works for me," Patrick said. "See you then."

Their call was brief, but most of their phone calls were.

Hunter returned to the previous task, and continued scrolling through the current website opened on his laptop. A delivery person broke his concentration, dropping the day's first package on Esther's desk.

"Need a signature?" Hunter yelled.

"No, all good," the woman called back, closed the door, and left him alone once more.

Hunter stared through his office door out to Esther's desk and smiled as he thought about the current state of their relationship. It was a nice distraction from the morning's endless search, and he again felt himself drawn to leaning back in the chair. It creaked loudly, almost defiantly, as Hunter pushed back against the resistance until he could relax his legs.

While their situation wasn't uncommon compared to other newly joined couples, he wondered how many worked together the way he and Esther did. He was her boss, yes, but technically, they had never really seen each other in such a light. It was more of a partnership, with each knowing exactly where their roles began and ended. But there was the question of children. Esther wanted their relationship had to be more than a partnership—she wanted them to be a family. The thought drove a shiver through him.

After a long day in the office reviewing files, Hunter drove to Patrick's home that Thursday evening, and he felt drawn back to the days when he was still part of what he'd once known as family. Since his father's death, Hunter often drew back inside when anything about family came up.

Hunter knocked, and the second Patrick opened the door, he could hear the ballgame already playing out in the den. Patrick greeted him with the standard clap on the back, half-pushing Hunter through the door.

"Just in time," he said. "Kick-off was just seconds ago." He closed the door, then rushed past Hunter to get back to the start of the game. As he followed him through, Hunter could imagine his brother quietly cursing him for making him miss the beginning of the match.

"Who are they playing? I haven't had a chance to check," Hunter said.

"Seahawks," his brother answered, his eyes fixed on the television screen. "Help yourself to a beer," and then added, "I'll have a refill," as he downed the last of his Goose Island Pale Ale.

A clinical psychiatrist, Patrick Hunter's world was measured. His routine was strict, his focus was strong, and his demeanor was restrained. That was, until one of his beloved Chicago sports teams began playing. Then the animal inside of him came out. Whether he was watching the Bulls, the Cubs, or the Blackhawks, his passion erupted, screaming at the players in regular bursts.

While he loved those teams, it was his Chicago Bears he admired the most. The devastating defense, the toughness, the grit and determination. He knew every player's name, every player's stats, and made it to Soldier Field for most of their home games, regardless of the weather.

The brothers sat and watched the game in almost complete silence, the noise in the room amplified by the occasional knee slap or 'darn it' from Patrick each time the Bears offense was stopped. Hunter sometimes enjoyed watching his brother more than the game, his many facial antics worthy of stage time at the local Comedy Central. Their pizza arrived twenty minutes in and was eaten through cheers and rants.

Half-time was the first moment the pair got into conversation, but it remained mostly centered on football. They worked through a healthy argument about who the better quarterback was between Jim McMahon and Jay Cutler, with Patrick putting forth a passionate case for the latter.

It wasn't until the game ended that Patrick finally switched from football to family. With the result firmly in the hands of the opposing team, Hunter saw his brother almost grieving as he turned the television off.

As if to drown his sorrows a little more, Patrick went for a refill after depositing the previous can's contents into the bathroom. Hunter agreed to another while chomping on the last of the pizza. Once Patrick was back at his spot on the couch, the conversation turned to where Hunter knew it eventually would—family.

"How're things with Esther going?"

"I couldn't imagine it going any better," Hunter said. "Great, in fact."

"Ah, young love," Patrick joked. "And what's next for you too?"

"That's the only problem we have," Hunter said. "She wants to have children."

"And you?"

"I don't know," Hunter shook his head. "Do I want to bring a child into this world? With our family name? That's not an easy task. It's never even really occurred to me."

"Our family name has been cleared."

"The mud sticks," Hunter looked down into his beer. "We didn't have the easiest upbringing."

"No, but ours was unusual," Patrick said. "After what you had to endure growing up, I understand your apprehension. Often people who experience traumatic events during their childhoods tend to go one of two ways—either desperate to have children and provide a better life than they had, perhaps determined to heal their own wounds, or they end up being reluctant to have children, desperate to have someone else avoid the pain they had to endure."

"Always the psychiatrist," Hunter laughed.

Patrick picked up a cushion and threw it at him, almost knocking the can from his hand. "It's what I know."

"It's good you know something," Hunter quipped, "Because you certainly don't know how to pick winners in football games."

A second cushion launched as the grin took hold, soon turning into laughter.

"Don't think you can come in here and slander my Bears." Patrick rose from his chair and went to come at Hunter, then held his hands up in surrender as his feet stumbled. "Maybe we can resume this argument when I've had less to drink."

"Drown your sorrows all you want, brother. Won't change the outcome or the season ahead." Hunter continued laughing as Patrick dropped back onto the couch, grabbed his beer, and drank deep.

"Someone filed a complaint to the psychiatrist board against me last week," he said in a somber tone.

"Was it legit?"

"No," Patrick shook his head. "After a brief investigation, they proved that the person was protesting against our father's case. They hadn't even met me, but they were angry that our father had been released. The complaint was thrown out. A lot of people still aren't happy with us. There's still a lot of hate out there."

"Yeah," Hunter said. "I've seen it, but with time, it'll ease off."

"Think he was happy at the end?"

Hunter thought about the question. "Happy? Maybe. Definitely relieved. Not sure how happy he was spending most of his life separated from his family."

"Maybe happy is a bad choice of words."

"I think our father knew early on that he had little chance of getting out. My guess? He made his peace with his life and the sacrifices he made."

Patrick nodded as he took another sip.

"You know, I like to think during the last night at the campsite, he made his peace with life and then went off to meet Mum during that amazing sunset."

"Maybe she was waiting for him," Patrick added.

They weren't religious men, but they knew enough to understand that there had to be something waiting for humanity on the other side.

They fell back into silence for a short time before the conversation turned to a few memories from the times before the shadow fell over their existence. Their mother came up more than a few times, as well as their many trips to the Platte River campground.

It was a great night for the brothers, the kind which they didn't share enough.

When Hunter finished his last drink, it was just before midnight, the moon lighting the city up with an almost complete face.

As he gave his brother a hug goodbye, Patrick stated another warning. "Be careful out there, Tex. Our past may now be buried, but there are still a lot of people gunning for our family name."

CHAPTER 21

MICHELLE LAW had spent more than a month in a self-imposed lockdown.

Her bedroom window had the best view of the streets below, and sitting on the sill had become her new afternoon pastime. With the sun shining brightly overhead, Michelle could feel the heat through the glass, but rather than fill her with joy the way a sunny day normally would, it somehow siphoned all the positivity from her. The rays of summer reminded her of all the things she was missing out on.

As she sat with her forehead pressed against the glass, she couldn't help feeling each emotion take hold as random thoughts crossed her mind. Any time a thought of the impending case rose, her stomach would cramp as the adrenalin kicked in. Thoughts of her doomed career seemed joined to her tear ducts, while the endless reminders of loneliness caused her fingers to shake.

Quite a life you've carved out for yourself, Ms. Law, she thought to herself as a taxicab honked impatiently directly below. She tried to see why, but with the window closed, she couldn't press her face close enough to the glass to see immediately beneath her spot.

Trying to ignore the impatient cabbie as he honked

again, Michelle looked up and saw a jetliner circling the sky in the distance. She imagined the people on the plane. Were they flying in for an amazing vacation or perhaps returning from one? She thought about all the exotic places those strangers could have come from, imagining herself sitting on the plane dressed in casual clothes. Her mind was filled with wonderful memories created on the sands of a distant tropical paradise. The Bahamas was her favorite vacation spot. The sun, the surf, the sea. If she was going to run away, she would find a way to end up there.

As the plane disappeared behind a building, Michelle pulled away from the window, feeling the sadness bubbling inside. She closed her eyes in an attempt to thwart the tears threatening to fall. The desolation was overwhelming, and she tried to refocus her mind on other things. Opening her eyes again, she looked at the wall, then imagined the face of the person sitting just a few feet from her, perhaps he was also suffering through a moment of loneliness. She knew it was James' child-free weekend, and he would most likely be sitting on his couch watching a game.

Feeling a sudden rush of destiny tap her shoulder, a knock on the front door echoed through the apartment, and Michelle held her breath. She froze as the coincidence gripped her and only relaxed when she heard a second knock.

She'd always been a cautious woman. She knew from years of serving as a prosecutor that she had enemies, lots of angry people she'd sent to prison over the years. Never in all her years had she ever opened her front door without first checking the identity of her visitor through the peephole.

Approaching the door cautiously, careful not to make a sound, she checked the peephole. It was James. She smiled, brushed her hair behind her ears, and opened the door.

James Heath stood in the doorway larger than life, holding a cake platter in one hand, a bottle of red wine in the other, and a huge grin on his face.

"I thought you might need some company."

She couldn't resist the smile which birthed the moment he spoke, feeling it pulling against the muscles she'd grown accustomed to remaining locked into place. But something fought her intuition, doing its best to turn the tide from what it knew her answer would be.

As if sensing her defenses kick in, he added, "It's just cake."

He looked and smelled fresh, like he'd just stepped out of the shower.

James had tried numerous times to build something with Michelle, but each time he had launched an attempt, she put up a wall between them. She'd only let him inside her apartment on one previous occasion, and that had been interrupted by a call from work, ending that meeting well before anything substantial eventuated beyond the required small talk. And yet, the man never strayed from his intentions. He remained the course and continued to try and get close to her.

Just before she answered, a second warning rose in her mind, and it was enough to briefly pause the smile still growing on her face. What if this wasn't real? She'd made plenty of enemies during her many years in public life. What if he had an ulterior motive, perhaps even paid for by someone like Walter

Charman?

No way, she thought as she did her best to push the idea aside.

"How did you know?" she said instead, opening the door wider. The response briefly surprised James, who remained frozen until his brain seemed to jumpstart itself as it set his feet into motion.

"Guess I had some sort of intuition," he responded. "Hope you like baked cheesecake."

Michelle's heart briefly jumped. "I love cheesecake, baked or otherwise."

"Good. My grandma will be pleased."

"You baked this?"

The question seemed to please him. "Yes, why? The thought of a man baking surprises you?"

"Well," Michelle began, her smile returning, "I guess, in a way, it does."

"Then you haven't been around too many versatile men," he replied, holding the dish out. Michelle happily took it, then shied away when he held out the bottle.

"I can't drink that," she said meekly, lowering her voice some. The comment surprised James.

"Oh? No, that's fine. I'm not much of a drinker myself, actually."

"Really?" Again, her self-doubt crept in, his answers almost sounding too good to be true. She couldn't work out if he was genuine or simply trying to tell her the things he thought she wanted to hear.

"You have no idea of the number of people who shy away from friendship because I don't continuously hold a glass of liquor at gatherings," James continued. "I don't need a beer to watch a ballgame. A soda is just fine."

"I know how that feels. Before all this happened, I was sober for two years," Michelle said. She felt a hint of color rise in her cheeks and turned to take the cake into the kitchen. "Let me cut this up for us."

She pointed James to the living area and the couches and went to the kitchen. She grabbed a knife and two plates and walked back to the couches. James was sitting on the main couch, one leg crossed over the other. Michelle briefly paused as she looked at her options. The only single chair had a pile of folded clothes on it, and if she had opted for that one, she would have needed to move it, leaving James thinking she was avoiding sitting next to him. If she had sat beside him on the couch, she might have come off as too needy, perhaps clingy. Stop it, she snapped to herself, set the cake down on the table, then sat next to him, careful to leave enough respectable distance between them.

"Allow me," he said, picking up the knife and cutting a slice before he shoveled a generous piece onto a plate and held it out to her.

"No, no," she protested. "That's way too much. I'll be carrying that around for—"

"My grandma is watching," he joked, the grin almost childlike. "She needs to see you eat it."

And I'm watching you, she thought to herself, James Heath, where have you been all my life?

The first taste practically melted in her mouth, and Michelle's face was all the confirmation James needed.

"She likes it, Grandma," he said, speaking into the air above them. Michelle laughed, snorted, then laughed some more. James joined in as he watched her.

The pair chatted as they ate, talking about everything except the looming cloud that was her court case. For Michelle, it again felt a little too perfect, and she couldn't quite decipher whether he was just genuinely likable in every way or simply working her over with a well-researched plan to gain her trust.

While James told her about a recent work trip to Boston, Michelle's mind again took a step sideways as she wondered why fate would make things so hard for her. If she had tried with James just a few years earlier, her entire life may have taken a drastic turn, and she wouldn't be in the position she was in today. Just a few years, James, she thought to herself. As if sensing her distance, he paused, then took it as a sign. He stood suddenly, catching Michelle off guard.

"I'd best get back. Still have some paperwork to catch up on." He smiled uncomfortably, then added, "Promised myself to get through it over the weekend."

Michelle thanked him for stopping by, then followed him through to the front door. Her mind raced as she wondered whether she had offended him or whether he had picked up on her curiosity about him and perhaps thought he'd better cut and run before she discovered he was a fraud.

"I really appreciate you stopping by," she offered, and then, as if wanting to give him the smallest of signals, she reached out and squeezed his wrist. James smiled, looked down at the remaining cake, and said, "Maybe we can finish this another time."

He didn't wait for a response and disappeared back into the hallway, leaving Michelle alone once more.

Her mind was awash, running rampant with thoughts of deception, companionship, loneliness, and deceit all rolled into one dark and stormy cloud.

Whatever his intentions, she needed to take the risk. It was time to let her walls down.

CHAPTER 22

AS HUNTER woke the day before the murder trial, two months after the arrest, he sat bolt upright, sweat pouring from his forehead.

His dream was fading into obscurity as he wiped the sweat from his brow. His father had been in it, as was Walter Charman. The dream faded into the shadows, leaving Hunter sitting in the dark, trying to recapture the image. He reached for his cell, checked the time, and considered whether to try for another hour of rest or give up and make the most of an early morning. Five am wielded that type of power.

Opting for an early morning, Hunter climbed out of bed, drawing back the curtains to see the late summer sun painting its soft orange haze over the city. A faint tightness gripped his left eye, and he groaned as the onset of a headache came on. Not today, he thought as he walked into the bathroom and reached for the painkillers. Crunching two aspirins between his teeth, he sipped handfuls of water from the faucet before stripping off and hitting the shower.

The water felt good, washing away the tension headache before it took hold. Standing under the shower, Hunter closed his eyes and thought about the days ahead, wondering how Michelle was handling the moment. He couldn't imagine the amount of pressure on her and hoped she would hold it together long enough for him to work some magic.

Esther sent a text through just after seven and offered to pick him up. Hunter agreed as he sipped his coffee, then turned the television on as he tossed the cell onto the couch beside him.

The early news had little drama, but his ears pricked when the case scored a mention just before a station break. A photo of Michelle flashed up behind the anchor, and Hunter listened in as she recalled the details behind the murder trial.

After finishing his coffee, Hunter dragged his briefcase back to the couch and pulled out the files.

Esther caught him off-guard a few minutes later when she let herself in. He'd temporarily forgotten the whole exchanging of the apartment keys ritual they had held a few weeks earlier and had to calm himself to catch his breath. Seeing him jump up from his seat set Esther off as she joked about the man getting caught with his pants down. Hunter looked down and realized he was still in his boxers.

"Not that I'm complaining," Esther winked, watching as he disappeared from the room after a quick kiss. "You've been working out."

Once dressed for the day, Hunter followed Esther back down to her car and climbed into the passenger side. It gave him the chance to close his eyes and forget about the world around him. Knowing he needed to zone out a little, Esther turned on the tunes, settling on a mix of classic 80s.

Traffic was heavy on the Monday morning, not surprising either of them. Once Hunter had enough time to get into the mind space of things to come, he turned the radio down and ran through a checklist of things for Esther to acknowledge.

"This is it," he mumbled once finished. "After two months, Michelle Law is finally going to have her day in court."

"The moment of truth," Esther added. "You know, I've been thinking a lot about sex recently."

Hunter turned to her and raised his eyebrows.

"Yeah. When there's three people in the bed, it's called a threesome. When it's just two in the bed, it's called a twosome." A grin washed over her face. "So, I guess that's why they call you handsome."

Hunter was unable to control his chuckle, the joke delivered with perfection. "Where did that joke come from?"

"Think I was born with it," she offered back. "Comedy runs in my veins."

Once at the building, Esther dropped Hunter by the front and said she'd meet him inside once she parked the car and grabbed two coffees for the morning. He was still smiling, thinking about her joke as he walked to the entrance, when another voice reached out to him.

"Hunter." Ray Jones waited by the entrance to the building, coffee in hand. "Ready for the first day tomorrow?"

"Ready as ever," he returned. "Should be quite the event. A prosecutor versus the State's Attorney's Office. We've got weeks of headlines in front of us."

"Well, I've got a few things for you." Jones followed Hunter into the elevator, where they were joined by five other people. The two tall men waited at the back of the tight space, remaining quiet until they exited and walked through the doors of the office.

Hunter took off his suit jacket and hung it on the hook by the door. Jones followed him in, sipping on his coffee, and leaned against the wall, one hand still tucked in his large bomber jacket.

"Everything just came together yesterday. It happens sometimes. You put in all the hard work, put the feelers out there, and then, snap," Jones clicked his fingers. "All the information arrives at once."

"Hit me with it," Hunter said. "If we need extra time before the trial, I can file a motion to delay."

"First, we know that Callum Strauss went to the Five Cocktails on Tuesdays. So, I got talking to all the business owners down the street, seeing who had footage of the night. The guy at the diner was helpful, but said a security company managed his footage, and he'd have to lodge a request for it. On Friday, he got a call back to say that they'd sent through the footage for a month before the murder. I spent a day going through the videos, searching for cars or people on the street, and I noticed that Callum was drove there on every Tuesday night for the last month before the murder, but not the night when Amanda Ford was murdered."

"That's because he got a lift with Michelle," Hunter added. "He left his car in the parking lot, and Michelle drove them to the bar."

"Right," Jones replied. "But that Tuesday, he didn't drive. If he planned to drug Michelle, why didn't he drive?"

"Maybe he would've taken her car?"

"Maybe," Jones nodded. "But looking at the footage, I saw Jake Berkeley walk past the diner that night."

"Berkeley?"

"That's right. I was surprised as well. Now, the diner is half a block away from the Five Cocktails, so it doesn't prove he was in the bar, but he was in the area. The footage from the diner shows he walked past at 11.15pm, and then walked back the other direction at just before 1am."

"That's great, Ray." Hunter's fist clenched in a small sign of celebration. "If I need to get him on the stand, then that's something to attack him with."

"But you're not going to like the second part of the news I have for you."

Hunter drew a long breath. "The day before a trial isn't the best time for surprises."

"You can blame your client for this one," Jones nodded. "My contact called me yesterday and said that Michelle Law was making a run for politics last year."

Hunter's eyes narrowed. "She didn't tell me that."

"A political contact told me that before your father's trial, she met with Walter Charman a few times. This contact said that people only meet with a lobbyist like Charman when they're ready to make a number of backroom deals and make a run for politics."

Hunter's fist clenched again, this time in frustration that he hadn't been told the whole truth.

CHAPTER 23

"YOU DIDN'T tell me everything."

Hunter stood at the end of the boardroom, arms folded across his chest, the anger in his tone clear. Michelle Law had arrived for their final briefing but was confused about his confrontation. She sat at the other end of the boardroom, a paler version of herself than she'd ever been before. Her clothes were wrinkled, she had no make-up on, and her hair, usually held back tightly, was loose and out of place.

"I don't know what you're talking about," Michelle shook her head. "What's wrong?"

"I thought we had an understanding."

"We do," Michelle said, her tone questioning his. She tilted her head as she looked at him. "What's going on?"

"Why didn't you tell me that you were making a run for politics?"

The change in expression on Michelle's face was instant, her jaw visibly dropping open as he revealed the news. "How did you—"

"How did I find out about it?" He shook his head. "And not only that, but you've also held meetings with Charman himself."

That brought Michelle's defenses up. "I wouldn't call them meetings."

"No? What would you call them?"

Her shoulders slumped forward as she rested her elbows on the table, putting her head into her hands. "Look, I did have a plan to get into politics, yes, that much is true. And yes, I may have had several 'unofficial' meetings with Charman."

"But?"

"But it was before your father's trial. I could see that there were going to be issues with the trial, and I wondered what I could do after it. Charman," she drew a long breath. "Charman said he was happy to help me make a run in politics, but on the condition that I saw your father's trial through to his death. Then I could make a run for politics because I was also tough on crime. Clean up the streets of Chicago."

"And?"

"Ok, well, that might be a small problem," she said, cutting him off. "I may have made some stupid comment to wind him up during our final get-together."

"What exactly did you tell him?"

"Ah," Michelle rubbed her hands over her face. "I might have told him that I would take him down." The silence was deafening and, as if sensing an oncoming outburst, Michelle tried to lessen the blow. "But it was just a stupid, off-the-cuff remark as I left the meeting. Nothing more."

"We go to court tomorrow, and I've just found this out. We should be focusing on how to present at the trial. We should be focusing on how you should sit, how you should react, and how you should dress. But instead, I'm still finding out new things that could change the investigation." He stepped forward, leaning his arms down on the table. "What else haven't you told me?"

"Nothing. I'm sorry. I honestly didn't think it mattered."

"You thought wrong."

Michelle sat dumbfounded. She stared at the table in front of them.

"You're not telling me something else," Hunter pressed. "What is it?"

"Nothing," she whispered. "That's all there is to know. There's nothing else."

He took a few moments to calm himself enough to continue with his previous schedule. He called Esther into the room and began the process of preparing for the first day before court.

But during the meeting, and over the course of the day, Hunter knew he hadn't received the whole truth about Walter Charman.

CHAPTER 24

INDICTMENT

IN THE CIRCUIT COURT OF COOK COUNTY, ILLINOIS COUNTY DEPARTMENT, CRIMINAL DIVISION
PEOPLE OF THE STATE OF ILLINOIS,
-vs-
MS. MICHELLE LAW, DEFENDANT

The Grand Jurors chosen, selected, and sworn in, for County of Cook, in the State of Illinois, in the name and by the authority of the people of the State of Illinois, upon their oaths present on July 15th that MICHELLE LAW committed the offense of murder in that she intentionally and knowingly killed AMANDA FORD without lawful justification in violation of 720 ILCS 5/9-1, first degree murder.

COUNT ONE
720 ILCS 5/9-1 Ch. 38, par. 9-1

Sec. 9-1. First degree murder; death penalties; exceptions; separate hearings; proof; findings; appellate procedures; reversals. (a) A person who kills an individual without lawful justification commits first degree murder if, in performing the acts which cause the death: (1) he or she either intends to kill or do great bodily harm to that individual or another, or knows that such acts will cause death to that individual or another; or (2) he or she knows that such acts create a strong probability of death or great bodily harm to that individual or another; or (3) he or she, acting alone or with one or more participants, commits or attempts to commit a forcible felony other than second degree murder, and in the course of or in furtherance of such crime or flight therefrom, he or she or another participant causes the death of a person.

FINDINGS

We, the Grand Jury, find that MICHELLE LAW is to be indicted under (720 ILCS 5/9-1) (from Ch. 38, par. 9-1) as amended.

*****

The first day of a murder trial carried an intensity like no other.

There was a crackle in the air, a desperation that Hunter hadn't felt anywhere else. Michelle Law knew that better than most. She'd been through the process. She'd experienced the desperate battle that occurred throughout a trial. She knew what lay ahead of them—bitter, hard-fought, and emotionally draining days, weeks, and sometimes, months.

The intensity of the courtroom wasn't helped by the media presence outside. The broader community had a waning faith in the system, they had a waning faith in the process, and they needed to know that their tax dollars were hard at work protecting them from crime. With the advent of true-crime podcasts and serials, the interest in the real-life drama of the court was high, and the media kept feeding the beast with constant stories from every possible angle.

The media pack was desperate for a new soundbite, desperate for a new slice of the action, and they pushed every question they could. The mainstream reporters, flanked by the podcasters, pressed Hunter for new information as he entered the courthouse that morning, but he strode past them, not offering a word. They questioned him about Michelle, about Amanda Ford, and about his father, but he ignored them all. He needed to focus. He needed to keep his strength for inside the courtroom.

On one hand, he told himself that Michelle deserved the best defense a lawyer could provide, and on the other hand, he wasn't sure of her guilt or innocence. Not even Michelle knew what happened. She'd blacked out, and only awoke to be told there was a body in the trunk of her car.

Had she been lying the entire time? He knew she hadn't told him the whole truth, but perhaps that was deliberate. A defense lawyer cannot lie for their client in court, and Michelle knew this.

The less she told him, the more he could say. The less he knew, the more he could argue.

Their trial strategy focused on the idea that Michelle had been involuntarily drugged that night. If she was involuntarily drugged, she could not be found guilty of murder. Manslaughter, at worst, but not murder.

Suspended ADA Michelle Law was nervous as she sat at the defense table, barely able to sit still. She looked like she was about to vomit at any second. The bags under her eyes displayed that she'd been crying for weeks, and her pale skin looked unhealthy, but dressed in her best black skirt and jacket with her hair pulled back tightly, she presented well.

Pradesh Baron and his team were organizing files at the prosecution's desk. Baron didn't greet Hunter as he entered, instead focusing on his opening statement, rehearsing the lines under his breath.

When the bailiff called the room to order, the crowd rose to their feet. The thick and heavy nervousness in the room was distinctive, filling the air with unease.

Judge David Bales walked into the courtroom, in no rush to begin the trial, and once he sat down, he looked over his notes and then welcomed the parties to the court.

They spent the first morning in voir dire, the jury selection process. When called by the bailiff, the potential jurors filed into the courtroom in groups of twelve. Judge Bales questioned them first, dismissing several people early. Both Baron and Hunter called for Judge Bales to exclude potential jurors with 'for cause' challenges. Baron used two peremptory challenges after the pool was whittled down, and Hunter used five.

The ones that remained were a mix of ages, a mix of education levels, and a mix of social classes. Five men, seven women. Five office workers, two retirees, a housewife, and four blue-collar workers. They were all educated, all focused, and all appeared keen to serve the legal system.

Once the jury was formed, Hunter studied their profiles carefully. He knew which ones to target with emotions, which ones to target with perceived facts, and which ones to maintain eye contact with. There were two clear leaders in the group, one builder who held himself well and one female manager who looked like no one could win an argument against her.

Before the opening statements, Judge Bales called a recess for lunch. Michelle Law was nervous, the sweat building on her brow. James Heath sat behind her in the courtroom, showing his support for his neighbor. Several reporters sat at the back of the courtroom, with their notepads ready, and two Deputy Sheriffs stood by the doors. Esther sat behind Hunter, and Jones next to her.

After the brief recess for lunch, Judge Bales instructed the bailiff to bring the jury members in. The bailiff walked to the door in the front left corner of the room, opened it, and directed the members of the jury to their seats. The twelve people who would decide Michelle Law's fate entered.

Judge Bales spoke to the jury about their responsibilities, explaining the charges, and what that meant, before explaining his role, "As the judge in this trial, I will act as a legal referee to ensure that proper trial procedure is followed, and I will issue rulings on points of law. While it is my job to determine the evidence available and to instruct you on the rule of law, it is you, the juror, that is responsible for deciding the facts, following the law, and rendering a final decision. Members of the jury, your duty will be to determine whether the defendant is guilty or not guilty based only on the facts and evidence provided in this case. The prosecution has the burden of proving the defendant's guilt beyond a reasonable doubt. This burden remains on the prosecution throughout the trial. The prosecution must prove that a crime was committed and that the defendant is the person who committed the crime. However, if you're not satisfied with the defendant's guilt to that extent, then reasonable doubt exists, and the defendant must be found not guilty. As jurors, you must only look at the facts in this case, and you must not be swayed by sympathy."

Once Judge Bales was satisfied the jurors understood his instructions, he invited the State to begin their opening. Pradesh Baron stood, buttoned his suit jacket, and walked to the lectern.

*****

"Your Honor, ladies and gentlemen of the jury. My name is Pradesh Baron, and these are my colleagues Maxwell Smith and Tanya Campbell. We're here to present the charge of murder against the defendant, Ms. Michelle Law. As mentioned by Judge Bales, in this opening statement, I'll provide a roadmap of what the evidence presented during this trial will show, as nothing I say to you now can be considered evidence.

We are here today, in this court, to deliver a fair and just verdict on the charge of murder. We're here to deliver justice. Justice. That's such an important word to the Cook County legal system. It's what we do, and it's what we strive to achieve. Justice. The definition of justice is the idea that the citizens of this great country are treated impartially, fairly, and properly. Justice sees people treated fairly by the law regardless of their background, and it sees that the accused receives a morally right consequence merited by their actions. A moral consequence. I need you to remember that as we go through this trial.

The defendant, Ms. Michelle Law, sitting there at

the defense table, is a woman of privilege. She is a woman who has coasted through life with every opportunity that life has to give. If she wanted something, she could get it. But more than that, more than that level of privilege, was the fact that Michelle Law was a lead prosecutor within the State's Attorney's Office.

She's managed hundreds of cases, she's seen hundreds of trials, she's been involved with hundreds of murder hearings. She knows murder inside out.

I need you to remember that.

This woman, the woman sitting there at the defense table, knows the system.

She knows the law. She knows how people get off murder charges. She knows how people avoid justice.

That's why I ask you to really look at the evidence in this case. Really look at it. Because no matter the background of the defendant, and no matter the background of the victim, you must make a decision that is impartial and just. You need to make that decision without regard for race, bias, or, most importantly in this case, privilege.

As an Assistant State's Attorney, I represent the great city of Chicago and the State's Attorney's Office. Along with my colleagues, we serve Cook County. I'm very grateful for my opportunity to serve this area of our great country. I'm grateful for the opportunity to keep this city safe. I'm very grateful for my opportunity to keep murderers off the street.

You, as jurors, are tasked with a great responsibility. You're tasked with assessing the evidence in this case. You're tasked with evaluating the evidence that I present to you. You, as jurors, are tasked with making a decision based on the rule of law.

The facts of this case are simple.

Ms. Michelle Law murdered Miss Amanda Ford. We know this because Amanda Ford was found in the trunk of Ms. Law's Audi sedan. Think about that. A deceased body was found in the trunk of her sedan.

Over the coming days, we'll present witnesses to you, and they will provide the evidence in this case, as anything I say now cannot be considered as evidence.

You'll hear from the people connected to this case, and these people will provide evidence for you to make a decision on the guilt of Michelle Law.

You'll hear from Chicago Police Department Officer Dennis Parker, and he will tell you why he pulled over Michelle Law on the morning of July 15th. Officer Parker will tell you that when he pulled the defendant over, he saw a bloodstain on the trunk of the car. He requested the defendant to step out of the car, and when he popped the trunk open, he found the body of Amanda Ford. He will tell you that Ms. Law stated she had been drinking heavily the night before, and that she'd 'blacked out.' Officer Parker will tell you that Ms. Law stated she couldn't remember anything about the previous night.

You'll hear from the Detectives who interviewed Ms. Law at the police station after her arrest.

You'll hear from experts in crime and justice. You'll hear from crime scene experts who will tell you their interpretation of the night in question.

You'll hear from Dr. Mary Stuart, an assistant Medical Examiner with the Cook County Medical Examiner's Office, who performed the autopsy, and she will tell you that Miss Ford died as a result of strangulation.

You'll hear from Mr. Callum Strauss, who will testify that Ms. Law was acting irrational and crazed that night. He'll testify that Ms. Law threatened to kill Miss Ford that night. You see, Mr. Strauss had taken Miss Law on a date on July 14th, but when he mentioned his on-again, off-again girlfriend Miss Ford, the defendant descended into a jealous rage.

You'll hear from other witnesses who will state that the defendant was acting crazy that night, including Ms. Rita Banks, and Miss Sonja Lovett, who will both testify that they heard Ms. Law shouting that she was going to kill someone.

Once we arrive at the end of this case, once you have heard all the evidence, I have no doubt that you will have enough evidence to convict Ms. Law of murder in the first degree. It was her intent to kill Miss Ford that night, and she must be punished for this inexcusable crime.

At the end of this case, I'll address you again and ask you to consider all the evidence we have presented and conclude that Ms. Law is guilty beyond a reasonable doubt.

Thank you for your time."

*****

Lawyers are competitive by nature.

Every court case was a battle, a challenge, and a test. It was a battle of wills, a clash of intelligence, an encounter between two teams, each well-educated, each well-prepared. Murder trials brought out the most competitive nature, and it brought out the desire to win at all costs.

Most murder indictments never made it inside the courtroom. Most cases were dealt out with long before opening statements began, but occasionally, a case made it through the process, making it before a jury. It was that moment, that pinnacle of competition, that lit a fire under the most competitive of lawyers.

In the weeks before the trial, Hunter had pushed Baron to present a better deal, but none came. The media was watching, the entire state was watching, waiting to see how the justice system treated one of its own. The online warriors cried out that the system would protect her, they shouted from their keyboards that Amanda Ford's family would never see justice. They typed on social media that the system would never find Michelle Law guilty and complained that the system was biased.

The internet was a problem for the justice system, a place where even the most absurd of voices could find a following.

The State's Attorney's Office felt that pressure.

They knew the outrage that would spill out onto the streets if they were lenient on their own.

Hunter stood, made eye contact with the jurors, and nodded. Five nodded in return. Standing behind the lectern, Hunter began his opening statement.

*****

"May it please the court. Ladies and gentlemen of the jury, Your Honor, my name is Tex Hunter, and

I'm a criminal defense attorney. I'm here to represent the defendant, Ms. Michelle Law.

Any loss of life is a tragedy. Any loss of life is a disaster. It hurts so many people.

But the pain, grief, and agony of loss does not justify putting an innocent person away. No matter how you feel, no matter how much empathy you feel for the victim, you have to remember that it does not mean you can find a person guilty without evidence.

And that's an important distinction—you need evidence to convict a person of guilt. You need evidence. You need proof. You need facts. Not ideas, or notions, or beliefs. You cannot listen to your gut, and you cannot make an assumption.

You must listen to evidence, and you must only listen to the evidence presented in this trial. You cannot listen to what you hear in the news, on social media, or hear from friends.

And if you do that, if you listen, really listen, then you will see that this case is filled with holes.

We do not know who murdered Amanda Ford. That's a fact. There are no witnesses that saw the murder of Amanda Ford. There's no evidence that ties the defendant to the moment of the crime.

There's no murder weapon, there's no witness to the event, and there's no footage of this occurrence. There's no evidence that shows who committed this crime, there's no evidence that shows who strangulated the victim, and there's no evidence that shows who was involved in her murder.

The prosecution has theories. They have concepts. They have ideas.

But they do not have evidence.

As the defense, we will present witnesses who will

confirm that there is no clear evidence of who killed Amanda Ford. We will present blood splatter experts who will show you that if the prosecution's theory was even close to correct, then Ms. Law would've been covered in blood.

We will present expert witnesses that will demonstrate that the prosecution's evidence is doubtful, at best. Other expert witnesses will tell you that there is no way that Ms. Law would've had the strength to overcome Miss Ford.

The onus of proof is on the prosecution. They must present evidence that proves Ms. Law committed this act. They won't be able to because the direct evidence simply does not exist.

In making your decision at the end of this trial, the only evidence you can consider is the evidence presented here.

Ms. Law did not murder Miss Ford. There is no evidence that she did, and you cannot convict her for it.

There are many holes in the prosecution's case, and when this case is drawing to a close, I will stand up here again and point to all the ways they've failed to prove their case. You will then be asked to make a decision on this trial, and you can only conclude that Ms. Law is not guilty.

Thank you for your service to our great justice system."

CHAPTER 25

WHEN THE first witness was called, the tension in the room was electric.

Hunter looked over his shoulder. Spectators had filled the gallery. In the dark brown chairs behind him, there were media, supporters, and regular on-lookers. Behind the prosecution team sat the Ford family, and their supporters filled the five rows behind them. Hunter could feel their anger, and they glared at him every time he looked in their direction. The bailiffs, armed for the occasion, stood at the front of the room, searching for any unusual movements in the crowd, ready to pounce on anything out of order. The air was stuffy, credited to the lack of air-conditioning and the sun burning in the window to the far side of the room.

Officer Dennis Parker entered the courtroom with his chin held high. His confidence was clearly put on, faking it to convince himself. In his Chicago PD uniform, the skinny man's elbows were splayed wide like a bodybuilder's, his chest puffed out, and his stride too long. Officer Parker's schoolboy blond haircut and soft skin made him look like the oldest member of the Boy Scouts in history.

All eyes turned back to Baron as he prepared to launch his case. The time for judgment was now.

"Could you please state your full name for the court?" Baron began, standing behind the lectern at the side of the room.

"Officer Dennis Parker," the witness stated. "I've been an officer with the Chicago Police Department for five years now, ever since my twenty-first birthday."

"Thank you, Officer Parker. Can you please tell the court what happened on the morning of July 15th?"

"I was following a suspect, but I lost him in the streets of The Loop." He wiped his brow. "As I was driving back to my station, I saw a woman sleeping in her white Audi sedan. Her car was in the parking lot of the Five Cocktails Lounge Bar in River North, and that's always a sign that someone may have been drinking heavily the night before and could still be under the influence of alcohol."

"And did you wake this woman up?"

"No, I let her sleep. It was a nice car, must've been worth a few dollars, so I thought I'd circle the block, see if there was anything else happening, and then come back to check on the car. After I drove around the block, I came back to see that the Audi was pulling out of the parking lot."

"And how long did it take you to drive around the block?"

"Not more than five minutes," he replied. "So, I followed her for a few moments to see if there were any clear signs of impairment in her driving. She barely made it to the end of the street before the car started to drift over to the other side of the road. That's when I decided to pull her over. I put on the sirens."

"And did she pull over right away?"

"She did."

"And what did you notice when you exited your car?"

"As I approached the car, I noticed blood smeared on the outside of the trunk. It was pretty clear because the white car was so clean, and the blood was so dark."

"And did you have your body camera on?"

"I did."

"Is this the footage from your body camera?" Baron turned to his assistant and nodded. The assistant typed into her laptop, and a photo appeared on the court monitor at the side of the room. The footage played for a minute, from when Parker stepped out of the vehicle to when he first saw the visible streaks of dark red blood on the outside of the white Audi.

"That is my footage, yes."

"And what did you do when you saw the blood?"

"At this point, as we've been taught in training, I drew my weapon and instructed the driver to show me their hands. The window of the Audi went down, and the woman put her hands out the window. I rounded to the front of the car and instructed her to exit the vehicle. The smell of alcohol was strong on her, and with the few words she said, her speech was very slurred. Once she was out of the car, I handcuffed her, called it in, and then asked her what was in the trunk."

"And what did she say?"

"Not much. It was hard to understand what she was saying because her words were so slurred." Officer Parker drew a long breath. "I then took the keys out of the ignition to the vehicle and popped open the trunk."

"And what did you find?"

"The body of a woman who was clearly deceased." He drew a deep breath. "Photos were also taken by the forensic teams."

"And are these the photos that were taken?"

Again, the assistant tapped several lines on the laptop, and a photo appeared on the court monitor. One of the jury members gasped. The photo of Amanda Ford, squashed into the trunk, was confronting. Her lips were blue, she had dried blood pooled on the side of her head, and her eyes were open and vacant. Valerie Ford, a heartbroken mother sitting in the front row of the courtroom seats, began to sob. The prosecution presented five photos in total, and with each photo, Valerie's sobbing only became louder.

"And at this point, did you arrest Ms. Law?"

"That's correct."

"Did you read her the Miranda rights?"

"I did."

"And did she say anything to you after that?"

"She said that she couldn't remember anything. She said she was drinking with a friend, and then she didn't remember anything more. I think—"

"Objection," Hunter said. "Speculation. No statement from the witness should start with 'I think.'"

"Sustained," Judge Bales said and turned to the witness. "Please stick with what you know, and not what 'you think,' Officer Parker."

"Yes, Your Honor," he nodded his head. "She said that she'd 'blacked out' from the alcohol the night before and couldn't remember anything."

"Those were her exact words? That she 'blacked out?'"

"That's what she said, yes."

"And is that statement on the body-cam footage?"

"It is."

Baron turned back to his assistant, and they began to play the footage from the moment Michelle stepped out of the car. The shock on Michelle's face was clear and evident the moment the officer popped open the trunk. She mumbled a few words, 'I don't know who that is,' 'I blacked out last night,' and, 'This isn't real.' Despite her legal knowledge telling her she shouldn't speak once arrested, she continued to talk, even after being told to lie on the ground and place her hands behind her back. She pleaded with the officer that it was a mistake and continued to say that the last thing she remembered was being at the bar with a man named Callum Strauss.

Baron stopped the footage once Michelle was cuffed and sat on the side of the road.

"Did you call for back-up?"

"Absolutely. Once Ms. Law was handcuffed, and I felt safe to do so, I called in and told them about the body. The second car arrived five minutes later, and we cordoned off the area. The lead detectives arrived ten minutes after that."

"Did you take Ms. Law to the station to charge her?"

"That's right. She rode in the back of my patrol car back to the 18th District station."

"And at the station, did she submit to a rape-kit test?"

"She did. She insisted on it. Another officer took

the kit," Parker nodded. "And the result was negative."

"Did Ms. Law submit to any other tests?"

"She submitted a blood and urine test as well." Parker shook his head. "And the result of those were negative for drugs, however positive for a high blood alcohol content."

For the next fifty-five minutes, Officer Parker detailed his actions that morning, guided by precise questioning from Baron. They were well-rehearsed in their delivery, and the jury sat attentive to every word of the testimony. It was a good start, one that presented Michelle Law as nothing other than guilty.

"Thank you, Officer Parker," Baron concluded when the picture had been painted of Michelle's guilt. "No further questions."

"Mr. Hunter?" Judge Bales asked. "Any questions for this witness?"

Hunter first thanked the judge but remained in his chair, looking down at his notes, keeping quiet, and allowing the tension in the room to build.

It wasn't that he needed more time. He wanted the cop to wait for him, to feel the building anticipation of the cross-examination. From his research, Hunter knew that Officer Parker had only presented in court twice before, and both times, he was made to look like a fool by a defense lawyer. With each passing second, the pressure would continue to build on Parker. Just as Judge Bales was about to ask the defense to begin, Hunter stood and stepped out from behind his table.

"Officer Parker, is it normal for you to be patrolling around in the River North community area?"

"Well, not usually."

"Have you patrolled there, say, during the past twelve months?" Hunter stood next to the lectern, leaning one hand on it and stepping closer to the jury.

"No, but—"

"How about during the past five years?" Hunter didn't bother waiting for an answer. "Isn't it true your actual precinct is over fifteen miles from that location in the 24th precinct, in Rogers Park?"

"I had followed a suspect's vehicle down from Rogers Park that morning and just happened to—"

Hunter didn't wait for the officer to finish, walking towards him and showing him a second photograph. The cop looked at it, dumbfounded.

"Do you confirm that one of the men in that photo is you?"

Parker nodded.

"The court needs a verbal answer, Officer Parker."

The cop looked up and as their eyes met, Hunter could see he was flustered. The nerves which had held up to that point were beginning to fray. "Could you tell us who the second person in the photograph is?"

Silence enveloped the courtroom as Hunter waited for the answer. He looked over to Michelle, who looked nervously down at the table. Finally, Parker answered, his voice low, as barely a murmur sounded from elsewhere in the room. "Callum Strauss. We went to school together."

"And does Callum Strauss know Amanda Ford?"

"Objection," Baron stood. "Relevance. Where is the connection to a murder trial here?"

"Your Honor, I'm showing the court that the detective has connections to the deceased woman."

"Overruled," Judge Bales stated. "But get to the

162

point, Mr. Hunter."

"As far as I knew, Callum Strauss was dating Amanda Ford, but they separated before her death."

"This photo of you and the victim's ex-boyfriend was taken from a security feed at a bar called Largo's nearly a week prior to the arrest. Doesn't that strike you as odd, Officer Parker?"

"Not odd. It's just a coincidence."

Hunter paused for a moment, and on a hunch, he pushed harder. "Officer Parker, I will remind you that you are under oath, and I remind you that a log of all calls is recorded." Hunter paused to build the tension before he continued. "Did Mr. Strauss call you on the morning of July 15th?"

Parker sucked in a sharp breath. He looked to the prosecution table, but Baron was expressionless.

"Officer Parker?" Hunter asked again. "Did you talk to Mr. Strauss on the morning of July 15th?"

"How would you know that?" he whispered.

"Answer the question," Hunter stated firmly.

Parker looked back to the prosecution, but again, they offered him nothing.

"Officer Parker," Judge Bales leaned across his chair to talk to the witness. "Please answer the question."

"Um, yes."

"Yes?" Hunter pushed harder. "Are you confirming that he talked to you or confirming that he called you?"

"I talked to him, yes." Parker's voice was quiet. "He called me."

"And what time was that?"

"He called me about 5am."

"5am. Two hours before you pulled over the

defendant. And where were you at 5am on July 15th when you took that call?"

"I don't remember."

"Officer Parker," Hunter sighed. "Need I remind you that the GPS location of your vehicle is tracked during your shift. So, can you please think a little harder and tell the court where you were at 5am on July 15th?"

"Ok. I think I was in Rogers Park." He wiped the sweat from his brow again. "Yeah, that's it. Rogers Park. That's when I spotted a suspect in another case and followed them south to River North. I lost the suspect in River North. That's what happened."

"Sounds very coincidental, Officer Parker," Hunter replied. "And when Mr. Strauss called you at 5am, what was discussed?"

"Nothing. He calls me when he wakes up sometimes. We just talked about the Cubs. Nothing else."

"You talked about baseball at five o'clock in the morning?"

"Yes. That's all we talked about. Nothing else."

"During that call, did your friend, Mr. Callum Strauss, ask you to drive to the Five Cocktails Lounge Bar and look around the area?"

"No," Parker shook his head quickly, the same way a child would when caught out in a lie. "No, he didn't."

"Did he ask you to look for Ms. Law?"

"No," Parker's head kept shaking. "No."

"Did he ask you to find a woman in the nearby park?"

"No, he didn't."

"Did he ask you to pull over a white Audi and

check in the trunk?"

"Objection," Baron called out from behind his desk. "Badgering the witness. The witness has already stated that they only discussed the Cubs in that phone call."

"Sustained. The witness has already answered the question, Mr. Hunter."

Hunter paused for a moment and looked at the jury before turning back to Parker. He waited a moment, staring at the officer. "No further questions."

CHAPTER 26

DR. MARY Stuart, an assistant Medical Examiner with the Cook County Medical Examiner's Office, was called to the stand to start day two of the murder trial. She walked into the court wearing a dark brown pantsuit, complete with shoulder pads, ready to detail her knowledge of the murder. She was a tall woman in her fifties, and she looked like she hadn't smiled once in those past five decades. Her brown hair was straightened, her glasses were large, and her make-up was heavy.

After Baron established her name and lengthy professional qualifications, he submitted her report into evidence. "Dr. Stuart, did you examine the body of Amanda Ford?"

"I did."

"And what did you find?"

"Miss Ford died as a result of strangulation. Strangulation is defined as the compression of blood or air-filled structures that impedes circulation or function. It's referred to as the compression of anatomical neck structures leading to asphyxia and neuronal death." She paused and fixed her glasses. "Pressure obstruction of the larynx primarily results in the inability to oxygenate the pulmonary vasculature. Systemic hypoxia quickly ensues, of which the most pronounced effects are rapid loss of consciousness followed by death."

"Is there any sign of what caused this strangulation?"

"The bruises on her skin were consistent with marks associated with a forearm pressing into the neck, which is usually associated with a rear chokehold."

"Was there anything unusual about this?"

"Unusual chokehold? No."

"And what time of death did you record?"

"Due to the temperature of the body when the forensic team first found it, we calculated the time of death to be between 12.30am and 1.30am on the 15th of July."

"Did she display any other injuries?"

"Miss Ford had been struck on the side of the head before her death, and we know this occurred shortly before her death because of the bleeding patterns in the wound."

"Was there any indication that the victim was under the effects of any substances at the time of death?"

"Only alcohol. Her toxicology report showed that her blood alcohol reading was 0.05, which is associated with being intoxicated. We ran toxicology reports, and all the reports were negative for other substances."

"There were no other substances found in her system?"

"That's correct."

"Thank you, Dr. Stuart," Baron stated and retook his seat. "No further questions,"

Hunter stood as soon as Baron finished, and once

asked by Judge Bales to begin questioning, he walked to the lectern, a file in hand.

"Dr. Stuart, in your professional opinion, was the victim struck while in the trunk of the vehicle?"

She looked at Hunter blankly, tilted her head to the left, thought for a moment, and then answered. "No, she was definitely placed into the vehicle after her death. There was no blood on the inside of the trunk and considering the wound to her forehead, she would have lost a substantial amount of blood after the initial injury."

"Do you believe she was choked in the trunk?"

"I can't comment on that, but I can say that it would've been hard to choke someone from the rear while in the trunk of a car."

"Thank you, Dr. Stuart," Hunter looked at his notes. "If the deceased had ingested the drug GHB, would it have shown on the toxicology reports?"

"If it had been longer than five hours since the ingestion, then it's not likely. GHB only stays in the blood for a very short period. It stays longer in the urine, however, by the time she had passed, we found that there was not enough urine in her bladder to test."

"So, if Amanda Ford had been drugged using GHB more than five hours before her death, say at 7pm, it would not have appeared in the toxicology report?"

"That's correct."

"Interesting." Hunter pondered the answer for a moment, turned another page in his file, and continued. "And if you believe Miss Ford wasn't killed in the trunk, what sort of strength would be required to move her body into the trunk?"

"Miss Ford weighed 115 pounds at the time of her death, and a dead body is a lot harder to move than a living one. To move that weight, a person would have to be capable of moving a 115-pound mass."

Hunter nodded, tapped his hand on the page, and ended the questioning. "No further questions."

CHAPTER 27

WHEN THE court reconvened after lunch on day two, the tension remained.

The courtroom seats were full. There was a buzz, a desperate racket, which hummed through the room before the arrival of Judge Bales. When he arrived, five minutes late, it took him three forceful hits of his gavel to quieten the room down enough to call the jury back into the courtroom.

For Hunter, the intensity of the previous days in court had caused a dull headache. He'd hoped four aspirins would help, but they had little effect. During the lunch recess, he sat at the defense table, reviewing his notes, distracted by the constant movement of Michelle Law next to him. She rocked back and forth a little, unable to hold her nerves. Hunter asked her to remain calm, to draw long, slow breaths, but it did little to help her.

When asked, Baron stood and called his next witness, "The prosecution calls Mr. Callum Strauss to the stand."

The courtroom doors opened, and Callum Strauss stepped through. He was wearing his best suit, his nicest shoes, and had his hair slicked back. Hunter got a whiff of expensive cologne as he walked past, and when he turned to look at the crowd, he spotted a snarl on the face of Ian Ford, seated behind the prosecutor.

"Mr. Strauss," Baron opened once the witness was sworn in. Baron needed to establish a motive for Michelle's actions, and Strauss' relationship with Amanda Ford was the key. "Can you please describe your relationship with the deceased, Miss Ford?"

Strauss drew a long breath and rubbed his hands over his suit trousers. "We were dating on and off for five months before she died. We also worked together."

"And what was that work?"

"We both worked as interns for Mr. Walter Charman as aides and were competing for the one job on offer at the end of the internship. Mr. Charman is a political lobbyist." He blinked a few times. "It was an intense environment, but Amanda and I found comfort in each other's arms."

"And is this where you met Miss Ford?"

"That's correct."

"And were you dating Miss Ford at the time of her death?"

"Kind of, but not really. It was really on and off with her. We were good together sometimes, but other times we weren't. There was never any real relationship between us, but we tried for about five months."

"When was the last time you saw Miss Ford?"

"On July 14th, at around 2pm."

"The day before her death?"

"That's right. We went out to lunch and had an argument, and that was the last time I saw her alive."

"And what was the fight about?"

"I told her that I liked someone else. We'd both

been working with this woman, and I told her over lunch that I would ask her out on a date. She didn't like that and threw a glass of water in my face. Amanda could be fiery like that."

"And who was this other woman?"

"Michelle Law."

"And did you go on this date?"

"I went into Michelle's office at about 5pm, and asked her out for a drink. She was keen, and I offered to drive out to the bar, but she insisted that she drive us there." Strauss sat up straight. "And so, she did. She drove us out to the Five Cocktails Lounge Bar in River North."

"Was there a reason you went to this particular bar and not one closer to the office where you both were working?"

"I liked the Five Cocktails. It's a good bar, very trendy and they've got great drinks, and I thought Michelle would've been impressed by it."

"Ms. Law is quite a bit older than you," Baron stated. "Around twenty years older, in fact. Was this normal dating behavior for you?"

"No, but I really liked Michelle. We were working closely together on a case, and we clicked. She's so smart, and she was young in spirit, and we just got along. We were a good match."

"What happened when you arrived at the bar?"

"Everything was going great after one drink. We were laughing and having a good time." He shook his head. "But then things got very strange. Michelle turned into a different person after one drink, and she was desperate to keep drinking. That's all she wanted to do. She didn't want to talk to me, she just wanted to keep drinking. It was like an obsession. And when

I told her that I'd been dating Amanda, she went crazy. She was very, very jealous. I've never seen anything like it. She started saying that she was going to 'get rid of her.'"

"Those were her exact words?"

"That's right, and when she started talking like that, I knew it was time to take her home. That was around 10pm." Strauss shook his head. "I told her that I would walk her out and find her a cab. But as soon as we got onto the street, she started talking about going to the park. We walked into Ward Park, which was across the street, but she was still going crazy. That's when she asked where Amanda lived. I told her, but she insisted I give her the exact address."

"And did you?"

"I regret it now, but I did. I didn't know she was going to murder—"

"Objection. Assumes facts not in evidence." Hunter's voice was firm.

"Sustained," Judge Bales agreed. "Mr. Strauss, please only talk about the details as you know them."

"Yes, Your Honor," Strauss nodded.

"And where was Miss Ford's address?"

"Just across the road. Only five doors down from the Five Cocktails. She had a ground floor apartment."

"And what happened after you gave Ms. Law the address?"

"She started vomiting into the bushes, and that was the last I saw of her. She stormed off through the park. I tried to stop her, but she yelled at me, so I backed off. She was so angry and I was scared of her."

"And did you hear from Ms. Law again?"

"No. The next time I heard her name was when the police informed me that she'd been arrested for murdering Amanda."

"Did you think Ms. Law intended to murder Miss Ford?"

"Objection," Hunter jumped up. "Calls for speculation."

"Sustained," Judge Bales stated. "You know better than that, Mr. Baron."

"Withdrawn. Were you surprised when you heard Ms. Law murdered Miss Ford?"

"Objection. The question assumes facts not in evidence."

"Withdrawn," Baron replied. "Did you feel Ms. Law could've murdered someone that night?"

"Objection!" Hunter stood again. "The question calls for a conclusion."

"Sustained, again. Mr. Baron, please choose your next question carefully. I don't want to have to hold you in contempt. You know better than this."

Baron nodded to the judge, having pushed his luck far enough. "Thank you for your time, Mr. Strauss. No further questions."

"Any cross-examination, Mr. Hunter?" Judge Bales said.

"Just a few questions, Your Honor," Hunter said. "Mr. Strauss, when you first provided a police report about that night, you said that you left Ms. Law on the street outside the bar?"

"That's right."

"However, when you just testified now, you said that you last saw her in Ward Park?"

Strauss sat back a little. "Did I?"

"You did," Hunter replied. "Can you please tell the

court if you were lying to the police then or lying to us now?"

"Objection," Baron called out. "That's an accusation against the witness."

"Your Honor," Hunter turned to the judge. "We're trying to establish if this witness is credible. He can at least tell us which version of the story he wishes to stick with."

"Agreed. The objection is overruled, however, step carefully with your language, Mr. Hunter."

Hunter nodded. "So, please, Mr. Strauss, where did you last see Ms. Law?"

"In the park. Ward Park. It was across the road from the Five Cocktails."

Hunter nodded. He waited a moment, then looked across at the prosecution team. "We have no more questions at this point, Your Honor. However, we reserve the right to recall Mr. Strauss as a defense witness."

"Noted. Witness, you may step down," Judge Bales stated and then looked at his watch. "Given the time, we will recess for the rest of the day and resume tomorrow at 10am."

After Judge Bales walked into his chambers, the crowd filed out of the rear of the room, an anxious murmur growing as they exited. Ian Ford stood at the end of the row of seats, jaw clenched, staring at Hunter and Michelle Law, holding his mounting anger until one of his family members guided him away. Valerie Ford fell into the arms of another person in the crowd, sobbing into her shoulder, walking out arm in arm.

After speaking with a nervous Michelle, Hunter exited the courtroom, followed by Esther. Ray Jones was waiting at the exit, standing against the wall in the hallway, a piece of paper in his hands. When he saw Hunter, he stepped forward and called out. Hunter patted him on the shoulder, and they moved to a quiet area, near the empty courtrooms away from the elevators. Jones didn't hesitate to drop a gem into Hunter's hands.

"Here, take this," he said, handing over a sheet of paper.

Hunter looked at it and saw a printout of a bank statement. "What am I looking at?"

"I think you might find this useful for the next witness, Rita Banks."

"Homeless woman," Hunter said, more so to remind himself of the name. "Claims that she saw Michelle Law on the street that night, and that Michelle was acting aggressively and threatening people, saying that she was going to kill someone."

"Indeed," Ray said. "I volunteer at a local shelter, helping out in the soup kitchen, and her name rang a bell. I ran a couple of checks, and there was a single transaction on the 20th of July." Hunter looked, ran his finger up the list, and found the transaction Ray was referring to. It was a single deposit, in the amount of $1500. Hunter looked up at Ray, shaking his head.

"I don't follow."

"That statement is from our homeless friend, Rita Banks. A good friend runs the homeless shelter and says that Rita was bragging about the money she received for lying to the police. My friend didn't worry about it at the time because Rita usually talks and talks and talks, and you never know what's real. But Rita showed my friend the bank statement and then left it behind one night. The contact filed in away under Rita's name. The bank statement might be a breach of her trust, but man, it's going to blow her testimony wide open." Jones reached into his other pocket and pulled a second sheet of paper out, as well as a photograph. "Here, check the date." It was a police report, signed by the one and only Rita Banks. The date at the very top, as well as beneath the signature, was the same as the date of the deposit. "The time of the deposit was exactly one hour after Rita Banks signed the police report."

"Someone paid her off to make a false police report?"

"It appears that way."

CHAPTER 28

DAY THREE was when most defendants fell apart.

After the intensity of the opening days, and after only listening to the one-sided prosecution witnesses, the reality started to settle in, and a lot of clients found themselves a mess of anger, sadness, and fear, drowning under a never-ending strain of worries and possibilities which refused to let up. Michelle was facing some of the worst emotions imaginable, but Hunter needed her to remain in control. The last thing he wanted was for her to have a sudden outburst of uncontrolled emotion that would show jurors a negative side.

"Just breathe deeply, and if it gets too much, try to think about something else."

She nodded, looked like she wanted to say something back, but snapped her mouth closed. Hunter gave her hand a squeeze and turned his attention back to the front of the courtroom. Even though she understood the ins and outs of the process, even though she'd been in the courtroom many times, nothing prepared a defendant for the rollercoaster of emotions they experienced.

The court rose to their feet again once the bailiff called the room to rise, then watched as Judge Bales returned. The judge winced as he took his seat before calling for Baron to summon his next witness.

"The State calls Ms. Rita Banks."

The crowd turned to see a disheveled woman enter the courtroom. She wore a pink windbreaker over a ragged sweater, her dark hair hanging in long and visibly knotted strands. When she passed by Hunter on her way to the stand, he detected the faint aroma of urine.

As he watched the bailiff go through the spiel of the witness swearing the oath, Hunter couldn't help but feel sorry for the woman he was about to discredit. She was a victim of circumstances, used as a pawn by those with more dollars than sense.

Hunter listened as Baron first introduced the woman, then asked for her testimony regarding the scene she claimed to have witnessed. The court heard her describe sleeping on a bench in Ward Park before waking up and hearing the defendant yelling that she was going to kill a woman named 'Amanda.'

If it was true, it could've even been convincing.

"Nothing further," Baron announced once he'd gone far enough.

Hunter didn't waste time getting to his feet. He wanted the insanity gone from the courtroom as quickly as possible. He knew the puppet masters were watching, those pulling the strings of the witness.

"Ms. Banks, thank you for coming in today," Hunter began as he neared the witness stand. Despite the odor coming from the woman, he forced himself closer for the sake of his client. "During the incident you described, were you scared at all?"

"It was scary," the woman said, her voice nasally. "But I didn't think she'd hurt me. She kept saying the name, 'Amanda.'"

"I imagine it was very scary. But which was scarier? The story you were told to tell the officers, or figuring out how to best spend the $1500 paid to you for the deed?"

A murmur arose in the room.

"Objection, Your Honor," Baron called, trying to make himself heard over the noise. "Accusation."

Judge Bales struck his gavel repeatedly until the crowd died down again, then turned to Hunter. Before he had a chance to speak, Hunter held up both the police report and the bank statement, asked for them to be admitted into evidence, and handed them to the bailiff.

Baron objected again before requesting a sidebar. Huddled next to the judge, Baron, and Hunter hashed out the details of the new evidence in a restrained whisper.

"Overruled," Judge Bales stated as the lawyers returned to their desks. "The witness may answer the question."

"Ms. Banks," Hunter returned to his table, "Can you please tell the court the date you made the police statement?"

"July 20th."

"And on the afternoon of the July 20th, did you make a deposit to your bank account of $1500?"

"What?" She looked around the room. "How do you know that?"

"Can you please answer the question, Ms. Banks?"

"I was…" She fidgeted with her top. "I was told not to put it in the bank, but I had nowhere else to stash that sort of cash, you know? That sort of money would disappear in a day on the street."

"Who gave you the money, Ms. Banks?"

"Some guy."

"Some guy, Ms. Banks?"

"Yeah. Some guy approached me in the park one night and asked me if I usually slept around there. I said yes, and then he asked me to testify about July 15th. He said he'd give me two grand for it." Her honesty was disarming, completely unaware of her statement's impact. "Of course, I said yes."

"And you were paid this money to make a statement to the police?"

"He said if I told the police I saw the defendant screaming the name 'Amanda,' he'd give me two grand, but then he only gave me $1500."

"Was it any of these men that gave you the money?" Hunter presented pictures of Walter Charman and Callum Strauss directly to her, away from the jury's eyes.

"No. But I don't know who it was."

"Are you sure?"

"I'm sure."

"Then who paid you, Ms. Banks?" Hunter pressed.

"I don't know," she shrugged. "I'd never seen him before, and I never saw him again."

"Did you see Ms. Law on the night of July 15th?"

"Yeah, I saw her."

"But did she say the things you said?"

"Not exactly."

"Not exactly?"

Banks looked away. "She didn't say anything. She was passed out on a bench next to the street that ran around the edge of Ward Park."

"And what did you do when you saw her?"

"Nothing, you know?" She shook her head. "I

tried to wake her up, but she was out of it. Close to an overdose of whatever she took, I reckon. I checked around to see if there were any guys around, but there weren't. Us sisters have to look after each other, you know? When I saw no guys around, I left her alone. I slept nearby, just to keep an eye on her, and she left early in the morning."

"Did she look capable of moving a dead body?"

"Nah, that woman wasn't going anywhere." Banks chewed the inside of her gums. "She was so out of it."

Hunter looked across to Baron, who had his head down, reading a piece of paper, avoiding any eye contact.

Hunter drew a breath. He turned his attention to the judge and said, "Your Honor, this witness has changed her statement while on the stand. I move to strike this witness and her testimony under Illinois Criminal Code 720 ILCS 5/32-2 which states, 'A person commits perjury when, under oath or affirmation, in a proceeding or in any other matter whereby the oath or affirmation is required, he or she makes a false statement, material to the issue or point in question, knowing the statement is false.'"

Judge Bales nodded, and it was clear that he was feeling sorry for the witness, but he had no other options. "Prosecution? Do you have any objections to striking this witness and her testimony?"

Baron shook his head. "No objections."

CHAPTER 29

HUNTER FILED a motion for a mistrial with prejudice, due to the damaging and improper statements made by the witness, however, Judge Bales took little time in rejecting the motion.

After the day had finished, Hunter gathered his team in the office for dinner and a discussion. He phoned in a takeaway order from the great Lou Malnati's pizza. The delivery came quickly.

Hunter loved Chicago's deep-dish pizza, and Lou Malnati's was the best of them all. Every pizza was handmade from scratch using the finest and freshest ingredients, even going so far as to hand-select the farm for the vine-ripened tomatoes for the perfect sweet and tangy taste. The spicy sausage, the Wisconsin mozzarella, and the buttery crust made for not only the perfect pizza, but the perfect experience.

As they sat and ate their delectable food, Hunter couldn't help but notice the strain on Michelle's face. He didn't want to come right out and say it, but from his years of experience, he knew the case currently sat at a fifty-fifty point, with the jury divided right down the middle in terms of a decision. They had a legal defense but not much to prove it. He watched Michelle eat as she sat across from him, knowing her own experience as a lawyer would also tell her the same.

They sat and talked long after the last slice of pizza disappeared. Hunter talked about his early childhood in Logan Square, Jones talked about his latest in a long line of girlfriends, while Esther shared a story about working for a fashion magazine photographer as a teenager. The only person not adding to the conversation was Michelle.

Knowing they still had weeks ahead of them, Hunter cut the night short. After both ladies left, Jones dropped something Hunter wasn't expecting.

"Sonja Lovett," Jones stated.

"What about her?"

"I couldn't tell you earlier because Michelle was around, but a friend of mine just sent through a report about one of the witnesses."

"And?"

"Sonja Lovett is testifying tomorrow. She was passing the bar when she saw Michelle and Strauss, but this is where it gets interesting—Sonja Lovett was previously known as Sandy Maxwell. And Sandy Maxwell was tried by Michelle Law fifteen years ago. Sandy Maxwell claimed she was innocent of breaking and entering, but Michelle went ahead with the trial, and she was sentenced to five years in prison. After five months of prison time, it was proven that Sandy Maxwell was innocent, and the conviction overturned."

"How did we miss this?" Hunter shook his head.

"Because she completely changed her name, her look, and had her conviction sealed off. There's no record of her conviction anywhere. And she looks completely different to the woman that was tried fifteen years ago."

"This should've been in the discovery information." Hunter shook his head. "She has a clear personal vendetta against Michelle."

"Even if it's struck from the record? If she lied to them, the prosecution might not even know themselves."

"This is good," Hunter nodded. "Get me the file, and I'll expose her on the stand."

CHAPTER 30

BARON ROSE and called for Sonja Lovett.

The woman entered the courtroom, dressed in black jeans and a nice blue shirt. She wore heels, which sunk into the freshly laid gray carpet as she walked, and her hoop earrings were large. She walked strong, her head held high, and made eye contact with Michelle as she passed.

"I didn't recognize her name," Michelle whispered as the bailiff swore Lovett in. "She'll say anything to put me away."

"Let's wait and see," Hunter replied, trying to reassure her.

Baron began by introducing the witness and asking her to recall how she knew the defendant. Lovett looked at the defendant as she spoke, a way of driving home her dominant status compared to where Michelle was sitting.

"Could you tell the court what happened on the night you saw the defendant?"

"Yes, of course. I was out with some friends, and we were walking past the Five Cocktails Lounge Bar in River North. We were going to another bar, a block down, when we saw a couple outside on the street."

"What time was this?"

"Around 10.35pm. I didn't recognize her at first, but then I heard her distinctive voice. I turned to see Michelle Law standing outside the bar with another young man."

"Did they appear to be having a good time?"

"A very good time. I was surprised to find Michelle Law was drunk, given her history, but then, when she looked at me, I could sense she was very intoxicated. She must've had so much to drink that night."

"Objection," Hunter called out. "Speculation."

"Sustained. Please, just answer the question, Mrs. Lovett. Only what you saw."

"Sorry, Your Honor. I should've said that Ms. Law was slurring her words and speaking very loudly."

Beside him, Hunter felt Michelle shuffle her feet uncomfortably.

"Did you hear the defendant say anything?"

"I heard her say that she was going to kill someone. I heard her say it. Her exact words were, 'I'm going to kill that stupid girl.' She said it over and over again."

Baron continued the questioning in a monotone voice, and the witness answered with perfect rhythm—yes, she saw the pair on the street. Yes, the defendant looked nervous when she spotted Lovett. Yes, they had words, and Michelle threatened to kill her as well. No, Strauss did not make any attempt to intervene. Yes, the defendant stated Strauss wouldn't be dating the victim much longer. No, she didn't elaborate on the statement.

It was a back-and-forth; one Hunter was powerless to defend against. As he sat watching the proceedings unfold, he could sense the apprehension building in the woman beside him.

When it came time for him to run through his own set of questions, he stood, ready to take down the credibility of the witness.

"Mr. Hunter? Do you wish to cross-examine?" Bales repeated the question from his bench, staring down at him with the same impatient eyes he'd seen on so many other presiding judges before this one. "Mr. Hunter?"

"Yes, Your Honor," he said, rising to his feet. "Mrs. Lovett, can you please tell the court if you've previously interacted with the defendant?"

"Not recently." She shook her head. "No."

"But in the past?"

"A long time ago."

"But you have interacted with her?"

"That's correct."

"And what was that interaction?"

"She was a prosecutor in a case I was involved in."

"Involved in?" Hunter questioned. "Do you care to elaborate further?"

"Not really."

Hunter squinted. "Are you sure, Mrs. Lovett?"

Hunter turned and looked at Baron, and Baron offered him a confused look, a sign that he had no idea where the questioning was headed. "Can you please describe your relationship with the defendant?"

"Like I told the prosecution, the case I was involved in is sealed, and I don't wish to go on about it," she said. "But if you must know, I was a witness in a trial."

"Just a witness?"

She nodded meekly.

"Mrs. Lovett, were you just a witness in a trial that

Ms. Law prosecuted, or were you a defendant?"

The witness stared at the prosecution table. Baron turned to his assistants, and they shook their heads.

"Those records are sealed," she continued. "And I tell people that I was a witness in a case."

"But that's not true, is it, Mrs. Lovett?" Hunter turned back to the prosecutors.

Baron's assistants avoided eye contact—their failure to thoroughly vet their client was an embarrassment, and their failure was being exposed on the stand.

"Like I said," Lovett's tone became firm. "Those records are sealed."

"Your Honor, I would ask you to instruct the witness to answer the question truthfully."

"Mrs. Lovett," Judge Bales' tone was firm. "Can you please answer the question put forth to you?"

Lovett squirmed in her seat for a few moments before conceding. "Alright. Fine. I wasn't a witness; I was the defendant."

"And is it true that you were sent to prison due to that court case?"

She drew a deep breath. "She sent me to prison, but I was innocent."

"And how did she do that?"

"She prosecuted me even though I was clearly innocent." The rage began to build in the witness, unable to be held back. "I told her that I didn't break into the apartment and steal the money, but she just kept pushing and pushing and pushing. The case made it to trial, and they convicted me, but I was innocent." Her jaw clenched. "Five months after I was locked up in that hell-hole of a prison, new evidence came to light that proved I was innocent."

"And did you approach Ms. Law after that?"

"I did." Her shoulders tightened. "I wanted an apology. I wanted to hear her say sorry, but she didn't. She just waved me away and then had the security guards drag me out of the building."

"How did that make you feel?"

"Angry. Furious." She raised her voice. "She had no remorse at all for what she did to me!"

"So, you wanted to get back at her?"

"Of course, I wanted to get back at her! I want to put her away like she put me away!" Her fist thumped the side of the chair. "I saw her on the street! That's not a lie. I was there. She was there. I saw her that night."

"But did you hear her talk?"

"I saw her on the street! She was there."

Hunter turned to the jury and raised his eyebrows. A few nodded in return, acknowledging the doubt that was now spread over her testimony.

"No further questions."

CHAPTER 31

"THE STATE calls Mr. Steven Hughes," Baron stood and called his next eyewitness to the stand.

Steven Hughes claimed he saw Michelle walking around in the parking lot of the Five Cocktails at 5am. She looked drunk, he claimed, barely able to stand up, stumbling all over the place, before she stepped into the driver's seat of her sedan. It was an entirely credible testimony; however, it was hardly condemning. He didn't see Michelle with a body, nor did he see any blood. Baron was clutching at straws, a desperate attempt to piece the case together. Hunter objected where he could, and after a short cross-examination, the witness was excused.

At five-past-four on day four, psychologist and expert in alcoholic blackouts, Dr. Mary Lee walked to the stand. She swore her oath and sat in the witness box without even the slightest of smiles. She sat with an uncomfortably straight back. Her black hair was tied back tightly. Her clothes were nice, and her jewelry was expensive. She presented herself as an expert, a specialist with knowledge of only the facts. Despite her lack of warmth, she had an unquestionable authority.

Baron began by confirming Dr. Lee's qualifications, which only added to the weight of her expertise. She was an MIT graduate. Widely published. Presented at talks and conferences all over the world. She'd testified in over fifty trials. The statement of her credentials was essential to establishing her ability to discuss the case as an expert witness. Unlike an eyewitness, who is limited to only discussing what they saw or did, Dr. Lee was charged with assessing the available forensic psychological evidence and rendering an opinion for the court.

"Dr. Lee, what does it mean to blackout on alcohol?"

"Blacking out is a period of alcohol-induced amnesia during which an intoxicated person actively engages in behaviors like walking or talking but doesn't remember doing so," Dr. Lee's voice was monotone, no sign of any emotion coming from her. "Blackouts are most commonly caused by a rapid increase in blood alcohol concentration levels, resulting in a temporary loss of memory. People normally experience a blackout when their blood alcohol levels reach around 0.14%."

"What happens to the brain during a blackout?"

"During a blackout, the hippocampus, which is responsible for long-term memories, experiences a neurophysiological, chemical disruption and completely shuts down. This shutdown creates a temporary void in the record-keeping system in the brain. These memories are lost and will never come back, as the information wasn't stored by the brain in the first place. When a person is sober, memories are formed after sensory input is processed in short-term memory. This process is called transfer encoding, and these memories are then moved through a similar process into an individual's long-term memory.

Alcohol interferes with receptors in the brain that carry signals between neurons, causing some brain cells to then manufacture steroids that prevent memory formation. When a person is blacked out, the brain continues to process information but is incapable of forming new memories."

"Is a person's decision-making ability impaired during a blackout?"

"That's correct," Dr. Lee confirmed. "Due to the high level of intoxication needed to experience a blackout, decision-making and other psychological processes are very likely to be impaired during this period. This is dangerous, as the person suffering the blackout may attempt to drive or perform other risky behaviors that can lead to harmful and potentially life-threatening situations."

"Including an increased risk of violence?"

"Yes. Due to impaired decision-making, a person has an increased risk of engaging in violent behavior. There have been reported cases of vandalizing property, violent outbursts causing deaths, and aggressive behavior. Some of these behaviors may not have been displayed before the blackout, however, alcohol brings them out."

"And is the person coherent during this time?"

"They can be."

"Is a blackout different from passing out?"

"That's an important difference to note, as the person is fully conscious when blacked out. In fact, anything a person can do when they are drunk, they can do while blacked out—they just simply won't remember it the next day."

"Thank you, Dr. Lee. That is very helpful," Baron said. "No further questions."

When asked by the judge, Hunter read through his notes on the legal pad in front of him.

"Dr. Lee," Hunter began, sitting behind his desk. "How long does an alcohol blackout last?"

"For as long as it takes for the person to bring their blood alcohol level back down under a reasonable level, usually under 0.14, but by this time, the person usually is passed out."

"And do alcohol blackouts differ from the effects of a GHB dosage?"

"Objection," Baron called out. "Relevance. There's no evidence presented to state the presence of GHB."

"Your Honor, Dr. Lee is an expert, and we would like to question her about her expertise, including how blackouts look different from the effect of other drugs."

"Overruled, for now," Judge Bales leaned forward and rested on his elbows. "But don't stray too far from her expertise, Mr. Hunter."

"Thank you, Your Honor," Hunter responded. "Dr. Lee, can you please tell the court if an alcohol blackout looks different from a GHB dosage?"

"Yes, it does. A person with an alcohol blackout can appear very normal, and function normally, however, a GHB dosage affects a person's ability to physically move."

"Such as…" Hunter looked down at his notes from Steven Hughes' testimony, "'Barely able to stand up?' As quoted by Mr. Hughes."

"That could either be an alcohol problem, or it could be a GHB dosage."

"And would a person suffering from a GHB dosage remember anything from the night before?"

"No, they wouldn't."

"Thank you, Dr. Lee. No further questions."
Hunter sat down. The defense's case was building.
And he wasn't done yet.

CHAPTER 32

AFTER THE first week in court ended, Michelle Law sat in traffic, desperate to leave another week behind.

She could feel her freedom slipping before her, but worse than that, she was starting to see the struggle in her lawyer's eyes. He was starting to look defeated. She had initially considered a different person to defend her, but she had faith in Hunter's integrity and work ethic.

Traffic continued to thicken as the hour wore on, and Michelle knew the situation would become clogged enough to slow her considerably. Looking to her left, she spotted a possible escape, a way for her to avoid most of the traffic and make it home within a respectable time. It was the entrance to Lower Wacker Drive; its dark cavernous eye beckoning her to tempt fate and take her chances in the deep bowels of the city.

Swinging the car out of her lane, Michelle felt the satisfaction of watching the speedometer climb above fifteen mph for the first time in almost an hour. Her stomach heaved a little as the front of the car dipped down onto the entrance ramp, then recovered as the rest of the vehicle followed. Soon, her headlights lit up as the darkness of the hidden world consumed her.

There were a few cars surrounding Michelle's, meaning it wasn't quite the traffic-free run home she'd been hoping for. With speed a little quicker than the world above, she let her thoughts return to the day which changed her life forever. She couldn't remember anything from that night, but it didn't feel like an alcohol blackout. She knew what those felt like. She knew the regret and despair that accompanied them the following morning.

As much as she tried, as much as she focused, she couldn't remember one single thing between the bar and waking up in the park, lying on the bench. Could she have blacked out and killed Amanda Ford?

She always had a dark side. When she was bullied in High School for being a perfectionist, she imagined stabbing her tormentors. It gave her great joy to imagine driving a pencil into the perfect cheekbones as they told her how pathetic she was. Those daydreams made her smile. When she started work as a prosecutor, seeing pictures of dead bodies and mutilated corpses didn't faze her. Maybe that dark side came out when her inhibitions were squashed.

The police kept her Audi for crime scene investigations, but she didn't mind. She could never drive that car again after what they found in the trunk. She leased a second Audi, a newer model, and was comfortable with it, but she hadn't opened the trunk once.

Slowly following a taxicab, she recalled why she chose Hunter as her lawyer.

Justice wasn't a job for him. It was an affair that spanned decades of his own life. With everything that had happened to his family, Hunter had stayed on course, always standing up for what was right, always defending justice, never stopping until he'd achieved the only result possible.

He was the right man for the job.

While others may have had more prestigious accolades to show off their vast experiences, none could share the battle scars of a warrior like Hunter, one she now needed to stand up in her defense.

She spotted a car move close behind her.

It had been trailing her since the courthouse, following half a dozen cars back to ensure its stealth remained intact. It wasn't the most inconspicuous car on the road, a large black pickup truck that towered over the sedans. The windows were dark enough to cast nightfall into the cabin. It had gained a couple of spots during the subsequent traffic jam, then fell back half a dozen more as cars were forced to merge due to a breakdown. Once the driver spotted Michelle's car changing lanes, it quickly closed in on its target.

The truck crept up on her, then touched the bumper enough to cause a sudden vibration through the car.

Michelle's first instinct kicked in, and she looked in the mirror. She turned to look over her shoulder. The driver sped up again, giving the Audi a second bump, hard enough to push Michelle back into her seat.

She didn't cry out, swallowing her surprise, and looked for options. There were none. The road was blocked on all sides—on one side by guard rails running along the road, and the other by the cars ahead.

As the lights turned green, she could see the road opening up slightly, with a sidewalk forming, but people were walking on the strip.

Michelle's heart pumped furiously as fear tightened within her. She fumbled for her cell when the truck sped up hard again, the squeal of tires echoing through the tunnel. It turned sharply, pushing Michelle's rear end out.

Her tires screamed for traction but lost all control as the car first spun one way, hit the concrete barrier, then turned the other.

The explosion of noise from the impact boomed as it reverberated in her confined space. With traffic opening up, the attacker didn't bother to check the damage, instead taking a sharp turn and disappearing down the road.

CHAPTER 33

ESTHER AND HUNTER had barely walked into Esther's apartment when Hunter's cell phone rang.

He answered, but struggled to understand as Michelle's voice charged through. Even Esther looked up from across the room, Michelle's voice loud enough to rise in the silent apartment.

"Michelle. Michelle, calm down," Hunter tried. He could make out single words, but the message wasn't coming through.

"Crash. They…" rose through the jumble, "Charman…"

"Michelle, you need to calm yourself," he tried again, waiting for an opportunity to speak through the onslaught of words. She was frightened, that much was clear, but was she hurt?

When she didn't calm down enough for the call to move forward, Hunter did the only thing open to him.

"Michelle!" he snapped, and finally, the voice paused long enough for him to speak. "Slow down and breathe. Take a moment. Are you hurt?"

She was crying, the sobs coming through in waves of untamed emotion. She fought them back, small bursts of resilience holding the fear down.

"No," she sobbed. "I'm not hurt."

"Good. Give me your location, and I'll come down."

She did. "Lower Wacker Drive. Near the Michigan Avenue entrance."

"I'm on my way. Just sit tight, and I'll see you shortly."

Hunter and Esther were back in the car within a minute, before navigating through back streets. The main roads were clogged with Chicago traffic, but with Esther's navigation skills, she could talk Hunter through a maze of side streets which cut the trip from her apartment to the entrance to Lower Wacker Drive by half.

The final stretch took the longest, with traffic moving slowly due to Michelle's accident, but once they were near enough to see her, Esther swapped with Hunter's spot at the wheel while waiting at a set of lights. He trekked the final stretch on foot.

Police were on-site and had the victim to one side as they questioned her. She wasn't a stranger to the force, but their feelings towards her were mixed. Some respected her, others hated her. But from the look on the cops' faces, Hunter could tell they had a lot of empathy for her current situation.

Michelle's car was a mess. The concrete barrier had saved her from personal injuries, and from the outside, she looked relatively unscathed. She'd also calmed herself, a glimpse of the prosecutor back in charge by the time Hunter neared.

"Are you ok?" Hunter said as he approached.

She nodded.

"We're pretty much finished here, Ms. Law," one cop said, flicking his notepad close. "You were lucky it wasn't any worse."

"Yeah, just shaken up. Thanks for your help," Michelle said before turning to Hunter. She sounded deflated, as if her ego had taken a hit. "I'm ok. Just a bit shaken up."

"Did you get a look at the car that did this?" Hunter asked, surveying the damage as her car was pushed onto the back of a tow truck.

"A black pickup truck. Dark windows, no plates. Not even a scowling face to report."

"They knew what they were doing," he said as Esther joined them, and then hugged the still-shaking victim.

The tow truck took her car away from the scene. Soon, the police left as well. Michelle leaned against the wall, hands on her knees.

"Do you need to get checked out?" Esther asked.

"I'm ok," she drew a deep breath. "But I would love a lift home."

"On it," Hunter said.

"I'm just not having much luck with cars," Michelle tried to make light of the situation, but the attempted joke fell flat.

There was no conversation as Hunter drove them back to Michelle's apartment, an uneasy silence hanging over the three of them. The traffic had eased, and the drive into the West Loop was quicker than expected.

"Listen, Hunter," Michelle began as they pulled up to her apartment. "Do you think you could chat for a few moments? I've got something I need to tell you."

Hunter looked at Esther, and she nodded. "I can wait here if you want to discuss it in the apartment."

Hunter agreed and stepped out of the sedan. Michelle thanked Esther and exited the car, leading

Hunter through the foyer and into the elevator to her fifth-floor apartment.

After more than a decade of working together, both Hunter and Esther knew that clients rarely opened up completely during those first few all-important interviews.

They nearly always held back to some extent, and it left a lot of holes in the case a defense attorney was trying to build. Quick clients, like those often seen by public defenders, never reached a point where they needed a serious one-on-one. Their cases were usually done and dusted in a single hearing. But cases such as the one Michelle had gotten herself tangled in? Weeks and months could be spent on the matter, and, at some point, the client always came around to a complete revelation, a moment where everything was laid out bare. Hunter recognized that now was Michelle's moment.

"Time to come clean," she whispered as she opened the door to her apartment.

She walked to the kitchen, poured herself a large glass of water, before returning to the living area, and sitting on the edge of the couch. "It's about Walter Charman."

Hunter sat down on the opposite couch, waiting for her to continue.

Michelle took a large gulp of water and then stared into the glass before breaking the silence. "It's strange how nobody actually influenced me to try and make the change into politics. That dumb decision was all my doing. I thought it was the path that everyone followed when they grew tired of practicing law. It was what we were supposed to do, right?" She briefly paused to sip her water and lowered her voice as if dismayed by her previous aspirations. "I actually believed I could do more good in politics than I could as a prosecutor." She let out a half-hearted laugh. "Boy, was I wrong."

Hunter waited for her to continue. He nodded a little, allowing her all the time she needed.

"It didn't take me very long to discover the road to women's rights and equality still had a long way to go in backroom dealings. That's where Charman came in. Do you know what that scumbag said to me?"

Hunter shook his head.

"I should've known better than to approach a man like that for help. People like him always have ulterior motives. If there's nothing in it for them, why bother? That prick said, 'Sure, I'll help you. But I'll be setting up shop in your purse for a long time to come.' He didn't even bother dressing it up."

"Sounds like him."

"The only decent thing he did was give me advance warning of his intentions to fleece me as much as possible if I used his connections. I would be paying for the favor a long time into the future." She sighed. "And after experiencing it firsthand, I have no doubt about the sheer number of politicians and officials he already has in his grip." She paused and sucked in a breath. "But I was in. I thought the time was right, and it was my turn to try and make a difference. Charman invited me to his hotel room for a late-night drink when we were both in New York for a conference, but I never thought I'd be walking into a trap."

"A trap?"

"It was 11pm when I arrived, after a day of talks at the conference. I was so stupid. I should've seen it coming," she shook her head at her own mistake. "He was in his robe when I arrived at his hotel room. That should've been my first clue that something wasn't right. That fat old fool was waltzing around in a robe, and I didn't see what was coming. I should've known. I should've turned around at that instant and walked straight back out the door."

Hunter studied Michelle, allowing her as much time as needed to work through to the truth.

"He offered me a glass of wine, which I refused, and then we sat on the couch. He talked about making sacrifices and how a pretty lady like me could get ahead in the game. After only five minutes, I could see what was happening, but I was powerless to stop it. He wields so much power behind the scenes that I didn't want to cross him. Nobody wants to cross him."

She tried to hold back the tears, staring at her glass of water.

"I've never told anyone because I was so embarrassed," she continued. "But he promised me he could land me any seat I wanted. On the City Council—check. Run for Mayor—check. Run for Senate—check. He said he was powerful enough to ensure that I win whatever I wanted to win."

"But everything comes at a price."

She nodded. "Once he finished talking, he just stood up and dropped the robe. He just dropped it in front of me. And there he was, standing right in front of me, fully naked. That fat, greasy, hairy, naked body is burned into my brain." She took another gulp of water. "I stood up and made some excuses, but I walked out of there. I told him he was disgusting and that I was going to take him down."

"I'm sorry to hear that," Hunter said. "That must've been terrifying."

"I almost vomited when he took his robe off. There was no way I could do it. If I wanted a run at politics, I needed his backing, but that was a price too high to pay. And that was the end of my political aspirations. The worst thing is that I did nothing about it. Even though I threatened him, I did nothing. I didn't report it. I didn't make an official statement. I didn't even tell anyone. Not a soul." She clenched her fist and lightly tapped it against her forehead. "And I know I wasn't the only one. I wasn't special. I was just another target. And when I heard that Amanda Ford attempted to lodge a sexual assault charge against him, I blamed myself. I could've stopped him. I was the symbol of justice, but when it really counted, I walked away with a whimper."

"You didn't tell anyone?"

"Not a soul, but some other people must've known." She shook her head again. "When I went to talk to Jake Berkeley a week after that day, he asked me how the hotel room with Charman was, and he had that stupid, sly grin on his face."

"How did Jake Berkeley know about it?"

"I didn't tell him, but he knew. Charman must've told him." She knocked back the rest of her glass in one long gulp. "And then I go to a bar where a guy spikes my drink? I must be a complete idiot. After all the sexual assault cases I've worked on, I should've known better."

"Are you sure you were drugged?"

"I'm sure of it now. The more I think about it, the more I'm sure of it." She nodded. "He must've drugged me. The way I felt when I woke the next morning had all the classic signs. No memories, painful to move, headache, dry throat. It was so much more than just a blackout. I've done cases where women were drugged, and that was how they described it."

She looked at him as she sheepishly shook her head.

"I should have checked my drink. But... I was embarrassed. I should've taken a cab home in the morning, if you want to get technical. And again, another stupid mistake. It was 7am, and I didn't need the world knowing I had been out for a drunken bender all night. All I needed was to get home. To climb into bed and forget the night ever happened. How was I supposed to know there was a dead body in the trunk of my car?"

"You weren't." Hunter drew a breath and stood. "Thank you for being honest, Michelle. I can't imagine how hard that was for you."

"So, what happens now?" She stood up as well. "A weekend of rest and recovery?"

"No," Hunter said. "I'm going to confront the man at the center of it all."

CHAPTER 34

HUNTER RAGED through the Berghoff restaurant in Downtown.

The grace and style of the iconic restaurant was no foil for his anger. The wait staff asked him to stop as he stepped in the doors, but he ignored them, stepping between the tables toward the back of the room. The restaurant was busy, all the patrons dressed to impress. Charman was known to attend most Friday nights, wining and dining with some of the city's most powerful.

The inside of the building was filled with old-world charm—subdued lighting, recently polished dark-wood paneling, dark leather on the dining chairs. A bar ran along the left side of the room, the restaurant to the right. The ceilings were high, the atmosphere noisy, and the smell of seared steak filled the air.

"I told you to leave her alone," Hunter said as he approached Walter Charman's table.

Charman slowly raised his eyes and then looked back at the two other men he was sharing dinner with. "I don't know what you're talking about."

"Michelle Law. You know what happened."

He scoffed and then looked at his watch before leaning back in his chair. "It's 10.05pm on a Friday night. If the court case is anything to go by, I imagine she was blackout drunk."

One of the other men laughed while the waiter came up next to Hunter, looking up at his towering figure. "Excuse me, sir."

He started to put a hand on Hunter, but the lawyer snapped his head towards him. "Don't touch me."

The waiter nodded sheepishly.

Charman looked around the restaurant—all eyes were on them. The distinguished patrons weren't used to someone yelling in the restaurant. Charman stood and lowered his voice. "I have no idea what you're talking about. Michelle Law? She's just a piece of dirt to me. If she got hurt tonight, then she deserved it." Charman nodded towards the bar at the end of the room. "Go and have a drink. It's on me."

"You know that Michelle Law is innocent, and you know something more about this case."

Charman scoffed again, shaking his head. "You really don't give up, do you? Your client is about to go to prison for a murder she committed, and you're still out here harassing me."

"I know you tried to have sex with her, but she rejected you."

Charman laughed out loud. "Is that what this is about? Ok, sure. I like women." He turned back to the other men at the table. "Guilty as charged."

"And I know you're connected to all of this. This case has got your fingerprints all over it."

"Now, why would that be?" He grinned, looking up at Hunter. "Would it be because Michelle Law made a lot of people angry when she let your father's case be dismissed? She let a killer walk out the courthouse doors, Hunter, and that looked bad for a lot of the people I know."

Hunter grabbed the collar of Charman's shirt, lifting it up. "Don't talk about my father."

"Alright, big guy," Charman held his hands out wide as the other men at the table stood up. "No need for any violence here."

Hunter released his grip, giving Charman a shove as he did. Charman stumbled against the table, leaning his weight against the edge.

Hunter pointed his finger at Charman. "I'm going to find out how you're involved, and then I'm going to take you down."

CHAPTER 35

DESPITE A methodical search, Hunter couldn't find a link between Charman and Amanda Ford's murder.

He issued Charman with a subpoena, hoping to pressure him into making a mistake, but nothing came out of it. Not a hint, not a clue, not even a lead.

Pradesh Baron spent the next week in court calling expert witness after expert witness, trying to build a mountain of evidence against Michelle Law. A forensic expert testified about the blood splatter patterns in the trunk, followed by a crime scene expert who declared that the body had been carried to the location, as there were no bloodstains around the area where the vehicle was parked overnight. Another expert testified about the suffocation and another about the car.

Then came the character witnesses. When they started to talk about Michelle and her behavior at work, it became a character assassination. Former assistants testified about her drinking during work hours, and a cleaner testified how she found empty bottles of vodka at her desk for years. Under cross-examination, they admitted they hadn't seen her drink in the last two years, but the damage was done.

Michelle Law was painted to be a frantic career

woman who escaped reality under the spell of the bottle.

Hunter spent the evenings after the trial working the phones, thinking of strategies, and reviewing the witness statements. He called Deputy Chief Tony Mann numerous times. After a week of phone calls, Tony Mann finally conceded that he could do something. Sit tight, he said, but give me another week.

Another week of the trial pushed past.

Hunter lodged several motions, slowing the case down, but they were dismissed with regularity. The jury looked convinced of Michelle's guilt, even nodding every time Baron alluded to it. Hunter had to admit that the parade of experts, followed by character witnesses, was convincing. Baron had played his case well.

Michelle suggested that she could take the stand, but Hunter shot that idea down in an instant. She remembered nothing about the night and would only be opening herself up to an intense cross-examination. After a little convincing, Michelle agreed it was a terrible idea.

The media continued coverage of the story; the audience gripped by the story of a prosecutor out of control. There were talks of a book, a podcast, and a movie. Michelle wanted none of that and said she would sue for defamation the second any work of fiction came out about her life.

After three weeks of bluster, after three weeks of evidence and witnesses, the prosecution rested their case.

The prosecution was in front. There was no doubt about that.

Hunter had a number of strategies, but the one he liked the most rested on Tony Mann's influence.

Walking out of his office, late in the evening after the prosecution rested their case, Hunter was surprised to see the number flash on the screen.

Thumbing the screen to accept the call, he pressed the phone to his ear and turned the volume up. The noises of the city street were at their peak, and as the voice began to speak, Hunter struggled to hear.

At first, he barely heard the caller. Hunter asked the person to speak up as he couldn't quite make them out. After several requests, they finally did, and Hunter's reaction was instant. A broad smile, reminiscent of the sun bursting through the storm clouds, dawned on Hunter's face. His smile broadened as he nodded, the case finally taking a sharp turn for the better.

It was the news he needed to hear. Tony Mann had worked his magic.

The case was back on.

CHAPTER 36

ON THE Wednesday morning of the fourth week of the murder trial, Hunter stood, ready to open his case. He looked to Michelle Law, gave her a reassuring nod, and then across to Pradesh Baron and his team.

Baron squinted and leaned back in his chair. He crossed one leg over the other, a small smile on his face, and waited.

"The defense calls Detective Jemma Knowles."

"Objection!" Baron leaped to his feet almost instantly. "This witness isn't on any defense witness list, and we have no indication of what this is about."

"On the contrary, Your Honor," Hunter stated. "The prosecution is well-aware of what Detective Knowles was investigating, however, they decided to leave that information out of the discovery material."

"Approach," Judge Bales waved them forward.

Baron turned to look at his assistants, who all shook their heads in confusion before he followed Hunter towards the bench. Both lawyers leaned close.

"Mr. Hunter, who is this witness?" Judge Bales lowered his tone to a whisper.

"The Chicago PD Detective had been investigating possible drug spiking in The Five Cocktails Lounge Bar, and only yesterday, made an arrest of the bar owner for buying amounts of GHB," Hunter explained. "The witness, Detective Jemma Knowles, is running that investigation, and this information has only become available to us last night. We could not have possibly known about this information before now as the investigation was confidential."

"And do you care to explain why this witness wasn't on your discovery material, Mr. Baron?" Judge Bales whispered.

"The Chicago PD investigation was confidential, and no arrests had been made. This morning is the first that we've heard of an arrest in this case."

"Then the court will recess for fifty minutes while you review the police report, and if you need more time than that, you can request it after the defense's questioning," Judge Bales tapped his gavel, and then announced his decision to the court. He waited until the jury was led out of the room before he exited.

Baron turned to Hunter and raised his eyebrows.

"Don't act surprised. You knew about the investigation," Hunter said. "But the arrest has come earlier than you would've liked."

Baron grunted, grabbed his laptop, and then proceeded to exit the room, followed closely by his assistants hurrying behind him.

When the court resumed fifty minutes later, Baron looked like he spent every one of those minutes stressing out. The wrinkles on his brow seemed to have grown deeper, his collar was slightly looser, and his fists were clenched.

When called for the second time, Detective Jemma Knowles walked to the stand full of confidence. Her suit fitted her tall, muscular frame, and she stepped forward with a confident and commanding presence.

Hunter moved to the lectern and began his questioning. "Can you please state your name and occupation for the court?"

"Detective Jemma Knowles. I've been serving this great city for over two decades, first as a police officer and now as a detective."

"And as a detective, have you made any arrests recently?"

"We made an arrest last night. As part of a team, we arrested Mr. Elliot Brady for possession of a controlled substance with an intent to distribute." Knowles moved in her seat. "He was in possession of 550grams of gamma-hydroxybutyrate, commonly known as GHB."

"And what does Mr. Elliot Brady do for work?"

"He's the owner, and the main bartender, at the Five Cocktails Lounge Bar."

A gasp went through the room. Hunter let the information sit with the jury for a long moment before continuing. "And what does GHB do?"

"It's commonly referred to as a date-rape drug. It's a depressant drug, which slows down the rate of messages traveling between the brain and body and can lead to blackouts and unconsciousness. It's a potent date-rape drug because it leaves the system quite quickly, making it very hard to detect usage. As a police force, we've committed to getting this terrible drug off the streets before it does real damage to the lives of vulnerable women."

"And why did you make this arrest last night?"

"We had information that Mr. Brady was going to distribute this new shipment of GHB to some of his customers, and we weren't going to sit around and watch a whole lot of young women be drugged. We had to act. We had no choice."

"And was it usual for Mr. Brady to distribute this drug to his customers?"

"We had sources inform us that he has been distributing it to his customers to use on women once or twice a month for years. The information we had said that he did this on at least one Tuesday night a month."

"But always a Tuesday night?"

"That's correct," Knowles stated. "From the information we had, we found that after Amanda Ford's death, Mr. Brady stopped distributing the drug for fear of being caught, however, we were tipped off that he had received a new delivery and was planning to distribute it last night. After he was arrested, he made a full confession to us."

"Did he tell you who he sold the drugs to?"

"He provided a list of names, yes."

"And was one of those names Mr. Callum Strauss, the ex-boyfriend of Amanda Ford, and the man that took Ms. Law on a date on July 14th?"

"That's correct."

Another gasp went through the courtroom.

"Did Mr. Brady say that he saw Mr. Strauss use the drug?"

"He said that Mr. Strauss bought a supply of GHB from him on numerous occasions."

Hunter turned to the jury, most of whom had their mouths hanging open.

"Did he state if Mr. Strauss bought a supply of GHB during the month of July?"

"Mr. Brady stated he sold Mr. Strauss a supply of GHB just before the 4th of July. Mr. Brady said that

GHB was in high demand around that time of year."

"Did Mr. Brady acknowledge that Ms. Law may have been drugged on July 14th?"

"Objection," Baron said. "Hearsay. Unless Mr. Brady claimed to have seen Mr. Strauss drug Ms. Law, then we cannot have that statement admitted to the court."

"Mr. Hunter?" Judge Bales asked.

"I'll withdraw the question, Your Honor, and ask a more direct question. Did Mr. Brady say that he saw Mr. Strauss drug any person's drink prior to July 14th?"

"Yes. Mr. Brady did say that he saw Mr. Strauss spike another person's drink."

"Thank you, Detective Knowles," Hunter said. "No further questions."

When instructed by the judge, Baron stood quickly. "Detective Knowles, can you please tell the court if Mr. Brady has been convicted of any offense?"

"Mr. Brady has made a statement of guilt through his signed confession, which we have acknowledged," Knowles stated. "What I've described in my testimony today is what I saw during the raid on The Five Cocktails Lounge Bar. I've made no claim about the guilt or innocence of Mr. Brady, and he will front the court tomorrow morning to enter his plea."

"And did Mr. Brady directly state that he saw Mr. Strauss spike Ms. Law's drink on the night of July 14th?"

"He said that Mr. Strauss had bought—"

"Please, just answer the question, Detective Knowles. Did Mr. Brady directly state that he saw Mr. Strauss spike Ms. Law's drink on the night of July

14th?"

"No, he did not."

Baron nodded. "No further questions."

Hunter declined the opportunity for a redirect, and he turned his gaze to the jury. Juror five in the back row nodded. It was a coincidence too big to ignore, and as much as the prosecution was trying to avoid it, the doubt was rising.

After just one witness, the case was turning in his favor.

CHAPTER 37

WHEN HUNTER called drug expert Dr. Katherine Beck to the stand, the direction of the defense's strategy was clear. Hunter needed to target the fact that Michelle had been involuntarily drugged and have the charges dismissed under the rule of law.

Dr. Beck walked to the stand with poise, as she had done many times before. She was a slight woman with long red hair and a bright sense of style. Her delicate features were attractive, and her pale white skin glowed with health.

"Thank you for coming to court today, Dr. Beck," Hunter stood behind the lectern. "Can you please tell the court your occupation and your expertise?"

"Hello, yes," Dr. Beck stated. "My name is Dr. Katherine Beck, and I'm a doctor and researcher at the University of Chicago, and my research has specialized in the study of the effects of so-called 'date-rape' drugs, including GHB, Rohypnol, and others."

"And how long have you studied this subject?"

"More than two decades," she responded. "Over that time, I've published many studies on the subject, spoken at many seminars, and testified in many court cases."

"And can you please describe to the court what are

the symptoms of a GHB use?"

"GHB slows down the rate of messages traveling between the brain and body, and can cause confusion, irritation and agitation, blackouts and memory loss, and unconsciousness that can last for up to five hours. While it's a very powerful drug, it also leaves the system within five to ten hours. This makes it very hard to detect usage. While hair follicle tests can detect GHB usage up to a month later, that testing is extremely unreliable."

"And after reviewing Ms. Law's police statement that she made on the morning of July 15th, did you find there were any correlations between a typical GHB dosing and her symptoms?"

"Very much so. As soon as I read that statement, I recognized that everything she described matched the symptoms one would expect if she had taken GHB. She displayed the classic symptoms."

"What is the best way to identify someone who has consumed GHB?"

"Because the testing window is so small, over the years, it's been identified that the best way to recognize a GHB overdose is by reading the person's descriptions of their symptoms. Urine and blood tests are the most accurate, but they must be taken between five to ten hours after the dosage, or it can't be detected."

"And hair follicle testing?"

"While the Guidelines for the Forensic Analysis of Drugs Facilitating Sexual Assault and Other Criminal Acts from the United Nations Office on Drugs and Crime has a low level of hair detection for long-term use, single dose usage is almost impossible to detect, and no test has been shown to be scientifically reliable. Because it's so hard to test for, we must rely on the victim's descriptions, which have been shown to be accurate over the years."

Hunter nodded and moved around the lectern, letting the pause sit in the room before he continued. "Given what you know and understand about the drug GHB, do you believe someone who has consumed GHB could overpower another person?"

"No."

"Do you believe someone that has consumed GHB could strike someone hard enough to knock them out?"

"No, I don't."

"And in your opinion, would it be possible for someone who was drugged with GHB to carry a body and put it into the trunk of a car?"

"No, I don't believe that would be possible."

"Thank you, Dr. Beck. No further questions."

When called, Baron stood for his cross-examination. He waited a moment, running his hand over a line of notes, and then lifted his head to look at the witness.

"Dr. Beck, are you aware if Ms. Law submitted to a drug test after she was arrested?"

"Yes, and the reading for GHB was negative in the urine and blood test, however, that's to be expected due to the fact that these tests were outside the testing window. Ms. Law took the test at 1pm the next day. She would've needed to take the test within ten hours of being drugged, at the most."

"And are you aware if Ms. Law submitted a hair follicle test?"

"I'm aware that she did, and I have read the report, however, I must stress that hair follicle test isn't accurate for single-dose testing."

"In that report, her reading was negative?"

"That's correct, but again, it's not an accurate measurement of testing for GHB use."

"Dr. Beck," Baron shook his head and looked at the jury. "Do you have any evidence that Ms. Law was, in fact, drugged that evening?"

"We have her statement that matches how someone feels after being drugged by GHB."

"Let me rephrase that. Apart from what Ms. Law told you, do you have any evidence that Ms. Law was drugged that evening?"

"That's a loaded question. I must stress that listening to a person's description of their symptoms is very valid and match that to a GHB usage."

"All you have is her word?"

"And her word is enough," Dr. Beck stated.

Baron looked at the jury, shaking his head, and sighed.

"Then we have no further questions for this witness."

CHAPTER 38

THE STRATEGY of the defense became crystal clear as the days progressed.

Hunter called expert after expert, specialist after specialist, all detailing the effects of GHB. He called colleagues of Michelle Law, who testified that she'd been sober for two years; he called a witness who stated that he saw her sleeping on the bench in Ward Park at 1am, and he called a character witness, another prosecutor, who testified about Michelle Law's commitment to law and justice. A medical expert testified there was no way someone under the influence of GHB could've suffocated Amanda Ford and then carried her into the trunk of a car. Another character witness from the State's Attorney's Office testified they'd never seen Michelle drink, let alone willingly take drugs.

Hunter considered calling Elliot Brady, the owner of the Five Cocktails Lounge Bar, to the stand, but it was too much of a risk. Brady was well-educated, clever, and would likely say anything to protect his friends.

During his onslaught of witnesses, Hunter noticed a curious presence in court every day during the fourth week of the trial, seated in the back row nearest the door—Jake Berkeley. Hunter went to question him numerous times, but he disappeared before Hunter could confront him. He called Berkeley's office repeatedly, but Berkeley never answered and didn't return his call.

Hunter was pushing hard for Michelle to be found not guilty under 720 ILCS 5/6-3, involuntarily drugged condition. All the clues were there, all the signs pointed to the defendant being drugged, but they didn't have any hard evidence, nothing that signed, sealed, and delivered the verdict.

Even with his ferocious display in the courtroom, the case remained fifty-fifty, at best.

As the fifth week drew to a close, the defense team needed to take the risk. Hunter discussed a trial strategy with Michelle before he closed the defense case, and she agreed.

The risk was to be staged in two parts—build the pressure with a high-profile witness and then land the final devastating blow with a witness who could crumble on the stand.

It was a risk, a mighty one, but it was one they had to take.

"The defense calls Walter Charman to the stand."

A murmur raced through the courtroom as Charman strode through the courtroom doors. As he stepped through the gate towards the bailiff, his reluctance was as apparent as his arrogance. His chin was held high, his shoulders back, and his cold stare said that he was angry about having to take the stand. He wore a tailored suit, complete with a dark blue tie and a dark blue pocket square.

Charman sat in the witness stand, leaning forward slightly, waiting to be questioned.

"Mr. Charman," Hunter began, leaning forward on

his desk. "Can you please describe how you know the deceased, Miss Ford?"

Charman sat up straight. "Miss Ford was working as my intern for around five months before her terrible death."

"And was Mr. Callum Strauss also employed as an intern for you?"

"That's correct."

"And were you aware that they were dating?"

"I was aware of that."

"And even though you were aware of that, did you make sexual advances on Miss Ford?"

"Objection," Baron called out. "Where's the relevance here?"

"Your Honor, I'm establishing the circumstances around Miss Ford's employment before her death, which I assure the court, will become very important in this trial."

"Overruled," Judge Bales stated and turned to Charman. "You may answer the question."

"I did not have sexual relations with Miss Ford, no."

"That's not what I asked, Mr. Charman," Hunter responded. He lifted a police file in the air to catch Charman's attention. It was a threat. A clear ploy by Hunter to state that he had statements by people who would testify that Charman had made sexual advances on the victim. "I asked whether you made sexual advances on Miss Ford?"

"What's in the file?" Charman nodded to the folder in Hunter's hand.

"Please answer the question," Hunter said and placed the folder down. "Did you make sexual advances on Miss Ford?"

"I don't see the relevance here." He sat up straighter, pulling his suit jacket across his chest.

Hunter stood. "Your Honor, permission to treat the witness as hostile. He's clearly not answering the questions put forth to him."

Judge Bales looked across at Charman and then nodded. "Given the reluctance to answer the question, permission is granted."

Hunter picked up the file and moved to the lectern, placing it in front of him before he continued. He opened the front page of the folder and then shook his head. "Did it make you angry that Callum Strauss was dating Miss Ford?"

"Objection," Baron called out, still seated. "Relevance. Again, Mr. Charman is not on trial here. Is there even a point to this line of questioning?"

"Overruled, but get to the point quickly, Mr. Hunter," Judge Bales stated, his patience growing thinner. "You may answer the question, Mr. Charman."

"No, I wasn't angry."

"How many times did Miss Ford reject your sexual advances?"

Charman drew a long breath, the thoughts turning over in his head. "Listen, Miss Ford was a very beautiful young lady. I would've been a fool not to at least ask her out on a date."

"Did you ask her out on a date?"

"I don't remember the exact scenario, but I probably asked her out." He shifted in his chair. "Politely, of course."

"And she rejected your advances?"

"We didn't go on a date, so I guess she did."

"How did that make you feel?" Hunter moved

around the lectern again. "A big, powerful man, her boss, was rejected by his intern?"

"It happens," he shrugged.

"It happens enough for you to hurt her?"

"Oh, come on. Objection," Baron stood. "Accusation. I don't know what Mr. Hunter is trying to imply here, but it's ridiculous."

"Sustained," Judge Bales conceded. "It's time to move on from this line of questioning, Mr. Hunter."

"And how about Ms. Law?" Hunter tapped his hand on the lectern. "Did you ask her out on a date as well?"

Charman drew a long breath and then exhaled loudly. "She came to me."

"For a date?"

"For advice."

"And did you invite her back to your hotel room while at a conference in New York?" Hunter continued. "And before you answer that question, I will remind you that there's video surveillance footage at the Park Hyatt, Midtown, New York."

Charman nodded in acknowledgment of the hotel name. "Ok, sure." He looked across at the defense table. "I asked her back to my hotel room to discuss her career."

"And did you disrobe in front of her shortly after she arrived, standing in front of her naked?"

"Objection!" Baron shouted. "Where is the relevance? How often does the defense need to be told that Mr. Charman is not on trial?"

"Sustained," Judge Bales stated. "Careful where you tread, Mr. Hunter."

Hunter nodded and moved back to his table. He picked up another folder, held it for a moment, and then moved back to the lectern, placing it in front of him. "And Mr. Callum Strauss, would you say he was a good intern?"

"He was very eager."

"Eager?" Hunter said. "Would he do anything you asked him?"

"I would say so, yes."

"Even if that request was illegal?"

"I don't do anything illegal, so I wouldn't know."

Hunter looked at the jury, most of whom were looking at him puzzled. He was fine with that. Charman was merely the set-up before he landed the sucker punch with his next witness.

"No further questions."

CHAPTER 39

BARON DECLINED to cross-examine Charman. He didn't see the point. There was nothing in Charman's testimony that was damaging, and there was nothing that shifted the case.

But Charman wasn't Hunter's target.

"The defense recalls Mr. Callum Strauss."

The courtroom doors opened, and Callum Strauss stepped through.

His nerves were evident as he stepped through the door, wiping his brow with the back of his hand. The police had already interviewed him earlier in the week in relation to Brady's confession about the Five Cocktails Lounge Bar, but his lawyer told him not to say a word. He felt comfortable with his lawyer next to him.

But on the stand, under the glare of the courtroom, alone in the witness box, he was vulnerable.

Strauss wore a blue pinstripe, brown shoes, and had his hair slicked back. He tried to appear confident, walking with his shoulders back, but it was the false confidence of someone trying to convince themselves of a lie.

Once Strauss was seated, Hunter turned to Ray Jones, seated in the front row behind the defense table. Jones exited the courtroom and, a moment later, returned with the young woman who claimed that Strauss had spiked her drink previously.

As he confirmed his oath, Strauss laid eyes on the woman, and his mouth dropped open. He looked at Hunter, then back at the young woman, and then back at Hunter. Hunter kept his stare on Strauss.

Strauss wiped his brow again and looked down at his hands resting in his lap. They were trembling.

"Mr. Strauss, thank you for returning to the stand and answering some more questions," Hunter began, standing behind the lectern at the side of the room. "In your work for Mr. Charman, would you say that you would do anything for him?"

"I guess so," he shrugged. "It was a very high-pressure environment that we were working in. If you didn't do what Mr. Charman asked, you were out the door. I was working for him for five months, and during that time, four of the six interns had been let go."

"And who were the two interns left?"

"Amanda Ford and I."

Hunter nodded, almost ready to deliver the telling blow. He was building and building, but he wasn't ready to deliver it yet.

"You're connected to a lot of people in this case, Mr. Strauss," Hunter said. "So, can you please remind the court of your relationship with Ms. Law?"

"I'd met her a few times working for Mr. Charman. We'd done some work together, and she'd been introduced to me at some functions. Even though she was older than me, we hit it off. She was a lead prosecutor, so I thought she would be a good person to know."

"And were you with her on the night of July 14th?"

He drew a long breath and blinked again. "Yes. I went to her office and asked her out for a date. I figured that if things didn't work out with Mr. Charman, then I might be able to work at the State's Attorney's Office with her."

"How romantic," Hunter quipped. "And can you please tell the court which bar you invited Ms. Law to?"

The witness began to visibly shake, the nerves becoming too much for him. He knew what was coming, and there was nothing he could do to stop it.

"We went to The Five Cocktails Lounge Bar."

"On a Tuesday night?"

He nodded, trying to hold it together.

"Please answer the question verbally, Mr. Strauss."

"Yes."

"And do you know Mr. Brady, the man who owns the Five Cocktails Lounge Bar?"

"I do. We went to school together."

"Had you ever bought drugs from Mr. Brady?"

Hunter turned to look at the young woman sitting in the front row, and Strauss' eyes followed. Strauss' hands shook further, and he looked like he was about to cry.

"Mr. Strauss, please answer the question."

"Yes," he whispered.

"Sorry?" Hunter's voice rose. "Can you please repeat that loud enough for the court?"

"Yes. I bought drugs from him."

"What drugs did you buy from him?"

"Ecstasy pills."

"Any other drugs?"

He looked away, staring into nothingness, and swallowing hard.

"Mr. Strauss." Hunter thumped his hand on the lectern. "Did you buy any other drugs from Mr. Brady?"

"Yes."

"And what was that?"

"GHB."

"GHB," Hunter sighed, looking at the jury and shaking his head. He paused for a long moment, walked back to his table, opened a file, and returned to the lectern. He was letting the silence sit in the room, telling the jury that this was important information. "Mr. Strauss, did you spike Ms. Law's drink on July 14th?"

"I don't…"

"Mr. Strauss." Hunter's voice rose again, his fist resting on the lectern. "Did you spike Ms. Law's drink?"

Strauss looked at his hands, unable to answer.

"Mr. Strauss!" Hunter's fist punched down on the top of the lectern. "Answer the question! Did you spike Ms. Law's drink with GHB on July 14th?!"

"I don't remember," he whispered.

"You don't remember!" Hunter shouted. "Mr. Strauss, you're under oath in a court of law! You need to answer the question!"

"Ok," he whispered. "I've spiked other people's drinks, but I don't remember if I spiked Michelle's drink."

"You admit, under oath, that you've spiked people's drinks with GHB?"

Strauss looked up at Hunter, a single tear running down his cheek. "Yes."

"Did you rape them after you spiked their drinks?"

"Objection!" Baron stood. "There's no relevance to this case. Mr. Strauss isn't on trial here."

"Sustained," Judge Bales said. "Stick to the current case, Mr. Hunter."

Hunter shook his head and looked at the woman in the front row. "On July 14th, you spiked Ms. Law's drink with GHB, and what happened next?"

"I didn't spike her drink," he said. "I was going to take her home, but she was acting very weird and tripping out, so I left her in the park next to the bar and went home by myself. I didn't rape her. I didn't touch her. I left her in the park."

"Mr. Strauss, your story has changed many, many times over the course of this trial. How can we believe a single word you've said?"

Strauss didn't answer, keeping his head low and avoiding eye contact.

"Mr. Strauss?" Hunter pressed. "How can we believe what you've said here today?"

He looked away from Hunter, staring at a blank space on the wall in the distance.

"Mr. Strauss, you need to answer the question."

"Because I didn't rape her," he whispered. "I left her in the park."

"I have no further questions for this witness." Hunter shook his head and looked at the jury. "The defense rests."

CHAPTER 40

"IT DOESN'T prove you're not guilty." Hunter leaned against the wall in the meeting room in the George N. Leighton Courthouse. "All it proves is that you 'could' have been drugged."

"And incapable," Esther added. "If you were drugged, there's no way you could've done it."

"It wasn't a confession," Hunter continued. "We were close but he didn't confess to spiking your drink. We were so close. He hinted at it, and we've got to hope that the jury believes that he did."

Michelle Law sat at the end of the dark wooden table, arms folded across her chest, leaning far enough forward that her head was almost touching the edge. The meeting room was small and tight, and still filled with the smell of the last attendee's lunch. The scent of fried chicken lingered in the air, enclosed in the windowless room.

"He's right, though," Michelle whispered. "It only proves that I could have been drugged, nothing more. There's no evidence that I didn't do this, and there's no evidence that I was actually drugged."

Hunter's phone pinged, and he picked it up.

"It's a message from Jemma Knowles." Hunter's eyes scanned the screen. "They've arrested Callum Strauss, along with five others, for spiking drinks at the Five Cocktails. The bar owner turned on them all in return for a lesser deal."

"Good," Michelle whispered. "I hope they slam the full force of the law on that rich little prick."

Hunter nodded. "That means the closing statement has to be focused on the fact that you weren't capable of suffocating Amanda Ford, nor lifting her body into the car. That's been our tactic this entire case, and if we can convince the jury that you were involuntarily drugged, you can walk out of those doors."

"But there's no evidence I was drugged. It's all just a theory," Michelle whispered. "If the jury doesn't believe it, then I will spend the rest of my life in prison."

"It's the best defense we have." Hunter nodded and looked at his watch. "It's time to present closing statements."

As he walked out of the courthouse meeting room, he wished Baron had been waiting for him, ready to offer a deal for manslaughter, perhaps a year in total. But there was no Baron, no prosecution team, and no hope for a deal.

Hunter led his team back into the courtroom, head held high and ready for action.

The spectator seats in the courtroom filled quickly after the brief recess. The crowd wanted to see the closing statements, see the final arguments from the lawyers, and wait for the jury's decision.

Before calling for closing statements, Judge Bales spoke to the jury about their civic duty and the legal definitions that had to guide their decisions, and when he was sure they were clear on their responsibilities, he called for the lawyers to begin their closing statements.

Baron stood, walked to the lectern, and made one

last plea for a guilty verdict.

*****

"Ladies and gentlemen of the jury, people of Cook County, thank you for taking the time to listen to this case. This process has been long, at times boring, and arduous, however, you must not forget why you're sitting in the jury box.

You're here to make a judgment on a person's guilt based on the evidence presented to you.

And because of that, I need you to remember one fact—the body of Amanda Ford was found in the trunk of Michelle Law's car.

That's a fact.

We've sat here and watched the video of Officer Parker pulling over the white Audi sedan. We've seen, with our own two eyes, the moment Officer Parker spotted the smear of blood. And we've seen the moment he popped the trunk to see the deceased's body.

The defense has suggested that she was drugged at some point, but they haven't proven that she didn't murder Amanda Ford.

You've heard from character witnesses who testified that Ms. Law had a problem with alcohol for many, many years.

You've heard from Dr. Lee, an expert in alcohol blackouts, describe Ms. Law's behavior as consistent with someone who blacked out from excessive alcohol use.

A person who is intoxicated is criminally

responsible for their conduct. Remember that—an intoxicated person is criminally responsible for their conduct. If she blacked out because of the number of drinks she consumed, she is still responsible for her actions.

Even if you believe she was drugged, even though there is zero evidence of that, the level of intoxication or drugged condition is such that it must deprive her of the substantial capacity to appreciate the criminality of her conduct.

And there is no evidence that her level of drugged condition reached such a point.

We are talking about a prosecutor who has served in that position for decades. Right and wrong are in her very bones. Even drunk, or high, she must know the difference between right and wrong.

When making your decision, you need to consider the facts of this case, not the stories. You need to consider the evidence, not the fanciful display of fiction from the defense. You need to make your decision based on the proof.

The cold, hard truth is that Amanda Ford was found in the trunk of the defendant's car. This occurred after the defendant said she was 'going to kill' Miss Ford. This occurred after the defendant admitted she had blacked out the night before. This occurred after the defendant went into a jealous rage.

The application of the law in this case is simple—if you find beyond a reasonable doubt that Ms. Law murdered Miss Ford, then you must return a guilty verdict.

It's simple—Ms. Law is the only person who had the motive, the means, and the desire to murder Miss Ford.

This is a chance for the justice system to convict and punish a murderer and let the city know that nobody is above the law.

This is a chance for you, the jury, to clean up the streets of Chicago. This is a chance for you to protect our city. This is a chance for you to protect our neighbors from violence.

The only reasonable conclusion you can make after this trial is guilty.

Thank you for your time."

*****

Baron walked back to his seat.

He avoided eye contact with the defense table, sitting down and crossing one leg over the other. He looked calm and confident, like a winner who had just finished the job.

Hunter made several notes across his closing statement and then stood, moving behind the lectern to begin his statement.

Baron's case rested on one fact—the body was found in the trunk of Michelle's car and there was no other reasonable explanation for it. Baron had focused on that during the whole trial.

Hunter had to do the opposite. He had to cast doubt over the events of that evening, and he had to convince twelve regular people that Michelle was not guilty.

*****

239

"Michelle Law is innocent.

After the weeks that we've had together in this courtroom, that should be clear to you now. The facts of her innocence are too large to ignore.

There's no evidence that Ms. Law was in Miss Ford's apartment. There's no evidence that Ms. Law met with Miss Ford that night. And there's no evidence that Ms. Law caused Miss Ford's death.

Let me repeat that for you so it's clear—there's no evidence that Ms. Law caused Miss Ford's death. None. And because of that, and because the prosecution has presented no evidence, the state has failed in its attempt to convict Ms. Law.

What are the facts of this case? The facts are that Ms. Law went to drinks with Mr. Strauss on July 14th. The facts are that Ms. Law awoke with a body in the trunk. Not one witness, not one, could tell you how that body got there. Not one witness, not one, could tell you they saw the murder.

And what does that leave us with?

It leaves nothing, no evidence, no facts, nor any proof, that Ms. Law was involved in Miss Ford's death.

We know that Mr. Callum Strauss asked Ms. Law out for drinks at the Five Cocktails Lounge Bar on July 14th. We've heard Mr. Strauss state they left around 10pm.

During this case, we've heard from Officer Parker. We've seen his body cam footage.

We also heard that Officer Parker received a call from Mr. Callum Strauss at 5am that morning. After that call, Officer Parker drove twenty-five minutes from Rogers Park to River North. This was very unusual behavior from Officer Parker, who admitted he hadn't patrolled that area in the last twelve months.

Is that a coincidence? I don't think so.

During this case, we've heard from Detective Jemma Knowles, who informed the court that the owner of the Five Cocktails Lounge Bar had been charged with possessing a controlled substance in GHB. The owner, Mr. Brady, admitted he sold Mr. Strauss the date-rape drug GHB.

Mr. Strauss admitted, in this court, that he'd drugged people with GHB.

We heard from an expert in GHB, Dr. Katherine Beck, state that Michelle displayed all the symptoms of a GHB dosing.

We've heard from experts who have testified that it would be impossible to murder and lift a body into the car under the influence of GHB.

Listen to the facts, listen to what the evidence is saying, because it all points to the innocence of Ms. Law.

If you believe there is not enough evidence in this case, you must find the defendant not guilty. If you believe that you have reasonable doubt over the evidence presented, you must find the defendant not guilty. And if you believe that she was involuntarily drugged to deprive her of the substantial capacity to control her conduct, you must find the defendant not guilty.

Thank you for your service to the justice system."

CHAPTER 41

MICHELLE LAW couldn't shake the feeling of guilt.

It was deep inside her somewhere, bubbling away, threatening to come out. She tried so hard to remember something about that night. She meditated, listened to YouTube memory experts, and researched brain behavior, but she came up with nothing.

The night was a complete blank spot.

After closing arguments, Judge Bales had spoken to the jury, at length, about their responsibility to justice. She knew the spiel, she knew what judges told the jurors, but it sounded different from the defense table. The words, although familiar, felt foreign from that angle.

Hunter had done his best to reassure her of a positive result. He talked to her about which jurors he thought would side with them and which jurors wouldn't. He talked about the deliberation time and what this meant to their case. He talked about the appeals process if the decision didn't go their way.

But none of it mattered.

She was caught red-handed with a dead body in her possession, and she couldn't remember anything about that night. If she was a prosecutor, if she was on the other side of the courtroom, she would've been pushing for first-degree murder.

As the anxiety continued to build, Michelle started

to think about giving in and accepting her fate. All those years of drinking, all those years of numbing her pain, had caught up to her. She deserved this, she thought.

After she'd left the courthouse, she was hounded by the media, but she provided no comment. It was almost over.

As the case came to a close, she returned to her car alone. Alone. Even the word itself felt dirty to her.

She drove home in silence, just as she had during most of the trial. Even if the radio volume had been turned to maximum, she'd discovered early on that it did nothing to silence the thoughts running through her mind. No matter the distractions she tried to employ during the long commute home, those same thoughts would always climb to the top and stay there for the duration.

On the first night after the close of the trial, Michelle couldn't sleep. The following Saturday morning, after a night full of sweating and stress, she wanted nothing more than to strip off and hit the shower. It was the only hideaway she'd found which offered a reprieve from her mind. She relaxed under the heat of the water, under the streams as they fell across her body, comforted in her escape from the world. Each trickle was another distraction she could focus on.

The water felt amazing as she stepped into the heat. She heard a tap on her front door just as she pulled the shower door closed, but this wasn't the time for visitors. This was alone time, a moment of self-pity, where she could weep in silence and let her tears be washed away.

As the fear of the unknown gripped her tighter

than usual, she felt her legs weaken, and she allowed herself to slide to the floor. Pulling her knees close to her chest, Michelle wept quietly, giving in to the confusion ripping through her.

She stayed there, under the stream of hot water, until she cried herself out completely. Her eyes stung a little once she dried herself, and as she dressed in sweatpants and a t-shirt, another knock broke the silence of the apartment.

It was him, the man she both wanted to let in and also avoid at all costs. She peered out through the peephole like a thief hiding in the shadows, then almost pulled back when he looked directly at her.

"Michelle?" James called through the door as he knocked again. He held something in his hands, but she couldn't make it out. "I know you're home."

James. How she so wanted to open the door, pull him inside, and cry into his shoulder. She needed him, craved his support, and yet felt unable to give in to her needs. He knocked again as she continued to watch him, then as he shook his head and stepped back. Finally, he disappeared from view as he returned to his apartment.

Michelle pulled away from the door and squeezed her eyes shut, doing her best to fight the battle raging inside. After a grunt of raw emotion, she pulled the door open, looked out, and called out to him.

"Hey," James said as he once again stood in front of her. In his hands was a casserole dish, the contents hidden by aluminum foil. He held it up a little. "Thought you might like some lasagna for lunch."

She grinned, amazed at how a man like that could still be single. She invited him in. He was exactly what she needed, and as she closed the door, she hated herself for the conflict in her life.

They ate as James recalled a client from his work, a man running an amusement park. Michelle heard his story but found herself distracted by the guest himself, caught up in everything from the friendliness in his smile to the warmth behind his eyes. He was an honest man wanting to spend time with a friend in need, and here she was judging not only herself but also him.

She wanted him. The realization didn't come as a surprise, nor for the first time. Despite doing her best to reject him on every level, she'd fallen for him, her heart torn due to the upheaval in her life.

After an hour, he asked about the court case, careful not to offend her. James sat and listened as she shared her fears of losing the case and ending up in prison for a night she couldn't remember.

Surprising herself, when she finished talking about the case, Michelle felt the flow of tears resume, unable to fathom how more could have been hidden after the recent session in the shower. But when James put his comforting arm around her shoulders, the sobs turned into outright crying, and Michelle felt unable to hold back any longer.

He held her close as she cried herself completely out, her body rocking with each release of emotion. There was no talk during those precious minutes. James knew words weren't what she needed to hear, and, for the first time, Michelle didn't cover up her darkest fears.

They sat like that for almost an hour, long after Michelle's pain evaporated for good. She had her head on his shoulder while his arm held her close. If it wasn't for Michelle's cellphone ringing, they might have remained like that for the rest of the day.

"I'm so sorry," Michelle began as she reached for the phone. James let go of her as he told her not to apologize. The caller came up as 'Private,' and Michelle thought about just ignoring it. But feeling an urge to end the teary session on the couch, she stood as she thumbed the 'Accept' button.

"Hello?" she asked, heading for the hallway. Rather than a voice answering her back, a laugh came through instead, a loud and throaty sound that oozed obnoxiousness. "Hello," Michelle demanded, trying to break through the wall of noise. When the sound continued to mock her unimpeded, she ended the call.

She stared at the screen, wondering if it was just a prank caller, perhaps one of the many haters that had made themselves known through her now-canceled social media accounts. When the phone began to ring a second time, Michelle almost screamed as it vibrated in her hand. Not knowing why, she thumbed the answer button a second time, raised it to her ear, and barked her greeting through with conviction.

The laughter was gone, replaced by an eerie silence. Michelle knew someone was listening. But just as she was about to cancel the call again, a voice spoke, one she recognized in an instant.

"Hello, Ms. Michelle Law," Charman mocked, his voice more gravelly than normal.

"What do you want?" Michelle snapped. She wanted to cancel the call, to shut the man up once and for all, but felt powerless to move.

"How does it feel to be nothing more than a passenger in your own fate?"

"What do you want?" she screamed into the

phone, the pain gripping her in spasms.

James jumped to his feet.

"I warned you not to play with the big boys, didn't I?" Charman said. "That'll teach you for insulting me."

He hung up, leaving Michelle alone to listen to the silence of her own nightmares. James reached for her as she stared back in terror. Her whole body trembled, unable to keep herself still.

And as she fell into his arms, Michelle instinctively knew her fate had been sealed.

CHAPTER 42

HUNTER COULD handle losing.

The relentless questioning of witnesses, both for and against his cause, were also things Hunter could ride with ease. But where his patience struggled the most was during the moments of nothing, the waiting game, when others took control of the boat, and he had no choice but to sit back and watch the journey.

Jury deliberation was the pinnacle of waiting games, and Esther also knew about Hunter's weakness. Deliberations could take anywhere from hours to days to weeks, depending on the complexity of the case. Michelle's had been one of the more complicated ones, and he knew the jury could take forever to decide on the technicalities of the law.

It had already been five days since the jury started deliberations. That meant there was doubt in the jury room, but Hunter wasn't sure which way the jury was leaning.

Esther awoke to the start of another day with a bounce in her step, waking Hunter by ripping the curtains back and bathing him in brilliant sunshine.

"We've got work to do," she proudly proclaimed, and he stared back in confusion.

"Work? What work?"

"You and I are going to plant some trees today."

Still confused, he sat up in bed and rubbed his eyes. "Wait, what? Trees? Work? I'm not following."

"You remember our trip to the Morton Arboretum a couple of years ago?"

He looked up, searching for the memory through the sleep fog. "Planting trees?"

"That's the one," Esther smiled. "They have a new section of woodland they've just closed off to the public, and they've asked for volunteers to come and plant some new trees. Looks like today is your day to give something back to the people."

He groaned, fell back onto the pillow, and pulled the blanket over his face.

"Really?" He couldn't sound more childlike if he tried, giving Esther another reason to giggle.

"Yes, Mister, we have to. Already signed and sealed. We're doing our bit for the environment." She walked back to the open window. "And besides... check out the day. Blue sky and warm weather."

"On a Friday morning?"

"That's right. Let's go. We won't get many more days like this before winter arrives."

He couldn't argue about the amazing weather gracing them, and, despite trying to change her mind, he eventually gave in and jumped into the shower. An hour later, they were grabbing the first lot of plants off the back of a flatbed.

Morton Arboretum was a sprawling 1700-acre public garden forty-five minutes from Chicago. It was a horticultural oasis, a diverse woodland that served families, walkers, and young lovers in abundance.

A team of twenty-five volunteers had arrived to plant trees, and the head volunteer sectioned them off into groups. Esther introduced herself and Hunter to another couple who had volunteered, and soon the four of them were following each other around as they spread the young trees along a pre-determined row.

Hunter put the shovel to work as Esther prepped the young trees, and soon, they had a mini production line happening. With the other couple on the plot line behind them, they set to work planting dozens of new trees along the side of a small path. While the work may have been more physical than he was used to, Hunter found himself swept up in the moment. Although he didn't get out as much as he wanted, he loved the outdoors. He often thought if he could move his desk outside in the woods, he would happily do so. The clients might not be as good, he reasoned to himself as morning ticked past, probably end up defending bears accused of mauling hunters. They'd get off on self-defense. He smiled as the ridiculous thoughts rolled around his head. Nature had that effect on him. In the city, behind his desk, his world was governed by rules and procedure, but in nature, out in the open, he could let his mind run free.

As Hunter was digging, Esther called out. "If a man takes two hours to dig one hole, what does he dig in an hour?"

"Half a hole," Hunter responded without thinking, driving the shovel back into the ground.

"You can't dig half a hole," Esther laughed. "He just digs a hole."

Hunter stopped, leaned on his shovel, and shook his head. "I heard that one in elementary school, and it still gets me."

"And he's the smartest guy I know," Esther leaned close to the other woman planting trees and pointed at Hunter. "And it only took him ten years to ask me out on a date."

The two women laughed together as Hunter smiled and then drove the shovel back into the ground. "You know, I was thinking about the shovel," Hunter called back to them, a smile rising on his face. "When the shovel was first made, it must've been a groundbreaking invention."

"So true," Esther smiled. "But the invention of the broom was what really swept the nation."

They worked hard for the next two hours, sweating, laughing, and losing themselves in the moment. The stress of the jury decision had been left behind. There was something about sweating in nature, being out in the open, and working hard. It felt like real work, like a homecoming.

By the time the complimentary coffee was served up for the morning break, Hunter had worked up quite a sweat.

"Do you guys have kids?" One woman asked. It was an innocent query, a conversation starter, but it hit them where it hurt. Hunter and Esther exchanged a glance, neither of them answering the question. "We've got two boys," the woman continued. "Max and Mitchell. They're twins, five years old. My mother is looking after them while we volunteer out here, but I hope to have them out here with us in a few years."

Hunter remained uncomfortably silent until his cell rang, and the familiar number repeatedly flashed on the screen. As Hunter held the cell phone up to Esther, she saw the caller's ID and paused, drinking her coffee.

"Perfect timing," she whispered, and as Hunter answered the call, she explained the situation to the couple.

"We need to get going," Hunter said he ended the brief call. "Decision time."

They packed up, leaving the others to continue, and raced back to Chicago. They returned to Hunter's apartment, showered, freshened up, and dressed for work in the city.

She could tell he was nervous, almost silent the entire journey.

While he may have appeared calm and collected, inside, Hunter was anything but.

It was time to hear the jury's decision.

CHAPTER 43

THE FOYER of the George N. Leighton Criminal Courthouse was humming with the noise of people conversing, debating, and deliberating.

The ever-present hum of action was only interrupted by the occasional screams of victims and their families about the failures of the system. The drone of the noise in the foyer was a recipe for a headache, but Hunter didn't want to be anywhere else. This was his home. This was where he felt comfortable. This building, this place, was where he chased justice.

After he stepped through the security line, he stood in the foyer and looked around. When Esther joined him, she rubbed his arm, bringing a sense of calm to his rising anxiety.

"Michelle has had the best possible defense available to her," she began. "Whatever happens in there, I'm proud of what you've done for her."

Hunter drew a long breath and nodded. "It's time."

Waiting in the foyer, near the elevators, was Walter Charman, looking as arrogant as ever, a smirk stretched across his face.

"Decision time," Charman noted. "I hope this is a lesson for you, Hunter."

"Excuse me?" Hunter said, holding himself back from lunging at him and wiping the grin from his irritating face.

"This decision should be a lesson to stay out of other people's business." Charman grinned and then looked at his phone, which had started ringing in his hands. "Just remember your place in this world. It's not good for your career to go digging too deep."

Charman laughed and then turned away to answer the call, walking back towards the foyer.

Hunter wanted to fight back, to throw his own insults at the man, but he resisted, turning to the courtroom instead.

Michelle Law was already waiting in the courtroom when Hunter arrived. Baron and his team were talking to the Ford family, seated behind the prosecution table. Half the seats were already filled with the Ford family's supporters, all falling quiet as Hunter walked past. More of the extended Ford family filed in after Hunter, along with friends of Amanda Ford. Soon, the seats were all filled; the audience bringing a nervous tension with them.

Michelle sat next to Hunter, the look of fear in her eyes evident. Esther sat next to Michelle's only supporter in the room, James Heath.

Michelle didn't say anything. She looked like she could fall apart at any moment. She had sprayed on an expensive perfume for the occasion, one full of floral notes, perhaps in her last moment of freedom. Hunter provided Michelle with a nod, but she offered nothing back.

The nerves were filling his stomach as well, afraid that he'd failed a woman who had placed her faith in him, laying her freedom into his hands. Had he done enough? The question plagued him as he waited.

There was no hiding from the tension hanging in the air. The buzz was a looming fear of the final revelation, the last play after months of stress. The game had been played, the race had been run, and the results in. All that was needed now was for the host to reveal the winners.

At five minutes past 2pm, the bailiff stood and brought the murmurs to a close. The people in the courtroom rose. All eyes watched as the judge shuffled out of his chambers and took his seat. Once he sat, the silence intensified.

Judge Bales asked the bailiff to call in the jury.

The five men and seven women walked in single file, each following the person in front until they were all seated.

"Has the jury reached a verdict?" Judge Bales said, his voice loud in the silent tension of the room.

The woman sitting in the front left seat rose and spoke as if she'd rehearsed her lines for days. "We have, Your Honor."

The bailiff stepped forward, took the slip of paper, and walked it back to the judge. Once Bales read the short note, he looked back at the head juror and waited for her to finish the sequence.

Her words punctuated the air. Hunter didn't need to hear them. Looking at the woman, the answer was clear. He closed his eyes, clenched his fists, and prepared himself for the inevitable.

"In the charge of murder in the first degree, we, the jury, find the defendant guilty."

CHAPTER 44

THE CROWD erupted.

Some cheered, some cried, others hugged. The reporters jumped to their feet and rushed for the exit to be the first to get the news back to their respective offices. The prosecutor stood, shook hands with his assistants, and looked pleasingly across at the losing party. The judge, despite attempting to regain control of his courtroom, gave up and simply voiced his final instructions methodically towards the microphone.

Michelle Law fell back into her chair, her hands covering her face. She was shaking as she sobbed, her head and shoulders bouncing up and down.

It was over. Michelle Law was a convicted murderer. She was going to prison.

Hunter could do no more than sit and stare at the scene unfolding before him.

He had failed.

As the guards stepped forward, handcuffs ready, Hunter rested a hand on her shoulder and said, "This isn't over. We will appeal." Not sure if she heard him above the roar of the crowd, Hunter repeated himself, leaning closer to her. "We will appeal."

She didn't appear to hear him, her uncontrolled sobs rocking her body as she was cuffed and pulled to her feet. Hunter could do little to help her, watching on as nothing more than a helpless spectator.

As she was pulled away, Michelle continued to sob. The officers ignored her, continuing to guide her towards the side door. When the door closed, her cries were finally cut off. Hunter remained where he sat, stunned by the turn of events.

Behind him, Esther didn't move. While the crowd slowly began to exit the room, their cheers echoing down the hallway, she remained in her seat, watching as Hunter stared at the empty bench where Judge Bales had sat. When he finally turned and saw her sitting there, Hunter slowly shook his head in despair.

"I failed her," was all he could whisper.

Hunter's eyes looked past Esther; his expression briefly paused before the eyes grew wider.

Walter Charman stood by the door, arms folded across his chest, a smile on his face.

Charman stepped forward through the now empty seats, standing next to Esther, leaning forward to deliver his comment. "Don't beat yourself up too much, Hunter. You never had a chance."

CHAPTER 45

FROM THE moment the verdict was read, Michelle's reality disappeared into a cloud of grief and pain. She lost all grip on the people surrounding her and reacted to each event on instinct alone. Feeling the cold steel of the handcuffs only pulled her further away from the real world.

After the second door to the courtroom slammed closed behind her, Michelle's sobs grew louder, the tears blinding her as she found herself led down a dark corridor. She could hear shouts in the distance, but despite coming from the cells off to her side, the voices sounded miles away. Perhaps they were, with her own soul now helplessly floating above her own body as it was led to her doom.

The cell she was first taken to felt more like an icebox, her shivers further fatiguing her. Trauma victims often shook uncontrollably, and Michelle couldn't stop shaking as she sat in near darkness. She sat in the corner of the cell, overwhelmed by the emotions rolling through her. She had always been so restrained, so measured, but now, there was no stopping the flood that was coming out.

The officer asked if she wanted the light on but left it off when no answer came.

The cell smelled like rank sewage, a stench that

only added to her anguish.

The sounds surrounding her came and went as if she was caught in the belly of a great beast, breathing the misery in and out with regular clarity. Michelle sat on the floor, clasped her knees close, and sobbed into the cloth of her pants. A woman sitting in the cell next to hers heard her weeping and began to cackle loudly.

"Watcha crying for, Honey? You ain't in Paris now," the voice jeered before sinking back into a guttural laugh.

Michelle squeezed her eyes shut, pressed the palms of her hands against her ears, and focused. A face began to form in her mind, taking shape within the swirling mass of emotion. It was a man she had tried to avoid, to push aside whenever he held a friendly hand out towards her. James had been a supporting anchor for her during the past weeks, and yet she'd still tried her best to cast him aside.

Why hadn't she let him in completely? He would have, without question. He wanted her, that much she knew. But just how committed was he really? If she had been back at her post, she might have had Berkeley check him out, run a background check to see if he really was disconnected from her life and those who wished her harm.

James' face disappeared into a swirling mist, the cloud awash like whitewater. A new face pushed in, summoned by her subconscious. It was Berkeley, grinning at her with seedy lust in his eyes. In the seconds it stared out at her, Michelle felt her stomach turn. Berkeley began to fade again, a new face pushing him aside, then consuming what remained like a parasitic leech. Charman mocking leer stared back at her, his eyes a sparkle of amusement as the man repeated the guilty verdict over and over again. Michelle pressed her hands against her head even harder, the scream building low before culminating into a deafening shriek of anguish.

The bang on the door brought her back into the moment, the guard's voice summoning her attention.

"Hey. Keep it down. You're not the only one in pain." A small portion of his face squeezed through the viewing trap. "We'll process you next."

He slammed the trap shut again, and Michelle listened as the chorus surrounding her cell resumed mocking each other, the guards, and any entity still present in the hellhole.

True to his word, the same guard collected her five minutes later, handcuffing her again and walking out of the cell to one of the counters to begin to process her into the system. The sequence was much faster due to her previous incarceration but still required several steps before she could be walked through the tunnels under the courthouse to the nearby Cook County Jail.

The guard asked several questions about her current situation, next of kin, and other details which might have changed during her brief taste of freedom. He updated her file with a new mug shot, then walked her to the strip room along with three other women.

Degrading was too tame a word for how she felt, as her very humanity was stripped away during the next few minutes. After removing all of her clothing, Michelle went through the emotional task of opening herself to the supervising officer in the most impersonal way imaginable.

Standing naked, she had to raise her arms, fingers,

and each breast to prove nothing was hidden in any fold or crevice. The final insult came when she was instructed to turn around and bend over.

Michelle felt like a passenger on a horrid rollercoaster, tied to the seat, unable to exit. Her words were ignored, the sobbing a mere inconvenience to those trying to process her. Nobody cared who she was, what she did, or the reasons behind her crimes. They didn't care about her physical state, mental state, or past traumas. To the staff, she was just another prisoner, a mere number, there to be flicked and ticked, then moved on to other staff members further along the production line.

Michelle Law the person ceased to exist as she silently donned the dull blue pants and top, an empty shell taking her place. How long this inevitable hell would last was still a mystery to her, and hope seemed impossible to wish for.

The officer handed her a set of flip-flops, then guided the group into a new holding cell. Moments later, they were cuffed and led through the tunnel, making the final journey to her future.

All she could do was watch life pass by, the reality of the final verdict consuming her completely.

CHAPTER 46

IT TOOK Hunter the rest of the afternoon, as well as most of the next day, to bring himself up from the throes of defeat and face reality.

He began work on the appeal the second he walked back into his office, but he had lingering doubts about whether it would serve to change Michelle's fate.

As he sat in his office, piles of paperwork in front of him, he called Jones and gave him instructions to use his own discretion and find him something, anything, which could be used against the prosecution witnesses. He asked him to dive even deeper into the powers standing in the shadows, including Charman. Especially Charman, he had highlighted.

Picturing the man's obnoxious victory grin from the courtroom was enough to rile his temper again, and he slammed his cell phone into the desk once the call finished. The sound was enough to bring Esther to the door, her head poking around the corner.

"Need me to pre-order a new phone now, or wait for that one to completely shatter?"

He looked up, wanted to snap back, then saw her face.

"I'm sorry," he whispered, rubbing his index fingers into his temples. "I need to get something going. Every minute we spend sitting here is another minute Michelle is spending in that hole."

"Then we might have something," she said. "Jemma Knowles just called, and asked if you were in and whether you could meet her at the Lincoln Park Conservatory."

"Did she say why?"

Esther shook her head. "No, but she said it was worth getting up there for."

Hunter checked the time. Five past five. "Tell her I'll be there in twenty-five minutes."

Hunter grabbed his briefcase and walked to the door. He stopped to give Esther a kiss on her forehead as he passed, and then in the elevator, he ordered an Uber. By the time he walked out of the foyer, the driver was waiting on the street.

He told the driver to move it, and the driver weaved in and out of the Chicago traffic like he was racing in Formula One. When they arrived at the Conservatory in under twenty-five minutes, Hunter thanked the man and left him a healthy tip.

He called Knowles, and five minutes later, she'd pulled up in front of the meeting spot.

"Let's take a walk." She didn't greet him as she stepped out of the car, instead leading him further down Stockton Drive, away from any prying ears. She checked over her shoulder to ensure nobody was following, before crossing the street, and stopping near the William Shakespeare Monument, which had been there since 1894. Knowles stopped at a park bench, tucked away behind an oak tree. She checked for anybody else around, and when she saw no one following them, she turned back to Hunter.

"Tough day?" She folded her arms across her

chest.

"Michelle didn't take it well," Hunter nodded. "She was a mess when the decision was read out."

"I heard. I heard she was sobbing the whole time, at least that's what they said on the news bulletin." Knowles nodded, checking her surroundings again. "I've got news about the case with the Five Cocktails Lounge Bar."

"Go on."

"The whole thing is a mess. All the boys have rich parents, and they've all lawyered up, but something came up in the investigation that you need to know. It's just a lead, and we'll investigate it, but our hands are full at the moment. We need time before we can work this lead." She drew a breath. "But I thought you needed to know straight away, even if it turns out to be nothing."

Hunter waited while Knowles checked her surroundings again. When she saw the coast was clear, she continued. "Did you check out all the jury members?"

"Of course."

"I thought so," she replied. "Listen, this was only flagged because we arrested Callum Strauss. His arrest brought up all the details we have in the system about him, and one of those links is his father, Stephen Strauss. I was looking into his file, and there are allegations of insider trading against him, but nothing ever stuck. But what was really interesting was his family connections. Stephen Strauss' sister married a man named Gregory Wallis, and they had several children."

"Wallis? That's the last name of one of the jury members."

"That's right. Robert Wallis was juror number five, serving on the case against Michelle Law," she said. "He's Callum Strauss' cousin."

Hunter groaned and ran his hand through his hair. "This is grounds for appeal, or even having the case thrown out. This changes everything."

Knowles nodded. "I know."

"And you haven't talked to them about it?"

"Not yet," she shook her head. "We haven't had time, and with all these boys lawyered up, then we have to tread very carefully. It'll take us months to even move a step forward in this case."

Hunter nodded. "Then it sounds like I need to talk to these cousins."

CHAPTER 47

PRISON LIFE is different.

It could be compared to living in another country for the most part, given the vast differences between it and reality outside the walls. The rules governing prison would seem strange to a newcomer, with a new dialectal to learn if one wanted to fit in. Breaking the rules of prison often attracted punishment, which was both instant and brutal, with very little room for mercy.

The first night Michelle had spent in prison was the night after her arrest. On that night, she had come close to getting an old-fashioned beating from the pod boss, watched two of her cellmates smoke drugs, then had another inmate ask to share her bunk and keep her warm. She ended up lying awake, terrified the entire night, watching as the rest of her cell partied around her.

This trip, some two months later, Michelle had been told that she'd be taken to solitary confinement due to her job as a prosecutor, however, there had been no such move made.

Michelle was returned after her guilty verdict, and she barely recognized her surroundings, caught up in her own internal turmoil, which continued to play out. One of her previous cellmates had seen her enter the pod in an almost catatonic state. She was barely carrying her mattress and bedding, dragging it behind herself as she walked in. The cellmate led Michelle upstairs and into a cell with a vacant bed.

There was no welcoming committee this time the way she had been inundated the first time. The other women quickly recognized their previous co-tenant, and went on about their business. For Maggie Levine, however, it was cause to celebrate seeing the stuck-up lawyer back.

Maggie, a fellow prisoner known as the pod boss, ran the female population of the unit with an iron fist. She craved the attention of the other girls and wasn't afraid to spill blood in her quest for dominance. At six-foot-one, she was also one of the tallest, a formidable opponent given her two-hundred-forty-pound frame.

The problem Michelle faced began on the first night, recognized for who she was almost the second she first walked through the pod's front door. One of Maggie's closest allies in the pod had a sister whom Michelle had sent to prison the year before. It was a red flag that should have been picked up by the prison's intel department but wasn't.

Once Maggie found out, she made it her business to get as close to Michelle as possible. She sent two of her 'starlets,' as she liked to call them, to relocate Michelle into a cell housing groups of violent women, giving them easy access to her.

Maggie's eyes lit up as she spotted Michelle entering the pod for a second visit and cackled in delight as she watched the former prosecutor walk the floor of the pod in a trance-like state. All it took was a nod, and one of her starlets manipulated Michelle's direction enough to land her in another cell of their choosing. This time, there would be no mistakes.

Michelle barely registered arriving at the prison at all. Her head was still awash with the trauma of the verdict, her mind continuing to play out those final moments during the jury's final delivery. As she climbed the stairs, the howls and laughter from other inmates echoed around her.

Once in the cell, Michelle dropped her mattress onto the only vacant spot, a lower bunk closest to the door, and lay down in a fetal position. Two other women sitting on top of an adjoining bunk paused their card playing and simply stared as the new arrival entered. Once they recognized her, they looked at each other with wry grins, waited for the woman to drop down, then continued drawing cards from the deck.

Michelle was tired, emotionally drained, and close to collapsing when she dropped down onto the bunk. A second later, her eyes squeezed shut, and not long after, faint snores rose from the bed. The two women glanced at each other, carefully climbed down, and headed off to find their leader as Michelle lay helplessly alone in silence.

But an attack didn't come that night. The timing of her arrival had given Michelle a short reprieve, with lockdown just a few minutes after she fell asleep. Maggie had called the girls off until the next day, wanting to ensure all who wanted to get their boots in would have a chance. They would wait until the following mornings unlock.

Michelle didn't wake once during the subsequent night, despite a couple of adjoining cells pulling all-night parties. While the laughter and ruckus kept the rest of the pod awake, Michelle didn't stir, her sleep deeper than she could have ever imagined.

Her state of mind didn't change much by the time she awoke the next morning. The shock of the verdict refused to subside. Her eyes, bloodshot with the remnants of the marathon weeping session from the previous day, blinked painfully as sunlight streamed in through the smallest sliver of window. Michelle sat up, looked around, and took notice of her new surroundings.

Knowing how the system worked, Michelle's most dominant thought was also one of the hardest to fathom, understanding how the rest of the case would turn out. If Hunter's appeal failed, she would face a sentence of no less than twenty years for murder.

Twenty years of this? The thought plagued Michelle as she looked up at the underside of the bunk above. Twenty years. It was too painful a thought to consider and one she couldn't fully accept.

She looked around again, staring at the rest of the women as they slept in the bunks surrounding her own. An arm hung down from one, a leg from another. Loud snores roared from the woman above her own bunk, while the lower bunk opposite kept twitching, as if the woman was swatting flies in her dream. A sudden pop echoed from somewhere above her, a throaty noise causing a chain reaction of bodies to begin moving under blankets.

The attack, when it finally came, didn't surprise Michelle.

She knew she would be a target the second she stepped through the door. It came with the territory of her profession. Of course, she would be recognized. She'd sent dozens, perhaps hundreds, of these women to prison, and some of them would surely have contacts inside the pod she was now forced to call home.

But while the attack didn't surprise her, the ferocity did.

What Michelle had expected was a one-on-one, the way civilized people handled physical violence. But this wasn't a place for standard rules, a prison pod more reminiscent of the Wild West. Perhaps even the Wild West wasn't wild enough compared to Michelle's new surroundings.

She started feeling her senses peak when the crowd inside her cell began to swell. While there were bunks big enough for eight, there were almost a dozen women standing around once she came back from eating her breakfast out in the common area. Up until that point, not a single person had spoken to her directly, simply eyeing her as she passed them by.

As she walked to her bunk, Michelle felt the air turn electric, the previous murmur suddenly dropping to near silence. Within seconds of entering the cell and walking to her bunk, she knew she was in danger and tried to think of a plan to get out of there again.

The only possession she had been given was a small bible during the previous evening's processing. A passing priest had handed it to her, saying he'd include her in his prayers. Michelle's plan was to retrieve the Bible from her bunk and take it back into the common area.

Attacks rarely happened out in the open.

Common areas were where the majority of cameras were located. Few blind spots existed, and it also gave opponents an open space to move in. Inside a cell, escape was much easier to prevent, and the lack of cameras meant more chance of not being identified.

Michelle had expected a confrontation, perhaps someone taking offense at her and then getting up into her face. A fight would follow, and she would be moved out of the pod for her own protection once she raised the alarm. That, however, was the thinking of a decent individual.

As Michelle pulled the Bible from under her pillow and turned back to the door, one of the girls sitting on the bunk above hers suddenly kicked out, the foot connecting with the side of Michelle's face. The surprise of the kick temporarily disorientated her. The kick acted as a signal, and within a split second, the rest of the women surrounded her. Fists and feet flew from all directions.

She fell to the floor.

Curling into a tight ball, kicks continued to rain down on her head and side. All she could do was weather the assault as her aggressors continued to scream obscenities throughout the attack.

The first officers entered the cell within thirty-five seconds of the attack starting. Another inmate had raised the alarm, itself a risk of retaliation.

Thirty-five seconds of endless punching and kicking, a terrifying onslaught of verbal and physical abuse from ten inmates.

Under a daze of concussion, Michelle was transferred to the prison's medical wing, covered in bruises, spit, and blood.

She'd sustained a broken rib, cut lip, fractured eye socket, and numerous lacerations.

It wasn't until the nurses cut away her top that one horrific revelation emerged.

During the attack, an inmate had stabbed Michelle in the lower back, perforating her skin, but not lodging deep. The puncture mark looked the width of a toothbrush handle, and, after locking the pod down, the weapon was found hidden in a bathroom stall.

It could have ended in tragedy.

Michelle didn't doubt that luck had been on her side, but despite surviving the attack, Michelle had no doubt it wouldn't be the last.

If she remained inside, her life would more than likely end with the next onslaught.

CHAPTER 48

HUNTER WAITED until he was back in the office before he called Jones.

Jones answered on the second ring. Hunter explained the revelation, then gave Jones instructions to locate Robert Wallis. If Wallis had been compromised by his relative, then he wouldn't be forthcoming with information. But, and Hunter knew it was a very big but, but if he'd been coerced, or perhaps even threatened, then his confession would come a lot easier.

"Bring him back to the office. We need to pressure him into telling us the truth," Hunter said. "I'm going to find Strauss and see what he'll give us. My bet is, not much, but it's worth the shot."

Hunter ended the call and opened his laptop to the witness files from Michelle Law's case. Strauss' address was listed as an apartment in Lakeview, twenty-five minutes north of his office. With Strauss' address on hand, Hunter jogged down to the parking lot, firing up his new BMW sedan.

He swerved onto the road from the parking garage, tires screaming for grip, questions running through his mind. Yes, he could threaten Strauss to tell the truth, but why bother? Strauss already knew what he was doing was wrong, which meant consequences didn't bother him, not when he had the backing of Charman.

But what if Charman was no longer on his team? Hunter rolled the thought around in his mind as he weaved in and out of the evening traffic, zipping through like a seasoned stunt driver. If he could make Strauss believe that Charman had turned on him, then Strauss may talk.

An accident clogged his way, and Hunter ducked down a side street as he continued to build the plan in his mind. When he thought of the two men, he couldn't get past how comfortable they appeared with each other. Strauss followed his boss around like a well-trained guard dog, while Charman looked ready to scratch the kid's ear at any moment.

"I'll wing it," he muttered to himself as he swung out ahead of the crash. Traffic was non-existent on the far side, and he coaxed the sedan up to speed in seconds. "Lawyers know how to wing it."

As the dusk started to bathe the area in an orange glow, Hunter pulled up a little further down from Strauss's apartment building. He entered the foyer of the apartment building, considering both the elevator and the stairs. Confronting Strauss in either would present their own problems, but he thought the stairs would provide a much better set of alternatives as opposed to the limited options of the elevator.

Hunter turned to the stairs, climbing them two at a time, but each set slowed him a little more, and by the time he reached the fifth floor, his heart was pounding hard. He took a moment to suck in the breaths, preparing himself for whatever confrontation awaited him on the other side of the fire door.

"Let's do this," he whispered to himself, feeling

the adrenalin starting to unload into his system as he opened the door.

The corridor was empty. There was a soda machine at the far end and doors lined along both sides, even numbers on the left, odds on the right. Apartment 505 was at the furthest end of the corridor, closest to the soda machine.

Hunter walked along the middle of the corridor, almost creeping as he walked. The sounds of the apartments he passed drifted out from behind closed doors as his focus remained fixed on the small sliver of the door ahead.

As he reached the apartment, the door was slightly ajar.

Hunter froze for a moment as he again considered his options. He looked behind to ensure the corridor was still clear, just in case someone saw him and asked questions.

Hunter thought about his two options: either knock on the door and confront Strauss or take his chances and push the door open, perhaps to gain as much advantage as possible. If Strauss entered whatever room existed on the other side of the door and found him standing there, he could close the door and keep the confrontation hidden from view.

He decided to go with the second option, slowly pushing the door open enough to peer through into the room beyond. The late evening sun had disappeared, and the shadows were already bathing the apartment in darkness.

Hunter could make out a living room, the couch facing the television, which sat in the furthest corner from the door. It was on, an old episode of Friends playing on mute.

Hunter turned to close the door again. He pulled his shirt sleeve down far enough to cover his hand and prevent leaving his prints.

The silence hanging in the air indicated an absence of life. Without needing to check every room, Hunter knew the apartment was vacant. For whatever reason, Strauss had left the apartment's door open and unlocked.

There was also a scent hanging in the air. It wasn't any single identifiable smell, but instead a combination of distinctive odors he thought he recognized. The first was gun smoke, its metallic stench strong enough to taste. The second was the unmistakable aroma of blood.

The two steps he took deeper into the apartment gave Hunter a better view.

He could see a foot positioned in front of the couch. The rear of the couch still blocked his view of whoever was lying on it, but now he could see enough to know there was somebody else in the apartment with him.

Taking another step forward, Hunter saw the full view of the person. The side profile looked familiar. Hunter took a final step forward to see the body of Callum Strauss lying on the couch. Blood covered his jumper, and both his hands were on his abdomen.

His skin was pale, and his eyes were open.

Hunter felt for the man's pulse and felt nothing but cold flesh. He stepped back. As he took another look at the surroundings, his cell began to vibrate. He pulled it from his pocket. It was Jones.

"What have you got?" Hunter whispered, afraid his voice might carry further than he anticipated.

"One dead juror."

The words froze him in place. "What?"

"I'm looking at Wallis's body. He's been shot in the chest. Looks like he bled out on his couch."

"I'm staring at the same scene here at Strauss's apartment," Hunter returned.

"The kid is dead?" Jones' tone matched Hunter's own surprise, and he took a step back to run the developments through his mind.

"I was about to call it in. You thinking of other plans?"

Hunter ignored him, options bouncing around.

"Hunter?"

Too many people would have seen him enter the building, and the security cameras would have placed him in the apartment.

"We'll call it in."

CHAPTER 49

OUTSIDE THE apartment building in Lakeview, Hunter waited by his car, hands in pockets, as police lights swirled through the night air. The temperature was cooling, a fresh breeze blowing from Lake Michigan, causing a shiver to run up Hunter's spine.

"You know I've got to ask you questions," Tony Mann approached Hunter, notepad in hand. "I need to rule you out of any possible involvement in his murder."

Hunter nodded, staring at the ground. "You're working as a detective on this one?"

"I like to step back into the fold from time to time, especially when things get complicated," Mann said. "Would you answer some questions?"

"Ask away."

"The time of death, while not official yet, looks to be around 5pm this afternoon. The neighbors reported hearing a gunshot, but when they called 911, they said the gunshot came from outside the building. A PD car came and checked it out but found nothing to worry about. So, Hunter, where were you at around 5pm?"

"My office. I left a five past five and caught an Uber to Lincoln Park."

"Can anyone verify that?"

"Esther, my assistant, was in the office, and the Uber receipt will show that they picked me up after 5pm and dropped me at the destination around 5.25pm."

"Most of the Ubers have passenger dashcams now, so we'll check that, but it sounds like you're in the clear. So, knowing that, tell me what you walked into."

Hunter drew a long breath. "I came to see Strauss and talk to him—"

"About?"

"About his connection to Michelle Law's case."

"More than what you questioned him on the stand?"

Hunter sighed. "This afternoon, after the decision was handed down, we got word that Strauss is the cousin of one of the jurors."

"Really? This is the first I've heard of it." Mann lifted his eyebrows in surprise. "And where is this cousin?"

"I had my investigator go to his place, and he was fronted with the exact same scenario. He's talking to the cops there now. The man's name was Robert Wallis."

Mann tapped his finger on his notepad and then took out his cell phone. He turned away from Hunter and made a call, speaking for five minutes before returning to Hunter.

Hunter waited, the thoughts rolling through his head. Charman was at the center of it all, but he had no evidence and no way to prove anything.

"I've just spoken to the Detectives at the scene of Robert Wallis' murder," Mann said as he approached Hunter again. "We're going to confer notes, but I imagine this looks good for Michelle Law's appeal. Looks like you might get a re-trial. A second bite at the cherry, so to speak."

"It should do," Hunter nodded.

"So, keep telling me what you walked into," Mann continued. "You said you came here to confront Strauss. What time was that?"

Hunter looked at his watch. "About one hour ago, at just after 7pm. I walked into the apartment building, took the stairs, and then walked down to his apartment. I noticed that the door was open, so I pushed it forward and called out his name."

"The door was open?"

"It was."

"Any sign of anyone else?"

"I didn't see another soul as I walked in." Hunter sighed again. "I entered and there was a smell in the air. It's hard to describe, but it smelled like dried blood. So, I stepped in closer, and I saw his foot dangling off the edge of the couch. When I continued forward, I saw that he'd been shot in the stomach and was lying on the couch."

"That's good, Hunter. That's going to help us. I imagine that someone around here saw something. At this point, we think that the shooter entered via the fire escape." Mann pointed to the alley next to the building. "And he probably left that way as well. We'll scour the place and look for clues, but I think we've got a start. If you think of anything that can help us, call me."

Mann patted Hunter on the shoulder and turned back towards the apartment building.

Hunter waited a moment, keeping his eye on the alley. After Mann had stepped away, Hunter walked towards the alley, approaching a shiny glint. There was something familiar thrown on the ground next to the dumpster. He tilted his head as he got closer, focusing on the object.

Hunter crouched down, removed his phone, turned on the flashlight, and focused on the empty bottle of Jack Daniels with blue tape wrapped around the neck of the bottle. It was tossed aside next to the trash, discarded like Callum Strauss' life.

And it was the answer to how he was going to break the case wide open.

CHAPTER 50

THE PIECES of the puzzle had fallen into place.

It was all there; all the information Hunter was after. He just needed to extract the truth from his target.

Hunter arrived at Jake Berkeley's office a little before 9pm. The door was open, and the light was on. Hunter walked up to the second-floor office, knocked on the door, and opened it. It was unlocked. As he stepped inside, he was instantly hit by the smell of alcohol.

Berkeley sat at his desk, feet up on the table, a bottle of Jack Daniels in his hand. The smell of pizza was overwhelming. Hunter looked around the room and saw a pizza box sitting on the floor near the window.

"I've finished it. No pizza left," Berkeley said. "I was surprised you called me. So, what is it you so desperately need to talk about, Hunter?"

"I need the truth about what happened to Amanda Ford."

Berkeley started laughing. "You're still going on about that? I thought it was all over now? Michelle's locked away forever. It's time to let that one go."

"Perhaps you'd prefer to talk about the murders of Callum Strauss."

The words had barely left Hunter's lips before the smile disappeared from Berkeley's face. His eyes scanned the guest instinctively, as if trying to see right through into his soul. Hunter stood by the door, a brown paper bag in his hand. "I thought that might get your attention."

"Why should it?" Berkeley asked. "Didn't know the kid was dead."

"It seems as if you're the common denominator between Robert Wallis, Amanda Ford, and Callum Strauss."

"You got nothing," he jeered. "You're all talk. That may work in a courtroom, but out here, in the real world, it does nothing."

Hunter opened the paper bag in his right hand and removed a bottle of Jack Daniels, blue tape around the neck of it. He held it up so Berkeley could get a clear look at it.

"Where'd you get that?"

"In the alley beside Callum Strauss' apartment building."

Berkeley lifted his chin, mouth open.

"I found Strauss in his apartment this afternoon, a bullet to the abdomen," Hunter said. "And then I found this bottle next to the alley."

"What about the cops?"

"That's the thing. I didn't turn this bottle over to the cops. I took it from the scene. I found it in the alley, next to the dumpster, presumably where you finished the bottle before going up the fire escape to put a bullet in Callum Strauss' torso."

"And why would you take it from the scene?"

"I don't care who killed Strauss. That arrogant man was going to cause a lot of trouble in his life, and

I'm happy he's off the street." Hunter placed the empty bottle on the table, searching for common ground with Berkeley. "I couldn't stand him. Just because he had a rich father, he thought he could do anything."

Berkeley made an expression of surprise and then nodded. He took his feet off the table and sat forward. "I hated that kid as well. Arrogant rich kid. I can't stand people like him."

"So, let's work out a deal."

"I'm interested," Berkeley stood and leaned against the wall at the back of the room. "But how can I trust you?"

"I've got the bottle, don't I?" Hunter reached for it again. "Or shall I turn it over to the police?"

"Wait," Berkeley said. "Let's talk about this like grown men."

Berkeley's hand reached for the back of his hip, presumably where he kept his weapon under his jacket. Hunter shook his head, pulling his jacket back to expose his hip holster and, more importantly, his Glock 17. Berkeley nodded in acknowledgment and took his hand away from his hip.

"I hope you've got a license for that," Berkeley smiled as he sat back down behind his desk.

Hunter closed his jacket.

"So," Berkeley stretched his arms out wide. "What is it you need?"

"The truth about Michelle Law's case."

"The truth?" Berkeley shook his head. "That's subjective, isn't it?"

"Not in a court of law."

"Alright, wise guy," Berkeley laughed. "The bottle for the truth, but this all has to be off the record. I won't repeat a word of this to the cops."

"Agreed. None of this will be on my records. I have Michelle Law's appeal coming up, and I need the truth. I need to know who killed Amanda Ford, why they killed her, and why Callum Strauss was killed. All I need is the truth. I can do the rest in court."

"Good, but you've got to do one thing first—turn your phone off, put it on the table, and then take off your jacket. I can't take any risks."

Hunter hesitated and then removed his phone, turned it off, and placed it on the table next to the bottle. He removed his jacket and handed it across to Berkeley, who checked the collar, the sleeves, and then the pockets. Once it was checked, Berkeley threw the jacket back at Hunter.

"Alright, you look clean. No recording devices," Berkeley sat back down. "So, you need to know who killed Amanda Ford? Well, you see, we've got a problem there because it was Callum Strauss that killed the girl. And he can't really argue about it because he's now dead."

"Why did he kill her?"

"Because he was a spoiled little rich kid. He thought he could get away with anything," Berkeley leaned forward on the table, drew a long breath, and then exhaled loudly. The smell of alcohol on his breath was heavy. "He took Michelle Law out for drinks and planned to spike her drink with that date-rape drug. He said it was because Michelle was an overbearing boss, someone who demanded action, and his fragile little ego couldn't take it. So, he was going to take her out, spike her drink, and rape her."

"To teach her a lesson?"

"That's right," Berkeley leaned back in his seat, shaking his head. "Now, I didn't like Michelle Law, but that was a step too far, even for a guy like me. Raping someone so that you can feel powerful? How messed up is that? The kid had a few loose screws upstairs."

"But she wasn't raped?"

"No. She had some sort of adverse reaction to GHB and started vomiting in the bar. Strauss said the bartender told him to take her outside, so he walked her across to the park, hoping she'd calm down, but then she started vomiting like crazy. Spewing up everywhere, so he just left her there."

"He just left her in the park? What a guy."

"I think we both know he was the lowest level of scum. And this is how I really know." Berkeley waved his finger in the air. "He thought he was going to get some that night, but he wasn't about to have sex with a woman that's vomiting, so he goes back to his ex-girlfriend's place."

"Who lived just around the corner."

"That's right. He still had her keys, so he let himself in, and when she said no to sex, he put her in a chokehold and suffocated her. He thought it was just enough to knock her out so he could rape her, but the stupid kid killed her." Berkeley sighed again, forcing out another waft of alcoholic breath. "In a panic, he calls Charman, who then calls me. I had to go and clean up the mess. And once the kid told me the story and that Michelle Law was passed out on a bench, well, it was too good an opportunity to miss. I went over, took her keys out of her pocket while she was sleeping on the bench, and then Strauss and I put Amanda Ford's body in the car. I raced over and put the keys back in Michelle's pocket."

"And then you called her at 5am."

"I was watching her. I was pretending to be a homeless guy across the street, and I watched her get into her car around 5am, but she fell asleep again."

"So, Strauss called his cop buddy to pull her over?"

"You got it," he snapped his fingers and pointed at Hunter. "It was the easiest dumping of a body I've ever done. Plus, I got that stupid prosecutor off my back. And then Charman lined up a whole lot of liars for the witness stand. It was legendary, in my books."

Hunter remained stoic, barely showing any emotion during the conversation. He was taking the information in, letting it roll around in his head. "And Strauss?"

"He was becoming too much of a risk for Charman. He was talking to the cops after the raid on the Five Cocktails, and he knew things about Charman that couldn't get out."

"Charman asked you to kill Strauss?"

"Asked me?" Berkeley laughed. "He didn't ask— he paid me to kill Strauss. But here's the great bit, I would've shot that prick for free."

Berkeley smiled, stood, reached across for the bottle, and placed it back in the brown paper bag. "Now, if you'll excuse me, it's time to get rid of this bottle."

Berkeley walked to the door of his office, opened it, but stopped.

Standing there, in the door frame, was Detective Tony Mann, with a police officer on either side of him. Mann tapped his phone and replayed the last part of the conversation. "It's all recorded, Berkeley.

It's over."

Berkeley swung back to face Hunter. "You played me."

Hunter stood. "Just like you said—you've got to do what you can to survive."

They had a killer. They had a murderer.

But they didn't have the man who pulled the strings.

Not yet.

CHAPTER 51

FRIDAY NIGHTS were always lively in the Berghoff restaurant.

The release after a week of hard work, the celebration of the weekend's beginning, the knowledge that they'd survived another week. For Walter Charman, the celebration was even bigger. He'd beaten the system, again, and still stood strong, proud, as those who challenged him fell away. Power was addictive, and Walter Charman had spent most of his life in its grips.

Charman smiled as he made a toast to Michelle Law, the five other men at the table, raising their glasses with him. Sitting with Charman was a City Alderman, a Senator, two building developers, and a real estate agent. He toasted to Michelle Law's expertise and laughed as he wished her well in prison.

His moment of joy was interrupted by the cars that parked in front of the restaurant.

He knew those cars.

He knew what they meant.

It wasn't a coincidence, and it wasn't by chance that the cars pulled up directly outside his dinner spot, double parking and blocking traffic.

Onto the sidewalk stepped Chicago PD Deputy Chief Tony Mann. The man stood tall as he nodded to the plain-clothed cop on the street, who then pointed into the restaurant.

"Uh-oh," Charman laughed and pointed to the front window. "It looks like one of us has done something wrong. The Sweeper is outside."

The men looked nervously at each other. Tony Mann could've been there for any one of them. They watched out the window as five officers stood next to Mann, listening as he was giving out instructions. Charman stared out the window, and the smile disappeared from his face as he watched criminal defense attorney Tex Hunter step out of Mann's black SUV. The message was clear.

Charman looked towards the exits. He nodded to the bartender, who then moved to the doors to slow the incoming people down.

"Excuse me, gentlemen," Charman said. "It looks like it's time I excused myself." He stood and pulled out his cell phone. "Pick me up around the back," he called his driver. "Now."

He stepped through the doors of the kitchen, making his way past the cooking stations, looking towards the exit. He was rushing as fast as he could, checking over his shoulder. He could hear a commotion from the restaurant. The cops were inside.

Charman moved to the exit, pushing open the heavy steel door.

But standing there, towering over him, was the tall figure of Tex Hunter, with Detective Jemma Knowles beside him. Her gun was drawn.

Charman stopped, took a step back inside, and when Tony Mann stepped into the kitchen, he knew he was cooked. His eyes drifted to the knife block nearby.

"Don't even think about it," Knowles grunted, her gun pointed at Charman's torso. "Don't move."

"Walter Charman," Tony Mann stated firmly. "It gives me great pleasure to clean up these city streets, and I'm honored to tell you that you're under arrest for conspiracy to commit murder."

"You think that's enough to bring me down? I own this town," he snarled. "You're not stopping me. I'll beat these ridiculous charges."

"You won't," Hunter stated. "Berkeley has rolled on you. He told us everything. That man would do anything to survive, including selling you out to save his own skin."

Charman's mouth hung open for a moment, and his eyes drifted back to the knives on the table.

"Don't be stupid," Knowles stated.

The cook in the corner of the kitchen moved, drawing the attention of everyone. Charman took his chance and went for the knives on the kitchen table.

He was a fighter to the end. Charman screamed, more from adrenaline than the act itself, and it was the scream which brought Knowles' attention front and center.

Charman lunged. Reached for the knife. Pulled it out. Turned towards Hunter. The defense lawyer.

If he was going down, he would take Hunter with him.

Before he could throw the knife, a shot powered into his shoulder.

Walter Charman fell to the floor, clutching his shoulder. It was over.

Whatever recovery he had to do, it was going to be in a prison hospital.

CHAPTER 52

MICHELLE LAW was asleep in her hospital bed when Hunter walked in the following morning.

He'd had no sleep. He sat by her bed and watched her sleep for a few minutes, wondering whether her dreams had served their purpose in such a horrible place. He thought he detected a faint smile at one point, then figured it was time to end her nightmare once and for all.

He rubbed her hand, whispering her name over and over until her fingers began to curl. A few seconds later, her eyes began to flutter and opened enough to see him. She smiled, but from where Hunter sat, he could tell it was forced.

"A nice dream, I hope?" He could see that it hadn't been. "You're free," he whispered.

She didn't answer at first, her eyes widening as she sat up. "What?"

"It's true," he said. "You're free to go. I'm here to help you get home. We've got to complete the paperwork, but it's over."

"But how? Why? What's happening?"

"Berkeley has admitted to moving the dead body into your trunk. He's signed a full confession to say that Callum Strauss killed Amanda Ford, not you."

"What?" The confusion flooded over her face. "Is

this a dream? Am I going to wake up soon?"

"No dream." Hunter tapped her hand. "You didn't kill anyone."

"What about Callum? Is he arrested?"

"Unfortunately, he died," Hunter said. "And Walter Charman has been arrested for conspiracy to Strauss' murder."

She stared at Hunter, the thoughts pounding through her head, trying to make sense of what he'd just said. She reached for her arm, pinching at the skin. She pinched herself five times before she turned back to Hunter. "It's not a dream."

It took another two and a half days for her to be processed, and she spent most of that time in hospital before she was taken to processing. There was hours of waiting, hours of lining up, hours of disbelief. She still felt it was a dream when she stepped outside the Cook County Jail walls at 5pm one night, looking over to Tex Hunter and Esther Wright, waiting by their sedan.

She hugged them, still in shock, and sat in the back seat.

She barely said a word the entire drive back to her apartment.

She embraced them again at the entrance to her apartment building, the truth of her release finally starting to sink in.

When she stepped inside the elevator to her building, she thought about going inside and making the shower her very first stop. There was a sense of prison smell on her, an invisible scum that refused to move without hot water and soap, but as she stood before her door with the key held out, she had another thought.

She turned and walked to the door further down the hall. She knocked and waited for a new beginning to invite her in. She listened as something rustled inside, then followed the footfalls as they came closer and closer.

When James Heath opened the door, he paused, surprised by the sight of her. She could see the shock in his eyes. But there was another look, one she had recognized a long time ago but had never acted on.

Before she had a chance to second-guess herself, Michelle stepped forward, threw her arms around his neck, and pulled him down for a kiss. As her lips touched his, she felt his own arms pulling her in, the warmth of his soul touching hers, and a future she was no longer afraid of.

Her emotional walls, forever so strong and so thick, were finally coming down.

CHAPTER 53

HUNTER ARRANGED to meet Esther for lunch at The Dock at Montrose Beach, twenty minutes north of Downtown.

Hunter arrived first, seated at a table close to the sand. Knowing Esther wouldn't say no to a chocolate frappe at the best of times, he ordered for the both of them, then sat back and waited to see who would arrive first.

The Dock was more than just a seat in the sun on the edge of Lake Michigan. It was an experience, with good food and good music, a sandy getaway from the stress of the city. Its holiday party vibe was always present, and the staff were always smiling.

Esther arrived just one minute before the drinks were set down before them. He leaned across the table and planted a kiss on her lips, pulled back a little, then returned for a second.

"Whoa, Mr. Hunter. Pace yourself," she giggled and, as if to defy him a little, stole a third. "You're happy," she said once he sat back down.

"More than happy."

"Have you talked to Michelle since we dropped her off?"

"Yesterday. You should have heard her. She was like an excited teenager with a fresh outlook on life.

Still a little banged up, but she's free."

As if to remind him, Esther leaned in a little. "You did that," she whispered. "You did what you do best. You never gave up, and you won the day for her."

He nodded. "I spoke to Tony Mann earlier. He sounded pretty happy with himself. Based on Berkeley's confession, Walter Charman has been charged with conspiracy to commit murder, and he's going to spend the rest of his life behind bars. They've kept it quiet so far, but they'll be holding a press conference tomorrow morning, and I imagine it'll be run across every news outlet for days."

"Charman has connections to so many politicians. They're going to distance themselves very quickly once this case hits the media."

"And Tony Mann is going to look like a hero. 'The Sweeper' who continues to clean up corruption in Chicago."

"And you're ok with that?"

"With him taking the credit? Absolutely. Without his backing and influence, Knowles wouldn't have made the arrest before the trial finished. He deserves all the credit."

"You deserve some as well," Esther said.

"I don't need it. I got what I needed—an innocent woman out of prison. That was my job, and I was happy to deliver."

"And Jake Berkeley?"

"Berkeley is going down for the murder of Callum Strauss and his cousin, Robert Wallis. For a full confession, he made a deal with the prosecution for a reduced sentence and a nice prison, but he's still going away." Hunter drew a long breath and looked back out at Lake Michigan. "But listen, I've been thinking."

"Oh? That must've hurt," Esther smiled as she sipped some of the frappe, dipped her finger in the cream, and licked it off.

"Funny," Hunter said. "But I've been thinking that there's a lot of bad people out there, and it's time to balance the scales."

"You seem to attract the worst of them. They come and find you."

"And it's time to even up the numbers." Hunter looked out across the sands, towards the deep blue waters as his mind wandered into the future. "And maybe, with your genetics, a child of mine might balance the scales in the world."

Esther stopped sucking her drink and raised her eyebrows. "A child of yours?"

"Well," he leaned forward on the table. "As long as the child had your genetics, I think."

"What are you saying?" she laughed.

"That I…" He looked at the table and then back out to Lake Michigan. "That I'm ready."

"For?" Esther smiled.

"You're going to really make me come out and say it?"

"You bet," Esther said. "I know lawyer talk when I hear it. You won't fool me. I need to hear the words come from your mouth."

"Ok." He sat up straighter, puffing his chest out. "I'm ready to start a family. With you. And have children."

Esther smiled broadly, moving a little in her chair as she sipped on her straw. "That sounds like the sort of plan I can get on board with," she whispered, then reached across and held his hand on the table. "Just as long as you promise me one thing."

"What's that?" he asked.

"Promise to always come home to me with the same passion in your eyes that you have right now."

"I promise." His smile grew as he leaned over the table again, this time Esther meeting him halfway.

"Wherever you go, I will be right there beside you, every step of the way."

"Together," he whispered, pulling her closer. They shared a kiss before drawing back.

Esther gazed into his eyes, smiled, and repeated the promise. "Together."

THE END

ALSO BY PETER O'MAHONEY

In the Tex Hunter Legal Thriller series:

POWER AND JUSTICE
FAITH AND JUSTICE
CORRUPT JUSTICE
DEADLY JUSTICE
SAVING JUSTICE
NATURAL JUSTICE
FREEDOM AND JUSTICE

In the Jack Valentine Series:

GATES OF POWER
THE HOSTAGE
THE SHOOTER
THE THIEF
THE WITNESS

In the Joe Hennessy Legal Thriller Series:

THE SOUTHERN LAWYER
THE SOUTHERN CRIMINAL

Made in the USA
Middletown, DE
19 May 2023

30967711R00179